THE LEGACY OF LEHR

KATHERINE KURTZ

THE LEGACY OF LEHR

A BYRON PREISS BOOK

WALKER AND COMPANY
NEW YORK, NEW YORK

Cover Painting by Michael Kaluta

Book design by Alex Jay/Studio J.
Special thanks to Sam Walker, Jr., Russell Galen, and Leo Hallen
Edited by David M. Harris

Library of Congress Cataloging-in-Publication Data

Kurtz, Katherine.
The legacy of Lehr.

Summary: The adventures of a husband and wife
team as they face the dangers of long distance space
travel and the evils that exist on various planets.
[1. Science fiction] I. Kaluta, Michael William,
ill. II. Title.
PZ7.K9627Le 1986 [Fic] 86-15899
ISBN: 0-8027-6661-7

15.95

For the original Mather Seton
and Wallis Hamilton
and for Nancy Berman,
who may never feel
the same about vampires.

CHAPTER

1

8

KATHERINE KURTZ

The cargomaster was sullen, the freight handlers were surly, and the spaceport's chief of security had been almost insulting earlier in the morning—though his insolence was carefully masked behind the veneer of officialese that seemed to be a requisite for backwater bureaucrats. Now a simple request for water for their precious cargo had been met with suspicion, endless forms to fill out, and a patronizing attitude that was the final affront after two days of waiting.

Nor was Wallis Hamilton reassured by the growing crowd of local malcontents gathering outside the spaceport gates to protest the export of this particular cargo. Neither she nor her partner-husband was exactly popular after the three-week stint on B-Gem. As she left the cargo area to the care of the Imperial Rangers, who had formed the backbone of the expedition—and who were taking home only the ashes of two of their comrades—she hoped Mather was having better luck than she was.

As expected, she found him closeted with the spaceport director: a brittle, officious little man named Irvin Vintar, who had given them nothing but argument since their return to the facility two days before. Some comment of Mather's had brought Vintar to his feet behind the cluttered desk, but for once, he was not even trying to interrupt as Mather continued to instruct him. Vintar's face was mottled with suppressed rage, his thin hands clenched rigidly at his sides, and Wallis had no doubt that a medscan would confirm an elevated blood pressure, too.

"Mister Vintar, we've been over this so many times, I should think that by now you'd know it all by heart," Mather Seton was saying in his low, quiet voice. "You can't still be questioning my authority. You verified it yourself before I had the *Valkyrie* diverted. Now, are you going to cooperate, or must I resort to more drastic measures that we both may regret later on?"

He did not look in her direction as she entered the room, but Wallis knew that he was aware of her presence as she slipped behind him to stand at his back. Outwardly, at least, Mather was as calm as Vintar was agitated, solid and imposing in well-cut gray naval fatigues. The insignia of a fleet commodore glittered on his shoulders and open collar, the crescent and trident patch of personal service to the Imperial House showing red and gold above the cuff of his right sleeve. The image conveyed was one of quiet control and competence, of unmistakable authority—which was, in fact, almost unlimited. That Irvin Vintar had continued to resist that authority for two full days, hindering their mission, was an unnecessary distraction. Wallis could see Mather's growing impatience in the slight tap-tapping of his right thumb against the desk top, even though he seemed to be at ease in his chair.

"Well, Mister Vintar? I'm waiting for your answer."

Vintar swallowed, desperate eyes darting here and there, even at Wallis, searching anywhere for an escape.

"I can't do it, Commodore," he finally said. "It's too dangerous. Bringing the shuttle ship as close to the terminal as you want it is—no! I dare not risk the ship, the crew, and this facility in a maneuver that is beyond our capability."

"It isn't beyond *my* capability," Mather retorted. "If necessary, I'll guide the ship in myself. But I do not intend to risk my cargo needlessly by dragging it across three kilometers of open landing apron. Not with the mood of the crowd outside. Do I make myself clear?"

"But—"

Vintar opened and closed his mouth several times as the full implications of Mather's suggestion finally registered.

"That's out of the question," he whispered. "I couldn't possibly—"

"Mister Vintar, I don't think I'm really interested anymore in what *you* can or cannot do," Mather interrupted impatiently.

"But, you're not qua—I mean—"

"Mister Vintar, are you saying that a fleet commodore in the Imperial Navy is not qualified to land a civilian shuttle by remote?" Mather asked—omitting to mention, Wallis noted, that he was officially retired from *that* service, at least. "My Academy training certified me for ship classes up to and including heavy cruisers. As long as I have the cooperation of you and your staff"—he paused just long enough for the emphasis to be unmistakable—"I think I can manage to bring a civilian shuttle in where I want it."

Vintar swallowed again, his eyes flicking involuntarily down Mather's ample frame to the commodore's shoulder boards, to the Imperial Staff emblem, then to the slight bulge of a needler beneath his fatigue jacket, and back to his face. The man's jaw tightened with the effort of biting back further argument, but it was fairly obvious that Irvin Vintar had reached the end of his resources. Wallis could almost feel the man's loathing.

"Very well, Commodore." He made a stiff little bow that ill concealed his anger. "But if anything goes wrong, you'll assume full liability for any injuries or damage—and I want that in writing."

"That was understood from the beginning."

As Vintar stalked out of the office, Mather heaved a heavy sigh, then glanced up and behind him at Wallis, giving her a grin of rare maliciousness—lost, fortunately, on the back of the retreating Vintar.

"Well, the bureaucratic bear has been wrestled and apparently bested, at least for the present," he said lightly, getting to his feet. "Now all we have to do is see whether I can deliver what I threatened. It's been a while. Is our cargo ready to load?"

Wallis, standing more than a head shorter than her husband, looked up at him with a slow grin to match his own. "Well, my problems were only bear cubs compared to yours—nasty ones, I'll concede—but, yes, I got things straightened out—I think. Do you know what it just cost His Imperial Majesty's government for water that should have been made available gratis?"

"His Imperial Majesty will be suitably appalled, I'm sure," Mather said, "though I suppose it's all reckoned as a part of the price of peace, in the end." He glanced out the plasteel viewing port that overlooked the B-Gem spaceport. The chromcrete of the landing apron stretched on for heat-shimmered miles.

"Well, Vintar said that the *Valkyrie* was due to make orbit about twenty minutes ago, so I suppose the shuttle ought to be here in another ten. Care to come and watch me bring her in?"

Wallis grimaced and shook her head. "No, I think I'll watch it directly. If you *should* put that thing down on our cargo instead of on the pad, I think I'd just as soon go up with the wreckage."

"Why, Doctor Hamilton, do you doubt my abilities?"

"Why, Commodore Seton, how could you even *think* such a thing?"

The holding zone outside the cargo area was crowded when Wallis returned. Starliners the size and reputation of *Valkyrie* rarely made unscheduled stops, especially at planets as far removed from the normal shipping lanes as Beta-Geminorum III, and the event had prompted a number of travelers to alter their plans and book immediate passage. The fax board at the entrance to the passenger lounge read: "The Gruening Line are pleased to announce the stopover of their Nova-class luxury liner *Valkyrie* . . . ," and went on to detail pertinent factors of cost, availability of accommodations, and further flight schedules.

Wallis suppressed a chuckle as she worked her way through the throng, wondering whether any of the two dozen waiting passengers suspected just how "pleased" the Gruening folk were, in fact. George Lutobo, the *Valkyrie*'s captain, had not been pleased. The *Valkyrie* had been engaged in a precision sprint from Tejat to Aludra, attempting—and about to establish—a new record for passenger service between those two systems. No, even if Mather Seton did have the force of the Imperial government behind him, Lutobo was not at all pleased at having to abort that record-breaking run and change course for Beta-Geminorum III.

The inhabitants did not call it that, of course. They called it B-Gem, if they did not call it Pollox III; and an earlier race, already dying out when the first Earther colonists arrived with disease organisms that finished the job, had called the planet Il Nuadi—a name that recently had begun to come into vogue again. Following the deadly Cruaxi Sweep, which had decimated human civilization throughout the known galaxy some three hundred years ago, B-Gem had been isolated for generations. The first recontact by an expedition of the Orion Cartel a quarter century ago had found a rich, verdant planet peopled by hardy folk of exceptional agricultural ability, well ready to resume a place in an intragalactic Empire.

And because B-Gem had started out as a company planet this second time around, carefully managed to make optimum use of its resources then and for the future, it remained relatively unspoiled. A young planet, far less developed than the world that had spawned humankind, B-Gem quickly became a magnet to zoologists and botanists from all over the Empire: an untouched wilderness of flora and fauna never catalogued before. And because an alien civilization had overlapped briefly with the arrival of the first humans, it also afforded an unprecedented opportunity for anthropologists and archaeologists.

But it was B-Gem's wilderness that remained one of the single, most attractive features for laymen. Here were vast areas of uncharted wilderness, jungles, and wilding canyons where man had never been before. And animal life: so wild, so bounteous, that in some areas, hunting expeditions were still permitted under almost unregulated conditions. Here was the opportunity to bag the trophy of a lifetime.

Interests of this sort had brought Mather Seton and Wallis Hamilton to B-Gem, though Mather's intelligence background and Wallis's medical training also qualified them for more esoteric pursuits than hunting exotic game. Except that they had come not just for *a* hunting expedition, but a *specific* hunting expedition, for game that must be brought back alive. Their quarry had been the fierce and elusive blue creatures called Lehr cats, of which hitherto only two had been in captivity, and those in the emperor's own menagerie.

Now four more of the creatures prowled the confines of separate plasteel cages in the cargo area adjoining passengers reception, their eerie cries setting chills on the hearts of those who heard them, whenever the connecting door opened between the two holding areas. Rather than mere zoological curiosities, these particular cats had become unwitting pawns in a game of intergalactic treaty talks: sweeteners for the proposal that an alien ambassador would take back to his planet-hungry masters. They had cost several lives already.

"Doctor Hamilton?"

Wallis raised a hand in acknowledgment of the young Ranger lieutenant who called to her as she entered the holding area. His dark green coverall was impeccable, as usual, but his thin face mirrored the fatigue and tension under which all of them had been laboring in the weeks since coming to B-Gem. From the other side of a glassite wall behind him, the four Lehr cats glowered in their cages, their jaws parting periodically in what would be ear-splitting screams without the insulation of the wall.

"What is it, Wing?"

The young man glanced beyond her at the passengers in the lounge outside, some of whom stared back in sullen sympathy with the demonstrators massed outside the spaceport gates, then beckoned her closer as he backed toward the door leading to the cats. Slight and wiry in the manner of his Asian forbears, still he had to look down at the diminutive Wallis.

"The cats are getting awfully restless, Doctor. I think you ought to have a look."

He slapped the door activator, and the increased volume of the cats' screaming assailed them as soon as the door began sliding back. As Wallis and Wing entered, two Imperial Rangers snapped to attention, needler carbines slung over their shoulders in readiness for any possible trouble, and four more roamed among the piles of equipment surrounding the cages.

"You see what I mean?" Wing had to raise his voice to be heard above the racket of the cats' howling. "They started up right after you left to find Commodore Seton."

"Hmmm, maybe they missed me," Wallis said with a wry smile, as she unsnapped a medscan pickup from her belt and held it closer to the nearest cage. "No one strange has been in there, have they?"

"Are you kidding, Doctor?" Our own people don't even want to be in here, with that caterwauling going on. My head feels like it's going to split right open."

She swung the medscan briefly in his direction, trying not to grin, then returned her attention to the cats.

"Take a headache tablet, Lieutenant."

"Thank you, Doctor, for that helpful advice."

The cats *were* more upset than usual, though. Wallis had no doubt about that. The male they called Sebastian bristled and spat when she leaned too close, his enormous ruff rippling like an electric-blue dandelion around huge golden eyes. Slender whiskers jutted from his cheeks like sapphire soda straws, quivering each time he roared. Wallis jumped back in reflex as the smaller female in the next cage suddenly leaped against the plasteel mesh and tried to bat at her with a melon-sized paw.

"Hey, easy, Emmaline! Have you forgotten Mama?"

She got only a snarl for an answer.

Unfortunately, Wallis suspected she already knew what the problem was—and there was nothing she could do about it for now. Ordinarily, the four cages were interconnected, end-to-end, allowing the cats access to the full length of the combined run and to one another. But just an hour ago, because of the imminent arrival of the *Valkyrie*'s shuttle, Wallis had ordered the Rangers to break down the cage system into four separate compartments again, for ease of handling. The cages were still sitting next to one another, in their usual configuration, but double plasteel divider panels now locked each cat into a separate compartment. It was necessary, of course, but the cats could hardly be expected to understand why.

"Maybe they just don't like being separated," Wing said, as Wallis consulted her scanner again.

"Oh, that's certainly a part of it," she replied. "And the're frightened. Of course, they're a little hungry, too, but there isn't a lot we can do about that, either, until we've moved them aboard the *Valkyrie*. They ought to calm down, once they're back together and fed."

"I sure hope you're right, Doctor," Wing murmured, making a notation on a tally board. "It's too bad we can't tranquilize them."

As one of the females shrieked again on an even higher frequency than before, Wallis could hardly disagree with Wing's observation, but they had learned the hard way that the cats were very sensitive to most medications. They had killed two with inadvertent overdoses before discovering that the drug used in standard needler charges was several times stronger than it needed to be: Even using the low-dose needles that all of them now carried, they had almost lost Rudolph, the smaller of the two surviving males.

And how the cats would react to unmedicated hyperspace jumps was anybody's guess, though she and Mather made unmedicated jumps all the time without ill effect—or at least *she* did. The cats simply would have to take their chances, for the standard jump medication was particularly toxic to them.

Not for the first time on this trip, however, Wallis almost wished she were a veterinarian rather than a physician. Not that anyone else from off-world knew much more about Lehr cats than she did. Presumably, the folk of Il Nuadi knew, since they had been living with the animals for several hundred years; but such zoologists as the planet had produced since its reentry into galactic civilization had left the cats strictly alone, relegating them to a complicated legend-taboo-myth cycle that forbade any interference with the creatures. That was what had drawn the crowd camped outside the spaceport gates and had nearly provoked a global incident when they brought the cats here after capture.

A deep rumble vibrated through the entire chamber, more felt than heard, followed by a jarring shake and then total silence. The cats were quiet for all of five seconds before taking up their wailing with renewed vigor.

"That has to be the shuttle ship," Wing said, rushing toward a darkened viewport where another Ranger was already hitting the polarizing controls. "The pilot must have set it down right on the roof!"

The wall went slightly transparent—clear enough to see the sleek, streamlined bulk of the shuttle ship now resting hardly twenty meters beyond, elegant and stylish in the murrey and silver livery colors of the Gruening Line.

"Well, well, Susmen Limited's latest model," the older Ranger murmured. "Gruening doesn't skimp, does it?"

"Aye, she's a beauty," Wing agreed, after a low whistle between his teeth. "I didn't know Gruening had such hotshot pilots, either."

Wallis had to try very hard not to laugh at the younger man's exuberance. He was the youngest of all their surviving Rangers—almost young enough to be her son—and still very green.

"They don't," she said with a grin, "though I suspect Mather would be flattered at the compliment. He might just have landed it on the roof, too, if he'd thought it would support the weight. That way, we wouldn't have to take the cats outside at all."

"Commodore *Seton* landed it?" Wing gasped, though the older Ranger only nodded knowingly. "And he must have done it by remote, too," Wing went on. "I'd heard he was a crack pilot before they made him retire, but you never really believe half the stories they tell you in the Academy."

"But you *can* believe *some* of them," Wallis murmured, almost to herself, as she hid a smile behind her hand and watched the ground grew already undogging the hatches, preparing for passenger and cargo boarding.

Aboard the *Valkyrie* an hour later, the return of the shuttle ship from planetside met with a variety of reactions, depending upon whether one was a passenger or a member of the crew. For the crew, it was hardly a matter for rejoicing, since the change in schedule had cost them the bonuses promised if the *Valkyrie*'s speed sprint had been successful.

Few passengers really minded, however, for the unexpected stop at B-Gem provided a welcome break in the monotony of long-distance space flight, even aboard a great luxury liner like the *Valkyrie.* Taking on new passengers and exotic cargoes was one of the highlights of any long trip, and an unscheduled stop at one of the Empire's outer worlds was almost guaranteed to pique the interest of even the most seasoned star traveler.

Nor was the management of the Gruening Line blind to this fascination. Long in the business of catering to the wishes of a wealthy and sometimes eccentric clientele, Gruening had provided an observation deck, above the shuttle bays, where interested passengers could watch the docking operations from behind safety ports and not get in the way of the crew. Less active passengers could even observe from the privacy of their cabins, via closed-circuit viewers. The ship's recreation computer correlated fifteen video channels, several having to do with routine operation of the ship, plus a wealth of library functions designed to amuse and inform.

Hence, the observation deck had attracted more than a dozen passengers for the B-Gem rendezvous. More might have come, but the ship's day had begun only an hour before, and many were still asleep in their berths. A handful of adults watched with casual interest, a few exotically clad aliens among them, but it was the children who had turned out in full force—who always seemed to know when a docking would take place. Five of the youngsters, fresh-faced and wide-eyed, clung to the railings behind the observation ports this morning; they obviously itched to go down on the loading docks for a closer look at the shuttle, the new passengers, and any interesting-looking cargo that might be coming aboard.

The new passengers disembarked first, each individual or party being met by a steward who conducted them to the purser's check-in, just inside the passenger reception lounge. The *Valkyrie*'s captain was also on hand to greet the passengers, though his motives were less of sociability than of vexed curiosity as he waited for the *other* passengers, one in particular, who had virtually commandeered his vessel. A man of impeccable abilities, and humors as dark as his handsome face, Captain George Lutobo was not likely to dismiss lightly the fact that he had been forced to mar the Gruening Line's reputation for precision scheduling—his mood was becoming darker by the minute. When a break came in the line of passengers waiting to check in with the purser, Lutobo drifted over to the foot of the shuttle ramp long enough to snap at a baggage handler bringing down expensive-looking luggage.

"One break in the normal routine, and the whole operation falls apart," he grumbled, pacing back toward the purser. "Mister Diaz, what *is* going on?"

The bleat of an all-clear signal in the adjoining bay drowned out his words, and Lutobo realized that the man could not have heard him. Diaz had piles of customs declarations, visas, passports, and other travel documents all over his desk, in an order that apparently made sense to him but probably not to anyone else. He was presently logging in a med chip for a family of three, asking the usual questions about any special requirements of diet or preferred environment.

"Mister Diaz," the captain repeated.

Diaz glanced up, nodding slightly as he saw that it was the captain.

"Good morning, Captain. How can I help you?"

The captain tried unsuccessfully to control a scowl. "This Commodore Seton—has he come aboard yet?"

"Seton? No, sir. I think he and his people are still with their cargo. Someone brought their papers, though."

With a grudging nod, the captain picked up the stack of passports and shuffled through them until he found what he was looking for: *Seton, Mather V.; Fleet Commodore, Imperial Navy (Ret.); Ph.D. linguistics, psychology; clearance 1-A-1*. The passport itself bore a codicil endorsed by Prince Cedric, the brother of the emperor, guaranteeing a credit line whose upper limit was not even specified, though Lutobo knew that the code letter after it would return an astronomical figure if he ran a credit check.

Lutobo harrumphed at that, glaring at the "retired" notation and glaring more at the 1-A-1 clearance, then dropped the stack of passports back on the purser's desk and strode purposefully toward the shuttle ship hatch. As he reached the foot of the ramp, two Imperial Rangers in dark green coveralls appeared at the top, carefully guiding an anti-grav dolly clamped under a huge plasteel container. A vaguely Oriental-looking younger Ranger with a tally board followed them, accompanied by a tiny, titian-haired woman who could have been almost any age from twenty on up. Lutobo had gone partway up the ramp to meet them before he made out what was inside the mesh-sided container and hastily backed down again.

"Coming through, Captain," one of the Rangers called.

The animal was curled into a tight, furry blue ball, but it still seemed to fill the cage. Lutobo guessed it might weigh close to two hundred pounds under standard gravity, but just now it was bobbing, nearly weightless, from the anti-grav dolly supporting its cage. The cage lurched a little as its handlers tried to ease it carefully off the end of the ramp, and the change of angle produced a cry—somewhere between a screech and the sound of metal being shredded—as the ball of fur suddenly was transformed into a bristling, spitting bundle of enormous blue cat. It was maned like an Earther lion around angry golden eyes, with pointy ears flattened to a skull suggesting extreme cunning. It lashed more than a meter of tufted tail hard enough against the side of the cage to make the cage and dolly rock, as it hooked razor-sharp claws into the floor mesh to catch its footing. The creature yowled again, blinking in the harsh light of the dock, and the sound sent a shiver up Lutobo's spine. The light also glinted off wicked-looking fangs, just before the creature closed its mouth.

The captain gulped, suddenly breathing hard, and backed off further as the cage passed, surreptitiously wiping clammy palms on the sides of his maroon uniform trousers—he had never liked cats of any sort—then resumed his previous scowl as a large, heavyset man in gray fatigues came down the ramp and started to join the others. Fleet commodore's insignia gleamed on his collar tabs, and the Imperial cipher on his sleeve. The name flash above the right breast pocket identified him as the very man the captain had been looking for.

"Commodore Seton, I believe?"

Mather turned to appraise the captain, a bland expression on his round, pleasant face.

"Yes, I'm Seton. You must be Captain Lutobo. I'm sorry we had to commandeer your vessel, Captain, but as I explained, we're acting under direct Imperial orders."

He stuck out his hand in the captain's direction, but Lutobo pointedly ignored it.

"You said that you were on urgent Imperial business," Lutobo said in a cold voice. "You implied that it was a matter of the utmost urgency. You did not say that it was to transport specimens for the Emperor's zoo! I don't know whether it's occurred to you or not, Commodore, or whether you even care, but the Gruening Line has a reputation to maintain. It cannot do that if officious Imperial procurers interrupt its schedules for frivolous purposes."

Mather had lowered his hand at Lutobo's outburst, and now he tucked his thumbs casually into the waistband of his trousers. Though the movement did not appear to be obviously calculated, it did draw the fabric of his jacket more closely against his side, outlining with frank clarity the butt of the needler he wore beneath his left arm. Beneath a shock of light brown hair trimmed slightly longer than military regulations prescribed, the hazel eyes were clear of any menace; the voice was calm and carefully neutral, but the promise of cold power was there, nonetheless.

"I hardly think that you're in a position to judge whether the emperor's 'whims' are 'frivolous,' Captain," Mather said quietly. "And while less flexible men than myself might feel obliged to take offense at your implied insult, I'm sure you reacted out of genuine concern for your own duties, just as I am trying to be faithful to mine. I assure you that my people and I will do everything within our power to help you make up the time you've lost by this unscheduled stop."

Lutobo blinked, taken aback by Mather's mild yet unmistakably firm reponse, and folded his hands behind his back, drawing himself up straighter.

"I apologize if I spoke a little hastily, Commodore," he conceded. "However, I'm afraid there's nothing you can do to make up for the delay. Aside from the fact that we've already lost our chance at the new speed record this time out and my crew will forfeit their bonuses, I cannot risk my passengers' comfort by making extra jumps, or by making scheduled ones too close together. The Gruening Line's reputation is built even more on passenger safety and comfort than it is on punctuality. My superiors would not support any action that endangered this reputation."

Mather spread his hands in a conciliatory gesture.

"I understand perfectly, Captain. However, it may be that I can assist your navigation staff to fine-tune a few of your scheduled jumps. It won't get you your record, but we might at least make up for some of the lost time that way. I—ah—have some acquaintance with the Margall-Seton drive."

"I appreciate the offer, Commodore, but—wait a minute! You aren't *that* Seton, are you?" Lutobo blurted.

Mather grinned. "No, but my aunt was. Seriously, Captain, I'd like to help, if you'll let me."

"Well, maybe we *could* manage to—"

But before he could say just what they might be able to manage, he was interrupted by one of the purser's yeomen, who came hurrying into his line of sight with a look of concern on her usually controlled face.

"Captain, there's been a disturbance up on the observation deck." She glanced over her shoulder, with both men's eyes automatically following the direction of her glance. "One of the passengers went into some kind of hysterical fit and started making a scene. He managed to get several other passengers upset in the process, and the deck officer had to close the observation level."

"What about the passenger?" Lutobo asked. "Is he all right?"

"That I couldn't tell you, sir. It was one of the Aludran pilgrims. You know how private they are. His mate apparently took him in charge and they went back to their cabin, but someone from Medical Section probably ought to check on him. One of the other passengers said the Aludran was screaming something about demons."

"Demons?" Lutobo said.

"He probably saw one of my cats," Mather muttered under his breath. "As I recall, Aludran demons are green rather than blue, but other than that, they do look rather a lot like Lehr cats."

Lutobo sighed. "I could have gone all day without hearing that, Commodore."

"Sorry, Captain."

Lutobo shook his head wearily and rubbed at the nape of his neck. "Well, we'll have to continue our conversation at a later time, I suppose. Will you excuse me?"

"Of course, Captain."

As Mather turned to go back up the ramp, where two more Rangers were bringing along the next cage, Lutobo followed the yeoman back to the purser's desk.

"Mister Diaz, how many Aludrans do we have aboard, this trip?"

The purser pushed a last folder onto the pile he had been building and shook his head. "Only five or six, sir. Did you want a list of names?"

The captain snorted softly under his breath, then shook his head as well. "Never mind. I'll have Doctor Shannon do it. I was going to stop by Medical Section anyway. This whole morning has given me a splitting headache."

"Sorry to hear that, sir." The purser raised a hopeful eyebrow. "But if you're going to Medical Section anyway, would you take these medical records on the new passengers? Doctor Shannon will want to get them integrated into the files as soon as possible."

With a shrug and a gesture of futility, Lutobo picked up the stack of chip cards that were the medical records and sighed, then began to make his way across the shuttle bay toward the crew lift. Behind him, Mather Seton watched his Rangers float a third cat cage down the ramp of the shuttle ship, its occupant screaming with a sound like ripping metal.

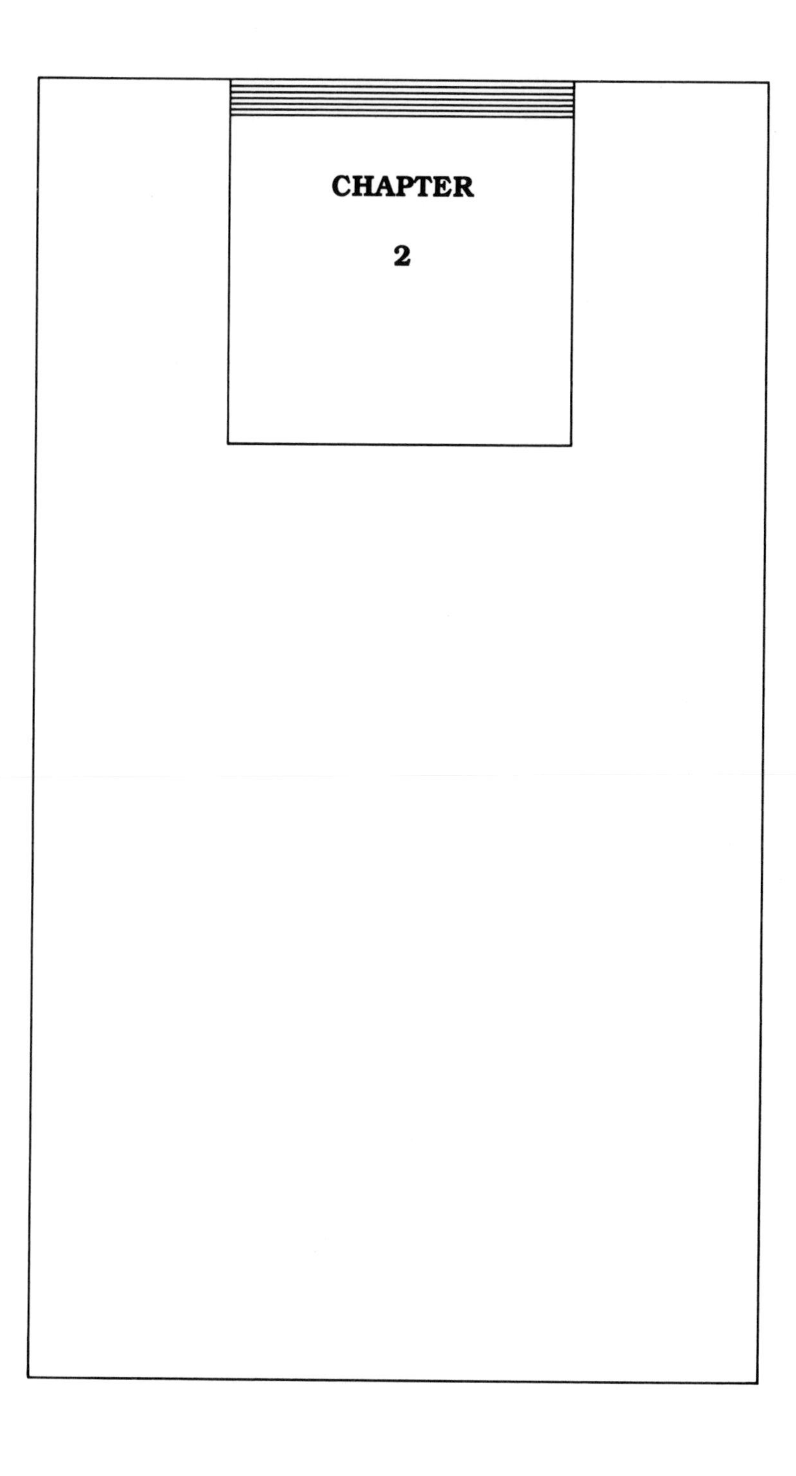

CHAPTER

2

KATHERINE KURTZ

"If they send me back to Tejat on the *Valkyrie*, I'm going to take you dancing, Doctor," said the legless man, managing a courageous grin as he made his antigravity harness lift him awkwardly off the treatment table. "I mean that, so you'd better start limbering up your dancing slippers."

Doctor Shivaun Shannon, Chief Medical Officer aboard the *Valkyrie*, gave the young major a wink and an answering smile and locked away the rest of the sanity-saving pain medication for another twelve hours. "I'll be looking forward to it, Major, but by then there are going to be dozens of other women just falling over themselves to dance with you. By the time you've got those new legs grown, you'll probably have forgotten all about me."

"You think I could forget you, Doc?" The major made his harness lift him to standing height and took one of Shannon's hands with his free one, trying to twirl her. "I'd dance with you now, except that the other passengers might get jealous. Besides"—they both laughed as *he* twirled instead of her—"this blasted harness won't cooperate! I'm going to keep practicing, though. I just might get it right before we arrive at the Med Center."

"You might," Shannon said lightly, taking advantage of his weightless condition to propell him gently in the direction of the door, "but I'm afraid it's only a briefly useful talent. You'll have new legs again before you know it. Seriously, though, if you exert yourself too much, your painkiller isn't going to last the full twelve hours, and you'll be hurting until I can give you the next dose. Run along now, and try to stay reasonably quiet."

"Spoilsport!"

"Yes, I know. I'm a cruel, heartless doctor, with absolutely no sympathy for a gallant war hero. Goodbye, Major."

" 'Bye, Doc."

Shannon was still smiling as the major floated off down the corridor, and the twinkle in her eyes softened even Lutobo's dour expression as he approached from the other direction.

"You're awfully cheerful this morning, Doctor."

"Well, it helps the patients feel better, Captain. Ah, I see that Mister Diaz has conned you into bringing me the records on the new passengers, hasn't he?"

Lutobo snorted good-naturedly as he handed them over. "Somehow, I always manage to forget that Diaz has as much blarney in his blood as you do—though you'd never know it by the name. At least yours got Major Barding smiling this morning."

"Indeed, it did. He's even promised to take me dancing on the way home."

She dropped the handful of medical chips into a holding bin on the reception desk and started to ask why *Lutobo* wasn't smiling, but decided to stick with the more neutral subject of Barding as the captain gestured toward her inner office with an expression that warned against further levity.

"Actually, Barding's doing pretty well—if he'd just stop overdoing things, so his pain medication would last the full time. The poor man goes through hell the last hour or so."

"And I'm going through my own hell right now, Doctor," Lutobo muttered, following her into the office and closing the door. "What have you got for a good, pounding headache?"

"Well, 'good' and 'pounding' are rather diametrically opposed when talking about a headache," Shannon said, sitting at her desk and opening a drawer. Controlling a smile, she added, "But then, I suppose that depends a lot on what caused it."

She shook a white capsule from a vial and handed it across to Lutobo, who gulped it gratefully before sitting down.

"Do you want to tell me about it?" she asked.

Closing his eyes, Lutobo rubbed both hands hard across his face and sat back in the chair.

"Do you know what the 'special' cargo was, the reason we diverted to B-Gem?"

"I'm sure I don't, Captain."

"It was *cats*!" Lutobo's tone conveyed all the contempt of the avowed ailurophobe. "Four big, hairy blue cats for the emperor's zoo. They scream like banshees. I don't know how Diaz and his people were managing to conduct business down there. Ugly-looking brutes—the cats, that is."

As Lutobo looked up at her again, Shannon raised an eyebrow.

"Cats, eh?" She started to chuckle but saw the warning gleam in Lutobo's eyes in time and managed to convert the chuckle to a cough. "Well, I—ah—can understand why you're concerned, Captain. We've lost a lot of time, haven't we? In addition to the bonus pay."

"Yes. And then, to top it off, there was some kind of disturbance on the observation deck. According to a yeoman, who got it from the purser, who got it from the deck officer, one of the Aludran passengers got hysterical, apparently over the sight of the cats being unloaded, and made enough of a scene that the deck had to be shut down. There was some talk of demons or some such nonsense. I'd like you to check it out."

"The Aludran?"

Lutobo nodded.

"Do you know which one?" Shannon persisted.

The captain shook his head. "Apparently his mate took him back to their cabin. But if we're going to have aliens berserking aboard my ship, I want to know why. I'd especially like to know what set him off. If it was the cats . . ."

Shannon sat forward in her chair and nodded. "I'll see what I can find out, Captain. As I recall, there are only six Aludrans, and they all have adjoining quarters. Anything else?"

The captain rose as a low, deep-throated chime sounded throughout the ship, signaling its imminent departure from parking orbit. The previous lines of pain in his face were already easing from the drug.

"Yes, you might check on those cats, when you finish with the Aludrans. Talk to this Commodore Seton, who brought the cats aboard. There's also supposed to be a doctor in his party. Maybe you can learn something from him. And don't let anyone distract you. Our first jump comes up in less than an hour."

Ten minutes later, Shannon was moving briskly down the corridor toward the Aludrans' quarters, a medical kit slung on her shoulder and a wealth of new information in her mind about these particular Aludrans.

She was already familiar with the racial type, of course. Fledgling physicians were required during their training to dissect cadavers of most of the major physiological groupings, and to complete certain survey courses in alien psychology and culture. The latter training had been augmented in even greater detail when Shannon came to work for the Gruening Line, since a starliner's medical officer might routinely expect to encounter a far larger variety of alien patients than most planetside doctors saw in a lifetime. In two years, Shannon certainly had seen her share.

Lutobo's remark about demons disturbed her, though, for she remembered that the Aludrans were a very mystical people, possessed of an ancient and intricate myth system, and actually believed in supernatural beings. They were also slightly telepathic among themselves, though not with other races—which meant that one terrified Aludran could infect all the others. Her quick review of their medical records confirmed that these particular Aludrans were religious pilgrims bound for a retreat on Tel Taurig, which was to have been the ship's next destination before they diverted to B-Gem. The leader, a *lai*—or priest—called Muon, was a noted lecturer at several major universities both on and off his home planet and carried the reputation of a respected and stable individual—though one could never be really certain when evaluating aliens by human standards. She remembered meeting him briefly at the captain's reception, their first night out, and being impressed.

Squaring her shoulders, Shannon paused in front of the first Aludran cabin and thumbed the call buzzer several times. Neither that signal nor several more produced any response. Nor did she have any better luck at the second cabin.

But as she approached the third, which was assigned to Muon and his mate, she could hear sounds of movement and an occasional sob or moan, even though the cabins were supposed to be relatively soundproofed. Pushing the buzzer this time produced sudden and complete silence but no acknowledgement from the intercom. When no one responded after several more buzzes, she took out an override key and inserted it in a slot beside the signal buzzer, pushing when it met resistance.

A circuit relayed, the buzzer sounded again, and a

green light came on in the buzzer button.

"This is Doctor Shannon, the ship's surgeon," she said in a low voice, speaking into the grille below the buzzer. "I've used a medical override because the captain asked me to be certain you were all right. I'm sorry to disturb you, but I understand that one of your party had an unpleasant experience a little while ago."

There was a short silence and then the scurry of feet and the sigh of a breath being drawn near the intercom.

"Please to go away, Doctor," piped a thin, reedy voice, thickly accented. "You can nothing do."

Shannon peered at the grille and at the blank vid screen beside it, wishing her medical immunity permitted her to override visual as well as audio circuits. In an emergency, she could override the door itself, but she would have to justify her actions later on, if the occupant complained. Thus far, she had no evidence of any real emergency.

"I don't mean to contradict you," she replied, "but if you won't tell me what's wrong, how do I know that there's nothing I can do? I realize that you're upset, but I have my orders. May I at least speak with Muon, your leader?"

"No!" came the emphatic reply. "*Lai* Muon not wish speak to anyone. I speak for him. I am his *laia.* This not concern you, Doctor."

"As a physician, it always concerns me if one of my passengers is in distress," Shannon said gently. "May I please come in, just for a moment? I promise you, I'll do nothing without your permission, and I'll leave if you want me to, as soon as I've been inside and confirmed that everyone is all right."

She heard a faint twittering in the background, quickly muffled as someone apparently held something over the microphone pickup, and then: "You go away then?" the voice asked plaintively.

"After I've been inside, of course I will."

She pulled out her override key as a faint click signaled the door circuit being activated. A puff of hot, moist air stirred her dark hair as the door slid back, and she felt her weight decrease slightly as she crossed the threshold. The Aludran atmosphere was oxygen-rich, tangy with some alien scent she could not identify, but she knew that nothing about the normal Aludran environment was harmful to humans. The thirty-degree temperature differential had her sweating immediately, though, and she hoped she would find no reason to stay in the Aludrans' cabin overlong.

"You come this way, Doctor," said the Aludran who had admitted her. "Muon over here."

The cabin was dim, but not so dim that Shannon could not see that the four other Aludrans were standing and kneeling around the chair of a distressed-looking elder. Though Aludrans normally were a colorful lot, especially the males with their iridescent plumage, this one looked almost monochromatic. Even the scarlet and yellow feathers of his crest seemed faded against the grayish down that covered his neck and the backs of his hands, and the skin stretched over the planes of his sharp, angular face was ashen. His eyes were closed, his head leaning against the chair back, and the fur-lined robes he needed to wear outside the warmth of his cabin had been thrown back to reveal a simple garment of amber crysilk that flowed from a scarlet scholar's collar and stole and partially covered his claw-toed feet. The female who had opened the door, rose-gowned to match her plumage, moved quickly to his side and knelt beside him, her delicate hand resting anxiously on the elder's, to face Shannon.

"This *Lai* Muon, Doctor. You see now, he unharmed and resting. You go now?"

Shannon, who had reviewed the basics of Aludran protocol when she scanned their medical records, gave careful salute in the prescribed manner of a healer to an Aludran elder, touching two fingers to her lips, to her breast, and then extending her open palm outward in the degree appropriate for near-equals. Several of the other Aludrans twittered among themselves in surprised approval at that, and the female kneeling beside Muon inclined her head cautiously in acknowledgement.

"You know our ways."

"Some of them," Shannon conceded. "Must I go immediately? I *am* concerned that *Lai* Muon was distressed."

The female returned a curt nod, but it was not one of dismissal.

"Please excuse, Doctor, but our people very frightened by what happen to *Lai* Muon, and most not speak your language well. I speak for Muon. He rests now, as you see."

Shannon nodded, casually letting her left hand drift closer to the scanner controls on her medical kit.

"Can you tell me what happened?" she asked. "My captain was told that Muon said something about—demons."

Unreadable emotion flickered in the female's face, but before she could speak, Muon himself opened sharp yellow eyes and shook his head slightly.

"Co-mekatta, Ta'ai," he chided the Aludran woman softly. "Doctor, I apologize if I have caused your captain alarm. Someone misheard me, I fear. Please, do not concern yourself. We can deal with what must be done."

Shannon looked him over carefully, her physician's eye evaluating the alien even as she moved slightly closer to him.

"Are you certain you're all right, sir?"

"I am certain, Doctor."

"You won't mind if I scan you, then, to see for myself?"

"If you must."

She scanned him, but a quick glance at the status tallies confirmed that what Muon said was true, at least as far as his physical health was concerned. With a sigh, Shannon let the scanner back down on its strap, glancing at the others in the room.

"Well, sir, you do appear to be in acceptable physical health. If only you would tell me—"

"Please, Doctor," Muon whispered.

"I know. I promised to leave, and I shall," Shannon replied resignedly. "But if there should be any further problem, I hope that you'll contact me. I want to help, if I can."

"Thank you, Doctor," Muon murmured in dismissal. "I should like to rest now, if you do not mind."

"As you wish, sir."

Shannon withdrew with a slight bow, reentering the cooler corridor with relief. She had not been aware of it in the cabin, but her uniform was stuck to her back, and perspiration crawled along her scalp and beaded across her upper lip. She resisted the urge to look over her shoulder as the cabin door slid shut behind her, and she concluded that whatever had riled the Aludrans was likely to remain a mystery for the present. Meanwhile, she decided that she had time to cool off and change to a fresh uniform before going below to look at these strange creatures that apparently had precipitated the aliens' distress.

And in the cargo hold assigned to the creatures in question—a square, high-ceilinged compartment perhaps twenty meters on a side—Mather's Rangers had already secured most of the equipment brought aboard from the shuttle. What was not battened down along the perimeter or stowed in storage lockers had gone into the small security room opening off the larger area, where two of the men were splicing it into the existing security system—much to the mystification of three men from ship's security. Just in front of the hold's exit door, Mather and two more Rangers were assembling something that looked very much like an airlock made of plasteel mesh. The other three, under Wallis's supervision, worked at jockeying the four cages into position for reconnection, one of them hooking up the big scanners atop each cage to switch from battery to ship's power—all to the raucous accompaniment of four disgruntled Lehr cats.

Actually, Wallis decided as she circled the long line of cages and took random readings with her hand scanner, the cats had weathered their transfer from B-Gem reasonably well, displaying real hysteria only when the anti-grav lifters were first attached to their cages and they began to float.

But terror had fast faded to apparent curiosity when weightlessness did not seem to harm. And when lessened weight did return once the cages were ensconced aboard the shuttle ship, Empire Standard gravity being lighter by a sixth than B-Gem Normal, the cats found themselves accordingly lighter, more agile, and almost a little intoxicated by the time docking was made with the *Valkyrie*. The only other anxious moment had come when the cats had been moved from the shuttle to the *Valkyrie* and vented their displeasure on the ears of everyone in the vicinity of the shuttle bay.

Not that the big cats had really settled down yet. Nor would they, until the cages were reconnected and they could be fed. Periodically, and for no apparent reason, one or another of them would let out a great roar—much to the chagrin of the three ship's security guards, who had even closed the door to the security office in an effort to shut out the noise.

But at least there was none of that frenzied clashing against the wire mesh, which the big cats had sometimes tried on B-Gem to amuse themselves. The two males looked quite befuddled by it all, and the female called Emmaline had even settled down sufficiently to nap, her oval topaz eyes shuttered to mere slivers beneath twitching, tufted ears. The other female had always been the least amiable of the four, and continued to pace back and forth in her cage, growling and lashing her tail against the mesh. She was also the one who seemed to be making the most noise.

"Well, old Matilda is certainly vocal enough," Mather said to Wallis as he came to look over her shoulder at her medscan readings. "Do you suppose she knows about hyperspace jumps?"

Wallis grinned and glanced sidelong at him. "You haven't been telling her, have you? *Some* people don't need jump medication to get them through, and *most* people don't react worse from the pills than they do from the jump. You'd better hope our little pets take after their 'mom' rather than their 'dad'."

"I'll settle for them making it through alive," Mather said. "Casey, are we nearly ready to activate that lock?"

A sandy-haired Ranger back at the entry portal gave a thumbs-up in response.

"Two minutes, Commodore."

"Good. Webb, how're we coming on the reconnections? I think that a lot of this caterwauling is going to stop, once they're back together again—I hope."

"Ready as soon as we've jumped, sir."

"Excellent."

As Webb and another Ranger continued to tinker with the cages and Mather drifted over to watch, Wallis continued to scan the cats. She turned, though, at the hail of one of the Rangers by the door, as a dark-haired young woman in officer's livery entered the hold and stopped inside the security lock, looking puzzled. Her insignia and the medical scanner slung across her shoulder identified her as one of the ship's medical staff.

"Is there something we can do for you, Doctor?" Mather asked, signaling Casey to let her through.

"Ah, you must be Commodore Seton," Shannon said. "Actually, I was looking for the doctor who's supposed to be with your party. I'm Shivaun Shannon, ship's surgeon."

"Ah, then, you're looking for me," Wallis replied, approaching the younger woman with a smile and an outstretched hand. "I'm Doctor Wallis Hamilton. Mather and I are in charge of this operation."

Good manners prompted Shannon to shake hands with both of them, but her attention had already shifted past the two of them, her eyes drawn irresistibly to the four caged cats.

"So, *that's* what's been wreaking havoc on our passengers' nerves and giving our captain headaches," she murmured, awed, though she immediately recovered and gave them both a conspiratorial grin. "Both are very dangerous occupations aboard this ship, you know."

Wallis shrugged and returned the grin. "What can I say, Doctor, except that I'm sorry. Who would have guessed you'd have Aludrans on the observation deck this morning? And as for the captain—well, unfortunately, I suppose our friends' shrieking *can* give one a headache, if one is so inclined."

"Well, our captain is, and he certainly did have one," Shannon replied. "It isn't really your fault. However, just so I can reassure him and anyone else who asks, I don't suppose there's any way they could get out?"

Mather raised an eyebrow. "Through plasteel and a Margall force field? Not likely, Doctor. No, I'm afraid the only danger from our furry friends is the possibility of jangled nerves—and even that should be minimal, once we get them settled down."

As if in support of the fact that they had *not* settled down yet, the smaller male let out an ear-piercing yowl that immediately was echoed in triplicate by his mate and the other pair. Shannon grimaced and covered her ears, then chuckled uneasily as the screams subsided.

"Well, I'll hope that's soon. Our first phase jump is coming up shortly. I suppose the medication will calm them down a little—or can you sedate them?"

Wallis shook her head resignedly. "Afraid not, Doctor. Unfortunately, they're allergic to the standard jump medication—deadly allergic, in fact. For that matter, we haven't found much that they *can* tolerate. The expedition before ours, which brought back the only other pair in captivity, lost five from bad drug reactions, nerves, and just plain cussedness. We lost two ourselves—even with the benefit of prior knowledge—not to mention two Rangers and several local people."

"Aren't you taking a big risk, then?" Shannon asked. "And why bother, especially with the vast expense involved?"

Wallis sighed. "I know it seems ridiculous. Unfortunately, the emperor's pair hasn't bred in captivity, and he needs these rather badly. I wish I could tell you why, but I can't. Actually, these are in far better shape than any of the others that have been captured alive. We hope they'll be able to survive the jumps without too much danger—though it certainly isn't going to be comfortable for them."

"Or for us," Mather murmured under his breath.

Shannon studied the cats thoroughly for several seconds, then turned back to the two scientists. "I take it that you'll be riding out the phase jump here, then, with the cats?"

"Yes, indeed," Wallis said.

She was interrupted by the discreet chiming of a phase warning signal; the lights dimmed and came back to full. Shannon glanced at a red light that had begun flashing insistently above the door and controlled a smile as she moved in that direction.

"Well, that's the five-minute warning. I was going to invite you to join me in Medical Section. We're testing some new suspension units that seem to be even better than drugs for getting people through jumps without discomfort. However—"

Wallis echoed the resigned shrug of her fellow physician. "Sorry. As much as we'd like to take you up on it, I'm afraid our friends may need us. Maybe Mather can try your new toy the next time, though. He hates jumping, and the standard medication makes him queasy."

"And *jumping* makes me queasy." Mather sighed. "A fine fate for a former starship commander, isn't it, Doctor Shannon? Neither the jumping nor the medication is debilitating—just damned uncomfortable. The unfair part is that Wallis jumps clean and isn't affected at all."

"You mean you jump without medication?" Shannon paused by the security lock. "I never heard of that."

"I hadn't either," Wallis said. "My mind just seems to click off during that instant of phase shift. I've tried to teach Mather how to do it, but—" She sighed and shrugged, giving Shannon an exaggerated expression of patient long-suffering, and Shannon shook her head in amused disbelief.

"Well, it's your headache. Incidentally, if Commodore Seton is still interested in food after an unmedicated jump, you're both invited to dine at the captain's table this evening. The purser asked me to tell you it will be formal."

If Mather had any misgivings about the probable condition of his stomach by dinnertime, his enthusiastic acceptance of the invitation did not show it. When Shannon had gone, Mather's mood was almost jovial as he set the security lock and dismissed the Rangers and ship's security guards to their jump stations in the adjoining security room. Wallis glanced at him sidelong as she positioned an oxygenator beside the cat cages.

"My, aren't we gallant today?" she remarked with a sly grin. "She *is* pretty, Mather, and probably very bright."

Mather found a spot between two steel stanchions and braced himself as the one-minute warning vibrated through the nearly empty hold.

"It isn't nice for a doctor to gloat over someone's future discomfort," he said in a tone of mock-injury. "If you're so great, why don't you find me a cure? And, yes, she did seem bright."

With a chuckle for an answer, Wallis flicked on the master scanners above each cat cage and set them to record, steadying herself with only one hand against a bulkhead as a pulse counted down the last ten seconds to phase-shift. Mather braced himself more substantially, feet apart and hands wrapped hard around the stanchions, and muttered something about its being her fault if he died.

Then, for an endless instant, there was a total cessation of sound, light, warmth, gravity—and a keening vibration that centered at the base of Mather's skull, only to explode agonizingly behind his eyes, as if all the cells of his body suddenly had been swapped end for end and jolted with a powerful electric charge.

He felt the familiar shudder of nausea and disorientation as weight and other sensations returned; he winced at the pain in the back of his head as he opened his eyes on the stabilizing light. Wallis, after a perfunctory glance to be sure that his reaction was no worse than usual, turned her attention to the cats, who were sprawled on the bottoms of their cages and beginning to mewl piteously. Mather, despite his own distress, was only a step behind her; it was he who began forcing oxygen into the cage of the smaller male, who was having trouble breathing, while Wallis checked on the other three.

After only a few minutes, the animal's breathing eased and he, too, began yowling with his fellows. Mather, with a sigh of relief, turned the oxygenator in his own direction and took several deep breaths.

"Poor old Sebastian. You know, I wouldn't be surprised if jumping is even nastier for these poor beasties than it is for me," he said. "How are yours doing?"

Wallis glanced at the medical tallies above the cages

and made a few minor adjustments.

"Well, at least we know that jumping doesn't kill them," she said. "They'll be back to their old roaring in no time. When the men come back to relieve us, I think I'll let them take the dividers out. They'll do much better with company. How are you doing?"

"Splitting headache, as usual, but it will pass," Mather said. "If you don't need me, I think I'll try to locate our cabin and lie down for a while before dinner. After all"—a vestige of the usual twinkle came back into his eyes—"I hear that the *Valkyrie*'s cuisine is excellent."

With a wordless chuckle, Wallis leaned up to brush his lips with hers, but as he headed for the door, she was already back to her scanners.

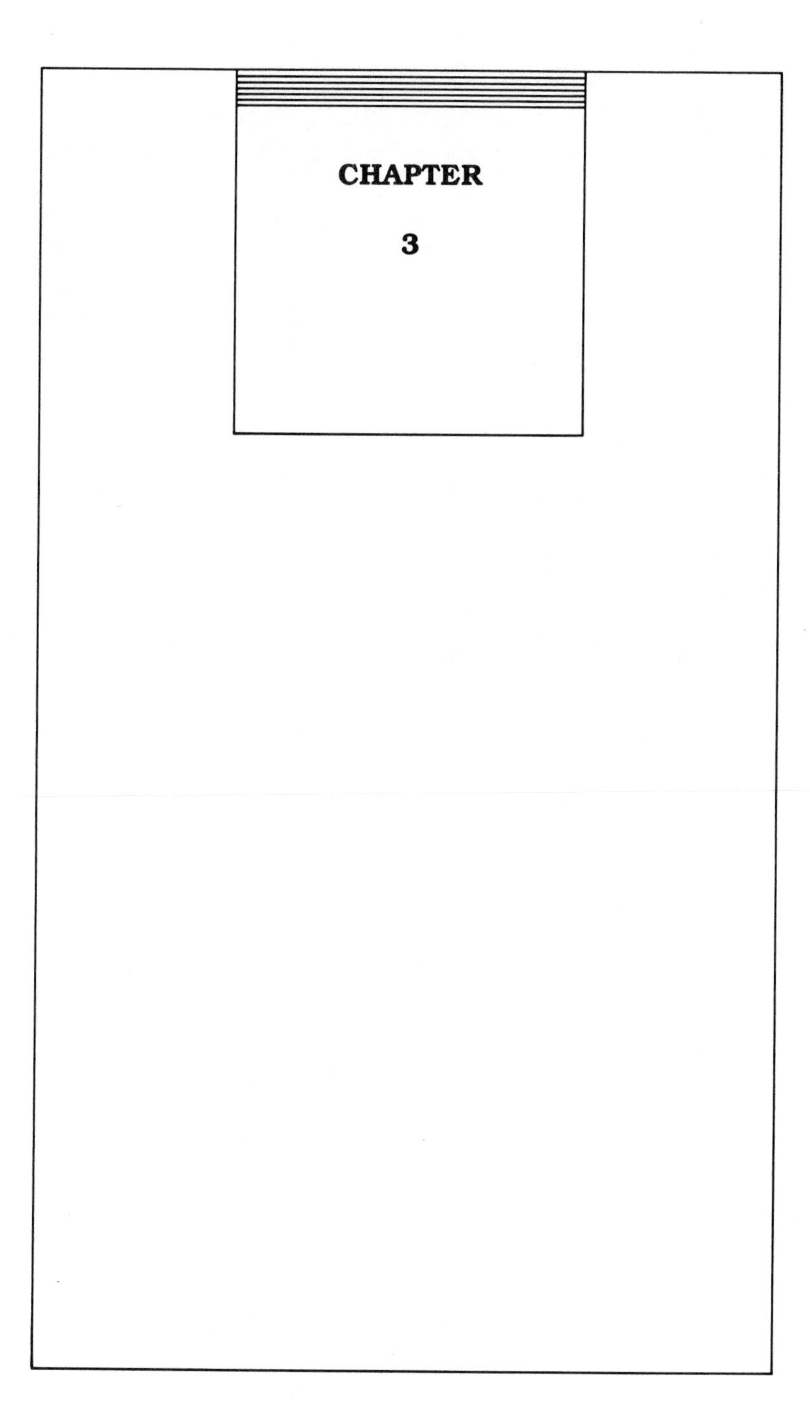

CHAPTER

3

"I've heard that Lehr cats are man-eaters, Commodore Seton. Is that true?"

The questioner was an aging hydroponics engineer sitting several places away from Mather at table in the *Valkyrie*'s grand salon. A diamond-pavéd badge in his lapel identified him as a retainer of the Derwal of Ain. The man had been asking inane questions since they'd been seated. Indeed, he was not alone in that, for by now most of the passengers had heard of the disturbance on the observation deck and knew that the cats were responsible both for the incident and the diversion to B-Gem.

As the stewards cleared away the soup course and began serving the entree, Mather found himself hard-pressed to remain a gracious table companion. Easing the high collar of his black dress tunic, he turned to glance amiably at the questioner. At his left, Wallis projected an image of classic serenity in a Grecian-style gown of shimmery white, her long auburn hair caught in a soft knot at the nape of her neck, but he could sense her irritation rising to match his own.

"Actually, it's never been proven that the cats favor human flesh, Mister Anderson." Mather said easily. "We feed our cats on fresh-frozen game that we laid in before leaving B-Gem. Fortunately, they adapted to the small animals that were brought in by the first colonists as well, so there'll be no problem keeping them supplied. Still, I doubt I'd put my hands in one's cage to find out whether he liked human fare."

Across the table, a hitherto silent young woman in turquiose shivered as she poked at her food with a fork. "Well, I haven't seen one yet, of course, but from their pictures, they certainly are frightening to look at. Are they as ferocious as lions? I saw a lion once," she added, almost as an afterthought.

Captain Lutobo, increasingly aloof at the head of the table, made no comment, choosing instead to pretend great interest in the vegetable dish that the steward had just presented for his inspection. An awkward silence settled over the table until Wallis turned to the other woman and smiled kindly.

"Well, there is a superficial resemblance to Earther lions, of course. In fact, they were first classified as *Felis leo caeruleus*—blue lion cats. That was the doing of Doctor Samuel Lehr. He described them as great, golden-eyed felines with dense blue fur, neck ruffs on the males, and tufted ears and tails. They're chiefly nocturnal, sometimes arboreal, definitely carnivorous—and they can be as vicious as a Furudite rock-spitter when cornered. Lehr was never able to capture one alive."

"But wasn't Lehr's expedition during the *second* discovery and mapping of the planet, Doctor?" asked a lean, intense-looking older man who had missed being introduced by arriving late at table. "If I remember my history correctly, the *first* expedition found a sparse native population of humanoids who revered the cats as messengers of a moon goddess—the changeable eyes and such, you understand. Unfortunately, the native population vanished during the years of isolation after the Cruaxi Sweep. Diseases brought by Earthers, I believe."

Mather turned speculative hazel eyes on the man. "You seem to know a great deal about B-Gem's history, Mister—"

"It's *Doctor* Torrell." The man's sneering arrogance—just in the way he picked up a glass and languidly twirled the stem between thumb and forefinger—almost brought Mather out of his chair. "It's Doctor *Vander* Torrell. And I prefer the older name for the planet in question: Il Nuadi, the Light of the Shining Ones. It has a splendid ring, doesn't it?"

"Indeed," Mather murmured, raising his own glass to drink, rather than letting himself get angry enough to show his contempt for the man.

At last he had a face to connect to the name. Vander Torrell was one of the most professionally renowned and personally disliked historian-archaeologists currently working with alien cultures. The Imperial computers had recommended Torrell above almost all others when putting together the B-Gem expedition, and Wallis had sent several increasingly pleading spacegrams to secure his services.

But Torrell had not been interested, even for the exorbitant fee offered by the Imperial government, and eventually had turned down an invitation, only just short of a command, from Prince Cedric himself. "Other pressing obligations," the final refusal had read.

Other pressing obligations, indeed, Mather thought, as he let a steward refill his glass. Though he had no way to check just now, he had an overwhelming suspicion that Torrell's "pressing obligation" was nothing more urgent than a desire to go on the *Valkyrie*'s speed-sprint—a pleasant enough prospect if one liked that sort of thing, Mather had to admit, and undoubtedly made the sweeter for Torrell by the statuesque blonde blowing kisses adoringly across the table at her benefactor—but there was such a thing as duty. Mather found himself taking perverse satisfaction in knowing that the *Valkyrie* would break no records this trip, thereby depriving Torrell of at least part of his pleasure.

He felt his wife's foot move slightly against his own even as he became aware of the almost empathic link they sometimes shared, and he sensed her concurrence in his opinion of the man. He was very tempted to follow through on the avenue that Torrell himself had opened and to expose the man for the hypocrite he really was, but before he or Wallis could act, Shannon put down her glass and leaned forward, handsome and animated in her stark dress whites.

"I've read several of your books, Doctor Torrell," she said, deftly turning the conversation to his benefit. "I especially enjoyed your work on the lost civilization of Wezen I. Are you planning any additional research in that area?"

Torrell inclined his head in as gracious a manner as he was likely to manage, but it soon became obvious that he did not want to talk about Wezen I.

"Thank you, Doctor Shannon, you're very kind, but Il Nuadi holds my true interest at this time. If only I had known that the *Valkyrie* would stop there, I might have rearranged my schedule to manage another visit."

If you had come with us, Mather thought bitterly, *you could be just concluding another visit—and with the thanks of the emperor, too. As it is, you probably cost us several lives.*

But he said: "Yes, I've heard of your work with the lost race of Il Nuadi, Doctor Torrell. In fact, you're probably the acknowledged authority in that field, aren't you?"

"In all modesty, I suspect that I am, Commodore," Torrell replied smoothly. "Did you know, for example, that there are curious parallels between your Lehr cats and the catlike creatures of at least three other vanished civilizations? Except, of course, that the other cat-creatures were looked upon as ravening demons and soul-eaters, not lunar messengers. A curious distinction, don't you agree? And I believe that the Aludrans, who are by no means extinct, also share that view."

The young woman who had spoken before gasped, her reddened lips agape. "Demons?" She glanced over her shoulder uneasily and shuddered. "You don't think that the Lehr cats might be—"

"Demons, too?" Torrell smiled unctuously. "I very much doubt it, dear lady. On the other hand, Commodore Seton never did tell us what happened to Samuel Lehr. You do know, don't you, Seton? Or you, Doctor Hamilton?"

Wallis suppressed a sigh, furious at the direction the conversation was taking and all but convinced that Torrell had set out to bait Mather and her from the beginning. She found herself disliking the man even more than she had before. And if he kept up this talk about demons and soul-eaters, he could start a wave of anxiety among the passengers. There was already too much talk about the cats.

"Of course Mather and I know, Doctor Torrell," Wallis said. "But not everyone here at the table is a trained scientist who can remain dispassionate through the most grisly tale. I simply didn't think it was something that the young lady would care to discuss over dinner."

"Why? Because Lehr was eaten by one of his cats?"

Wallis lowered her eyes uneasily, acutely sensitive to the effect Torrell's words were having on an increasing number of those at table. Beside her, visible only from her unique vantage point, Mather had begun methodically crushing the napkin that lay otherwise unseen across his lap.

"Oh, come now, Doctor," Torrell continued. "Animals kill to survive. So do humans, for that matter. Besides, I'm sure that the good Doctor Lehr had taken his toll of the cats. What fate could have been more fitting?"

A wave of nervous comment rippled around the

table much to the dismay of Wallis and Mather. But before they were forced to respond to this latest sortie, rescue of a sort came in the guise of a steward who bent to whisper briefly in Shannon's ear. The younger physician listened intently for several seconds, conversation dying around her, then put aside her napkin and smiled reassuringly.

"You must excuse me, ladies and gentlemen, but a doctor is always on call, I'm afraid. Captain, I don't think it's anything serious, but I like to be sure."

"Of course, Doctor. I'll stop in later for a report."

"Thank you, Captain."

As Shannon rose, she glanced at Wallis. "Doctor Hamilton, perhaps you'd care to join me? You might find our medical facility of interest. And Commodore, I can show you those new suspensor units when we're finished, if you'd like."

It must have been obvious to all that Shannon's invitation went beyond mere professional courtesy, but even Torrell was not rude enough to point that out publicly. When Mather had added his own apologies to Wallis's, the two of them followed Shannon out of the grand dining salon. Not until they had stepped aboard a staff lift and the doors had closed did Shannon look directly at them.

"Thank you for playing along," she said. "I hope you don't feel that you've been dragooned into anything, but Muon apparently is having another anxiety attack. He's the Aludran who panicked when you brought your cats aboard this morning," she added, at their looks of question. "I thought you might be able to help me reassure him that the cats aren't going to eat him—or whatever it is he's afraid they're going to do. You speak Aludran, don't you, Commodore? Aren't you a linguist?"

"Among my other dubious talents," Mather said with a nod. "I'll be glad to help, if I can."

"Thank you. In any case, the steward said Muon

was delirious," Shannon went on. "He keeps ranting about devil cats and demons in the dark—exactly what Torrell was talking about over dinner. My assistant is with him now, but he's only a student intern. I don't think he's experienced enough to handle something like this."

Shannon fell silent as the lift came to a stop and the doors opened. She cautioned curcumspection as she led Mather and Wallis down a corridor, for other passengers were about. The door to the main Aludran cabin slid open almost before she could thumb the call button, however, the youngest of the four male Aludrans admitting them with a bow.

"Good you come, Doctor," the alien said haltingly. "Muon, he plenty bad. You make well, eh?"

The hot, humid air closed around the three of them like a moist hand as they crossed the threshold: it was especially oppressive to Mather and Shannon in their high-collared uniforms. Across the room, Deller and a harried looking medical technician were gesticulating futilely at a hysterically weeping female who Shannon recognized as Ta'ai, Muon's mate. Deller had a hypo in his hand and seemed to be trying to persuade Ta'ai to let herself be sedated, but the alien woman only planted herself the more firmly between them and the farthest berth. Someone—presumably Muon—was thrashing frenetically in that berth, and the shadowed forms of other Aludrans appeared to be having no luck soothing the occupant. Nor did Deller, the technician, or another male Aludran seem to be having any luck in getting through to the distraught Ta'ai.

"Doctor Deller, why don't you let me take over now?" Shannon said quietly.

Her voice cut through the thick, humid air with quiet authority, and the intern's head whipped around in a glance of relief.

"Doctor Shannon, am I ever glad to see you!"

Leaving his reluctant patients, Deller crossed to

meet Shannon and the others, his plain, serious face sheened with perspiration. "He's having some kind of seizure, Shivaun. He was almost convulsing a little while ago, but she won't let me near him, and I didn't dare force the issue. Maybe you can reason with her."

"*Laia* Ta'ai," Shannon said, brushing past Deller to confront the alien woman, "Doctor Deller was only trying to help. And pardon me for saying so, but you are not helping, so long as you continue to weep like a child and refuse to let us help *Lai* Muon."

"They will kill us! They will eat us all!" Ta'ai wept, shaking her head frantically. "Muon has seen it. Muon knows!"

"What has he seen, *Laia* Ta'ai?" Shannon asked, quietly reaching one hand behind her for the hypo that Deller had been trying to administer. "No one aboard this ship is going to eat you, I promose. You're perfectly safe."

Despite Shannon's caution, Ta'ai saw the hypo change hands and shook her head, backing away wide-eyed.

"No, I must not sleep! *He* must not sleep! The Screamers in the Night will—"

But before she could tell them what the Screamers in the Night would do, one of the other aliens came from behind and pinned Ta'ai's arms to her sides, nodding for Shannon to move. Ta'ai screeched and hiccuped and tried to twist away, but not before Shannon pressed the hypo firmly to her throat, quickly confirming the setting before she triggered it. Even as the hiss of the hypospray died away, Ta'ai was slumping into her captor's arms. The alien deposited her in an empty berth opposite Muon's, then motioned Shannon closer to the weakly thrashing elder.

"I am Bana, brother to Ta'ai," he said haltingly as the med tech moved in to monitor Ta'ai's condition. "You help Muon now?"

"I will, if you can tell me what's wrong," Shannon

replied exchanging the hypo for a medscan pickup that Deller handed her and bending closer to run it along the length of Muon's body. As Wallis and Mather edged a little closer, Bana swallowed visibly and bowed his head.

"I think we all in very great danger, Doctor. Muon is seer. He has second sight." He glanced up cautiously, as if expecting a rebuff, and added, "Is true."

"I don't doubt it for a minute," Mather murmured. "Please go on."

Bana glanced nervously at the gold bullion crowns on Mather's shoulder boards and collar, then at Shannon.

"Is—is all right to talk in front of crown man?" he ventured.

"Yes, he's a friend," Shannon said. "And the lady is another doctor. Tell us, Bana."

"I—I tell." Bana sighed. "Short while ago, Muon go into—worship trance. I not know your word, but that is close to idea. Muon fine at first. He one of best seers I know. But soon see devils in dark, with eyes like fire sparks—and fangs. And devils in dark named Death. Muon very afraid."

"What do the devils look like, Bana?" Mather asked, afraid he already knew all too well.

"You should know, Crown-man-*Lai*," Bana returned. "You bring devils on board ship. Maybe you not know. But soon, too late for all of us."

"Why don't you step over here and tell me what you mean by that?" Mather said, taking the uneasy Bana firmly by the elbow and drawing him aside. "Muon will be fine with Doctor Shannon."

The other aliens clustered closer as they reazlied Mather had shifted into their own language to continue questioning Bana, leaving Shannon and Wallis to examine the still delirious Muon in peace. The elder alien had stopped his violent thrashing and was now merely moaning and rolling his head from side to side, eyes closed.

"He's going to burn himself out, if he keeps this up," Shannon said, frowning as she clamped one hand to Muon's thin wrist and carefully lifted an eyelid with the other. "Del, let's give him three units of Suainol. Even for an Aludran, his heart rate and pressure are too high, and there's something else going on that I don't begin to understand."

"He still in worship trance," Bana stated firmly, craning his neck to see what Shannon was doing before Mather recalled him to his questioning.

As Deller passed another hypo to Shannon, Wallis's hand shot out to close around her wrist.

"Wait," Wallis said. "I have an idea. Give him only half that dose for now. If you give him all of that, he'll be out for a full sleep-cycle—maybe even longer. I'd like to try to find out more about why he's so frightened."

Shannon glanced pointedly at her hand, and Wallis slowly released it. Though Shannon withdrew the hypo casually, she made no move to change the setting.

"I'm responsible for this patient's physical well-being, Doctor Hamilton. I'm afraid that my responsibility has to come before your curiosity."

"It's more than curiosity," Wallis replied. "Look: Mather and I are somewhat familiar with this worship trance that Bana was talking about. I think we can use it to our advantage. There's been an implication that our cats are responsible for Muon's condition, and Muon himself has given a warning. I respect the Aludrans' abilities far too much to discount that warning without further investigation."

"Are you saying that your cats *are* Devils in the Dark, Doctor?" Shannon said. "Come, now. That's superstitious nonsense."

Wallis shook her head. "Perhaps part of it is. But I think it's worth a little investigation to find out what triggered this particular superstitious response in this particular Aludran. They don't normally succumb to emotional scenes, Shannon—especially a *lai* of Muon's caliber. If you merely brush it off, you'll be doing him and us a great disadvantage."

Shannon sighed and glanced down at the still moaning Muon, at her medical scanner, then reluctantly slapped the hypo into Wallis's open palm and stepped aside.

"You leave me little choice, don't you, Doctor? If I were to refuse at this point, your husband probably would invoke the authority of the Imperial government and you'd still have your way." She folded her arms resignedly as Wallis readjusted the instrument. "At least the half dose should bring his vital signs closer to normal, which is the critical factor right now. I guess it can't hurt to try to talk to him."

The hypo hissed against the inside of Muon's thin wrist. "No, and it might help," Wallis said. "Mather, I'll need you in just a minute."

Mather, who had continued to converse quietly with the other aliens while his wife and Shannon argued, came closer as Wallis took Shannon's scanner, checked its readings, then administered a small additional amount of medication. The other aliens crowded in behind and around Mather as he pulled a chair closer to Muon's bedside and sat.

"He should be ready," Wallis murmured.

Mather nodded. "Okay, let's give it a try. *Lai* Muon, my name is Mather Seton. Bana said it would be all right if I talked with you. Are you more comfortable now?"

Muon nodded slightly, his eyes peacefully closed, the hawklike features relaxed. Mather, with a quick glance at his wife, then at Shannon, let one hand lie lightly across Muon's wrist. With his other hand he shaded his own eyes, resting his elbow on the chair arm.

Lai Muon, I am going to ask you a few questions. I want you to relax and listen to what I say. To make it easier for you, I will speak your language. *Essa di?*"

Again, the slight nod.

"Farsh. Durada-dan i?"

"Muon Vai-di-Chorrol, Lai Murrata gogorros e-do."

"Farsh. Sura-kei?"

The dialogue went on for nearly a quarter hour, Mather speaking in a soothing monotone and Muon responding at first in monosyllables, then in more complicated patterns of which Wallis caught the general drift, even if Shannon did not. Finally, Mather sighed and raised his head, then stood and signed for Wallis to give the rest of Shannon's previously prescribed medication. The other aliens gave him respectful nods as he glanced at them before turning back to Shannon.

"You might ask Doctor Deller or one of your other people to stay with him through the night. He's been through quite an ordeal today, between his visions and my questioning. I'm afraid I pushed him pretty hard."

Shannon nodded. "I can't spare Deller for very long, but Jacy can stay," she said, nodding to the med tech. "Did you find out anything useful, after all that?"

"We can talk about it on the way to the hold," Mather said, making a slight bow to the Aludrans as he began moving toward the door. "I'd like to check on the cats again, before turning in."

With a nod to her assistant, Shannon followed Mather and Wallis out into the corridor. The normal ship's temperature was like the cold of deep space by comparison, and their fatigue came sinking down on them with the return of normal gravity.

"Well?" Shannon asked, as they headed again toward the crew lift.

Mather managed a weary smile. "I'm not sure how much of this is going to make sense to you, Doctor, but it explains a lot to *me*, and I think it will to Wallis. It fits in with what Torrell was saying at dinner, too, though I'm not about to tell *him* that. Apparently the Aludrans have a mythic tradition—call it a racial memory, if you like—in which large, catlike creatures figure as the local equivalent of devils. They're actually more green than blue, and they have tiny tentacles instead of proper cat whiskers, but the similarity is close enough, when one is dealing with the subconscious."

"Then you think that this . . . racial memory was triggered when Muon saw the cats this morning, and that's what brought on the attack?" Shannon asked.

Mather nodded. "But that doesn't explain tonight's episode, at least not directly. Oh, seeing the cats earlier certainly didn't help, and it's possible that this worship trance that Bana mentioned somehow allowed Muon to do waking dream work of some kind—and in this case, all the terrors associated with the racial memories came flooding to the surface."

"But to let such superstition take control of him," Shannon said thoughtfully. "Muon is an educated man, Commodore. What does he think the cats are going to do to him?"

"You said it yourself, Doctor, though I don't think you realized how true it was," Wallis said. "He thinks they're going to eat him. Ta'ai said it, too. So did Muon. I understood enough to catch that much."

"But that's ridiculous," Shannon said flatly. "The Lehr cats aren't demons. There's no way they're going to get loose and go on a rampage on this ship."

They stepped into the elevator, and Mather cocked his head in Shannon's direction as she pushed the button for the cargo level.

"You know that, Doctor, and Wallis and I know that. But we aren't necessarily talking about rational responses, when dealing with the subconscious. And don't forget that Muon is a seer among his own people. They believe he is, and we don't dare discount that belief. As to how he thinks our cats are going to do it, I couldn't even speculate, and I doubt if he could, either."

"He'd probably say it was magic!" Shannon said with a snort. "What do you mean, he's a seer? That he can see the future?"

"Well, glimpses of future factors, perhaps," Wallis said. "I know it sounds farfetched, but you must remember that the Aludrans are a semitelepathic race among their own kind, with highly developed skills in several areas that we ordinarily classify as other than 'science.' Of course, Muon sees in symbols that he then has to translate into language, and Mather might easily misinterpret, especially since he isn't Aludran himself. But even if Muon isn't talking about physical death at all," Wallis went on, "I'm not certain that mental or psychic death is a great deal more appealing. Why don't we take another look at the cats, just to be sure?"

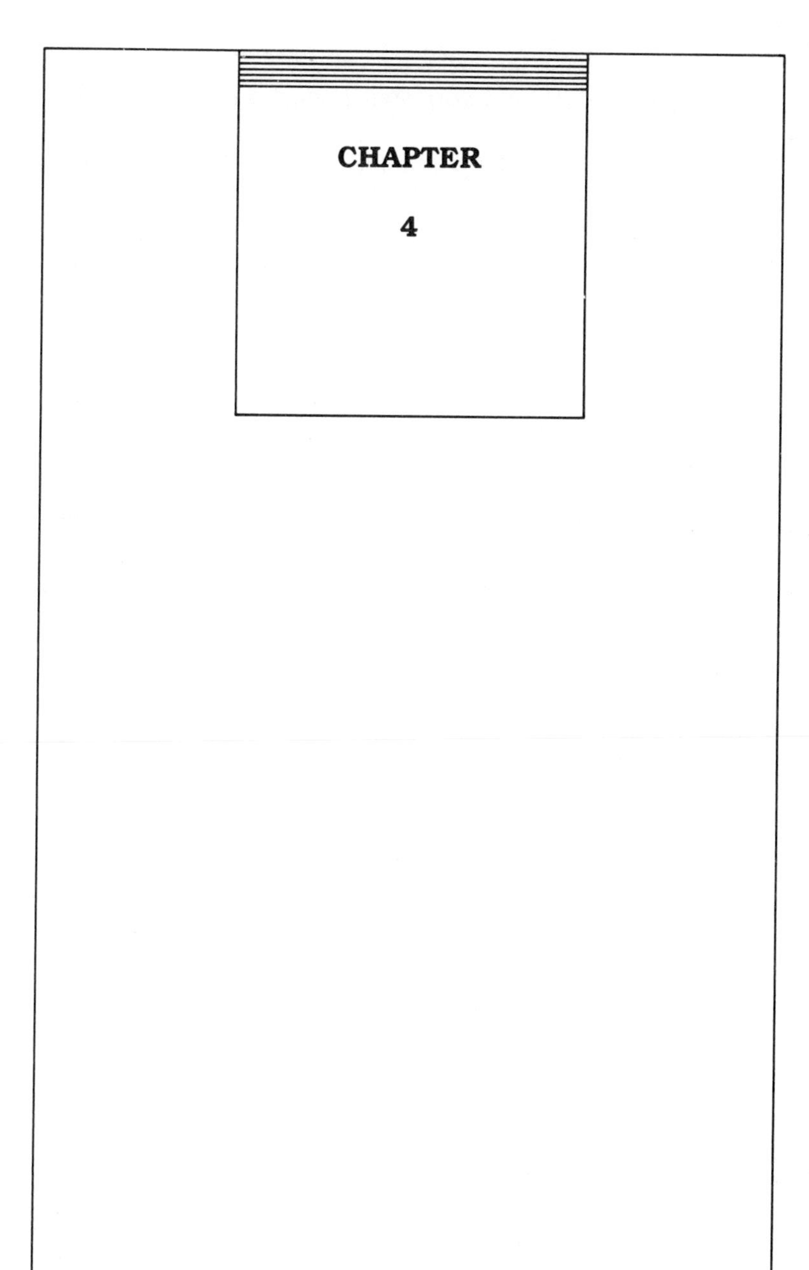

CHAPTER

4

They heard the cats' screaming long before they reached the hold where the animals were being kept. The sound assailed them from the instant they stepped off the lift at the opposite end of the cargo deck—which was all but deserted, for nonessential personnel had already found pressing reasons to quit that deck in favor of duties elsewhere.

Physically, at least, the cats' hold seemed to be secure enough. Safe behind the double security lock that guarded the only entrance, the animals prowled back and forth restlessly in the plasteel cages that were now reconnected into one long run. But their screams were almost deafening, running a shrill, three-plus octave range that grated even beyond hearing.

"Good God!" Mather said, drawing the Ranger named Perelli into the relative haven of the adjoining security room, while Wallis went to the scanners with Shannon. "How long have they been doing this?"

Perelli grimaced. "Long enough, sir. They started right after we reconnected the cages, and they haven't really stopped since."

"Well, did someone pinch their tails or something? They sound like they're in pain."

"If they are, it isn't from anything that shows on a

medscan," the man replied glumly. "They're together, they've got fresh food and water, the cages are clean. We've about decided they just like to hear themselves scream. Peterson even tried singing to them."

Even Mather had to laugh at that, for Peterson's voice was notably deficient in any quality that might soothe the savage beast. While Wallis ran repeated medscans on each cat, Mather reviewed the security tapes, looking for some anomaly that might account for the change in the cats' behavior—such as some outside visitor who might have stirred them up. But after nearly half an hour, they were forced to conclude that, for want of a better explanation, the cats simply preferred screaming, just now. And whatever had caused Muon's most recent distress, the cats seemed to have had no part in it, at least directly.

"Well, I'm sure *I* haven't any idea what it all means," Shannon said when it became apparent they were not going to find an easy answer. "Give me human patients, any day—speaking of which, I suppose I ought to get back and see whether any new crises have arisen in the last hour, before I turn in. I'll also look in on Muon. Let me know if there's anything I can do to help."

After a last inspection of the security arrangements in the hold, Mather and Wallis, too, returned to their cabin. Mather was almost fidgeting as he sat down in front of the library console and began tapping in a query, pausing only to open the stiff collar of his dress tunic.

"Mather, we've already read everything in print about Lehr cats," Wallis said, coming to read over his shoulder as she began taking down her hair. "If it wasn't in the Menkar Banks, I doubt we're going to find it in a starliner's library."

Mather only nodded and kept on typing. "Maybe not. But we haven't talked to this particular computer before. Maybe it will be able to suggest a new logic pattern for us. The whole thing might be so simple that we're not seeing it."

"You really think so?"

"No."

Wallis shook out her hair and began brushing it, watching as the green letters of Mather's query crawled across the screen.

Reference: dominant life forms of Eta Canis Majoris II. Cross-reference parapsychic makeup of principal humanoid species, commonly called Aludrans, with that of dominant life forms of Beta Geminorum III (Il Nuadi), especially species known as Lehr cats. Respond.

The library's response was almost immediate.

Humanoids of planet Eta Canis Majoris II, hereafter called Aludrans, reported possessed of limited telepathic abilities within own species. A spoken version of the written language persists from pre-telepathic days and has been revived since the advent of contact with other races. (See "Aludran language.")

Dominant life form of planet Beta Geminorum III (Il Nuadi) is homo sapiens, inhabitants descended from human stock seeded on planet during earth expansion period preceding Cruaxi Sweep. (See "Cruaxi Sweep"; Alien encounters; etc.) Extensive evidence remains of a pre-Cruaxi native race, briefly coexistent with the first human colonists, but no further sign following recontact by the Lawry Expedition in A.I. 42. (See Lawry, Sir Gregory. The Imperium Expands: An Account of the First Rediscovery Expeditions in the Former Fernmeyer Consortium. *Menkar: The Imperial Press, A.I. 51. See also Torrell, Vander.* Lost Alien Races. *Ravanah, Hyadum Primus IV: The Dursah Free University Press, A.I. 92.)*

Mather's hand hovered over the cancel button as the Torrell citation ticked up the screen, but he restrained the impulse as the reference continued.

Native life forms originating on Il Nuadi display

varying degrees of advanced psychic development in area of empathy, especially among carnivorous species. No known contact between Aludrans and life forms of Il Nuadi until recent times.

The readout continued, but it soon became clear that the information was becoming more general rather than less. Perplexed, Mather cleared the keyboard and glanced at Wallis, but she had stopped her hair brushing to focus elsewhere, apparently grappling with some nuance of possibility suggested by the reference. After a moment of contemplation, Mather hit the query button again and began tapping out another question.

Reference, Lehr cats. Are they included in description just given of native life forms of Beta Geminorum III? Respond.

The response came back at once.

No further data available on psychic abilities of Lehr cats. Though Lehr cats were first discovered and classified in A.I. 43 by Doctor Samuel Lehr (q.v.), no successful research has been—

Resignedly, Mather hit the cancel button with his fist and swiveled to glance at Wallis. She had resumed brushing her hair, returned from wherever she had gone on her mind wandering.

"Well, what do you think?" he asked.

"That the cats are screaming telepathically? It *is* possible, I suppose. In fact, it would be a handy talent for a predator whose main source of food is other empathic animals. I've never gotten any readings that would indicate telepathic sensitivity in the cats, but I wasn't looking for it, either. There's a lot we don't understand about the mechanisms of psychic phenomena."

"That much is certain," Mather agreed, thinking of his own off-again, on-again psychic abilities. "Is there any way we could find out for sure? About the cats, I mean."

Wallis thought for a moment, then said, "I could probably rig some kind of testing device and give it a try. We might be able to borrow the necessary equipment from Doctor Shannon. I can't promise any results, though."

"That's understood."

"On the other hand," Wallis continued, "after so many years of watching your hunches turn out to be correct, I'm definitely inclined to follow up. I'll get an equipment list to Shannon first thing in the morning."

Mather nodded and shut down the console, yawning hugely as he undid the rest of the fastenings on the front of his tunic. "Sounds good to me. Meanwhile, I suppose we ought to get some sleep, while we can. At least we know the cats are secure; and Muon isn't going anywhere for the rest of the night."

Wallis nodded and yawned in response, slipping her arms around his neck from behind to lay her head wearily against his. "That's the best idea either of us has had all day."

"Doctor Deller, I think the head steward poisoned me."

The voice coming from the treatment room next to Shannon's office was strident and irritating, making Shannon very glad that it was not her turn to handle sick call this morning. The all too predictable exchange about to run its course in the next room would be good experience for the younger Deller, but Shannon wanted no part of it other than to eavesdrop through the slightly open door, to see how well Deller handled it. She pretended to be absorbed in updating her medical log as Deller murmured some neutral response. The scenario had been nearly the same every day since Jacob Carvan had come aboard.

"You think I'm joking, don't you, Doctor?" the voice went on. "Well, I'm not. He *has* poisoned me!"

"Now, Mister Carvan, why would Mister Verley do

anything like that? I'm sure you just have a hangover."

"A hangover? Doctor, do you think I don't know what a hangover feels like? I tell you, I was poisoned! I want you to put the medical findings in my records."

"Drink this, please, Mister Carvan."

A slight silence. Then: "This isn't going to do any good, you know. I've been poisoned, and I know there isn't any antidote. If I should somehow manage to survive, I intend to press charges against—get him out of here!"

The sound of an outer door closing was followed by the voice of the chief steward himself, not at all amused.

"I found this in his cabin, Doctor Deller. According to the serial number, he bought the bottle from ship's stores only yesterday. If he drank it all last night, no wonder he thinks he's been poisoned."

"Now, see here, young man!" That was the passenger. "If you're trying to imply that I can't hold my liquor, then you're a liar as well as a poisoner! I felt fine last night until you brought me that Tauci toddy. You tried to poison me, and you can't wiggle out of it that easily!"

"Furudite whiskey and a Tauci toddy?" the steward mumbled under his breath. "Well, no wonder. Doctor, we had no way of knowing he'd be foolish enough to mix the two. He's still not sober."

"I am as sober as—as . . ."

Abruptly the voice trailed off, followed by the unmistakable sound of a body slumping to the floor.

"Orderly," Deller called.

Shaking her head slightly, Shannon leaned back far enough in her chair to peer into the next treatment room, where Deller and the steward were holding up an unconscious Jacob Carvan. A heavyset orderly was bringing in an antigravity floater from the outer corridor.

"Everything all right, Doctor?" Shannon asked, grinning a little as Deller glanced in her direction.

Deller sighed and made a wry face. "When are *you* going to start covering morning sick call again?" he said as he helped lift Carvan onto the floater. "Yesterday, it was Darroweed and Tejat brandy, and he was convinced he was going to dissociate on the spot. Today—well, I guess you heard. And tomorrow, who knows what new combination he'll dream up? One of these days, he *is* going to poison himself."

"You have to admit, though, it's good training for *you.*"

"Yeah, I get all the luck," Deller said ruefully, though he started chuckling as he watched the unconscious Carvan taken out of the treatment room. "You don't suppose he *likes* having his stomach pumped, do you?"

Shannon was still considering the amazing ill judgment of some of their passengers a few minutes later, when Mather and Wallis arrived.

"Well, good morning," she said, switching off her log as she motioned them to seats. "Should I assume, since you're here so early after last night's little escapade, that you've come up with some more ideas about our Aludran friends? You can close the door, if this is apt to get complicated."

Mather closed the door, but he shook his head. "It isn't complicated, and it isn't even directly about the Aludrans," he said, taking a seat beside Wallis. "We've come up with a theory we'd like to test on the cats."

"Well, they're your cats." Shannon paused a beat, then added, "What kind of a theory?"

"More like a conjecture, actually," Wallis said, giving Shannon a folded piece of paper from her jumpsuit pocket. "This is a list of equipment we'd like to borrow, if you've got it. Or, if you haven't got some of the things, we may be able to improvise. We think the cats might be slightly telepathic, especially on the sending end. The Aludrans are, you know."

"Hmmm, I remember reading that," Shannon said,

a little preoccupied as she scanned over the list. "But, I don't see what that has to do with—"

As her desk console shrilled an alert, a red light flashed beside the screen. Shannon punched the receive button in an automatic gesture, without looking up.

"Shannon."

"Deck Three Security, Doctor. We have an emergency coming in for you: two passengers in shock or hysterics and a DB."

"A body?"

Shannon gasped as she looked up at the expression on the face of the security guard. Without taking her eyes from him, she slapped the signal button for Deller and the nursing staff to stand by for an emergency.

"What happened?" she demanded. "Who died?"

"A passenger—we think his name is Fabrial. And he didn't just die; he was murdered."

"Murdered?"

"That's right. The other two coming in found him. They're too shaken up to give us a statement, so we're going to let you handle that when you get them calmed down. We'll send the body as soon as we've finished the on-site investigation."

"You're sure he's *dead?"* Shannon insisted.

"Oh, yeah, he's dead, all right."

A commotion in the outer office announced the arrival of the passengers in question, and Shannon dashed to assist. Mather and Wallis glanced at one another, at the face of the security officer just before he cut off, then moved into the doorway to watch and listen. Two stewards were bringing in a weeping woman of about thirty, Deller directing them into an adjoining treatment room and calling for a nurse. A dazed and shocky-looking middle-aged man had paused just inside the door to the outer office, a security officer supporting him under one elbow. There was a smear of drying blood on the back of the man's hand

and across the front of his expensive tunic and another barely visible on the guard's maroon sleeve.

"Lord Elderton and his wife," Shannon murmured under her breath. "Just what we needed. Del, that's Lady Elderton—I think her first name is Anne. Just sedate her and stabilize until I can come and get a statement."

As she turned her attention to Lord Elderton himself, she was not pleased to see that her instructions had elicited no response whatever from him.

"Matt, is he injured?" she asked the guard, gripping Elderton's wrist to find a pulse—which was racing but strong—but getting no sign of conscious awareness. "What happened? Did you see anything?"

The guard shook his head. "Not really, Doctor. The victim was already dead when I got there. Lord Elderton was kneeling beside him, just moaning and rocking back and forth on his heels, and the lady was screaming. That's what brought us running. He wouldn't say much, but I got the impression that he saw at least part of what happened. I'm pretty sure he got to the victim before he died."

"Is there any chance he did it?" Shannon asked, passing her hand back and forth in front of her patient's eyes without getting even a blink.

"None," the guard said flatly.

"All right, let's get him inside," Shannon said, leading them briskly through her office and into the adjoining treatment room, where Mather joined in helping lift their listless patient onto the padded table. When Wallis pitched in, swinging standard diagnostic equipment into position from above, Shannon began loading a hypospray. Elderton's eyes continued to stare blankly.

"I'll take over from here, Matt," Shannon said to the guard. She consulted the scanners while calibrating the hypo. "Thanks for bringing him in. Make sure someone notifies me as soon as the body arrives. And if the captain hasn't already been informed, make sure he is."

"Right, Doctor."

As soon as the man closed the door behind him, Mather and Wallis moved closer to the other side of the table to watch what Shannon was doing. Elderton had closed his eyes.

"I think we can safely assume, for now, that this is the victim's blood," Shannon said, gesturing at the smear on the tunic before injecting the man over the right jugular. "I'll turn the lab loose on it after I've stabilized him and gotten a statement. You realize, of course, that you shouldn't really be here for this."

Mather raised an eyebrow. "Would you rather we left?"

Shannon managed a strained smile. "I guess not. Frankly, I'd be grateful for your assistance. Forensic medicine is not an area that's stressed in the training one gets for starliner practice. I know the basics, of course, but—well, in your line of work, I'm sure you've witnessed this sort of thing many times. I think I can handle a simple statement without any problem, but remind me if I forget anything."

"Glad to help," Wallis said.

While they talked, Elderton's medication had made him relax, his vital signs settling to those of repose. Shannon gave him another few seconds, checking the medscan readouts again, then reached above the table and pulled down a recording pickup, positioning the microphone near the patient's mouth and aiming the camera with a dim green light. A touch to a test circuit, a minor adjustment of the alignment of the camera, and then she was drawing back to lean the heels of both hands on the edge of the table and watch her patient's face.

"Can you hear me, Lord Elderton? Just relax and let your medication take the edge off. I know you've just been through a terrible experience, but you're perfectly safe now, and you're going to be just fine. We do need a statement from you, though. Do you think you can tell me what happened? Just nod your head if you think you can."

The man's chin moved slightly as he wet his lips, and then he nodded.

"Very good." She glanced at the microphone and drew a deep breath before going on.

"Let the record show that this is a medical interview and preliminary statement of passenger Robert, Earl of Elderton. Attending physician is Doctor Shivaun Shannon, Chief Medical Officer, Gruening Novaliner *Valkyrie*. Witnessing: Doctor Wallis Hamilton and Fleet Commodore Mather Seton, Imperial Service."

She glanced across at them and raised an eyebrow, continuing at Mather's nod.

"Patient Elderton was brought to Medical Section this date suffering from severe emotional shock, allegedly caused by witnessing some portion of a murder. Stabilization was achieved by administering .5 cc pentomerisol over the right jugular vein. Interview follows.

"Lord Elderton, can you hear me? Answer, please."

Elderton managed a weak, "Yes."

"Very good. Now, I want you to tell me what happened up on Deck Three that upset you so."

Elderton wet his lips again and started to shake his head weakly from side to side, screwing his eyes more tightly shut.

"God, I can't! It was too terrible! I don't want to remember."

"I know it isn't pleasant, my lord, but we have to know what you saw." Shannon's voice was quietly insistent. "Think back to just before it happened now. You're walking down the companionway on Deck Three." She paused. "Where were you coming from?"

"I—I'd been in my cabin. I was on my way to breakfast."

"That's fine. You're doing just fine. Was there anyone with you?"

"My—my wife, Anne. But—oh, God, don't let her see it! It's awful!"

"Easy, my lord. Your wife is perfectly safe. Just relax. There's nothing to be afraid of now. It isn't really happening again. It's only a memory. Now, you're walking down the companionway on Deck Three with your wife, on your way to breakfast. Did something unusual happen then?"

Elderton swallowed noisily, but he went on. "I—I heard a scream. Only, it wasn't really a scream—it was more like a—a gurgle, like someone drowning. Oh, God, I don't want to remember!"

"You must remember, my lord. It's important. Now, you heard a scream, or some strange sound that frightened you. Then what happened?"

"I—I came around the corner by the luggage storage room, and there was Gustav, lying in a pool of blood. We—" He choked back a sob. "We'd had dinner with him, just last night."

He covered his face with his hands and started to shake, but Shannon gently pulled the hands away, continuing to hold them loosely on his chest.

"I'm so sorry, my lord. Can you tell me the rest of Gustav's name?"

"It's F-Fabrial—Gustav Fabrial. We—went to school together. He—oh, please! No more!"

"Shhhh—just relax now," she crooned. "It isn't really happening now. I'm sorry to have to put you through this, but please try to tell me the rest. Did you see anyone around him?"

Elderton swallowed and shook his head, apparently calming a little under Shannon's touch.

"N-no."

"All right. This is going to be the hardest now, but I need you to tell me about Gustav. Was he still alive when you found him?"

Tears streaming openly down his face now, Elderton nodded. "He—he was on his stomach. He—was moaning. I ran to him and turned him over— God, there was blood all over the front of him! And on the carpet under him! And he was gasping something about blue, and eyes—eyes coming after him—golden eyes! Only, he c-couldn't really speak, because his throat—oh, I can't!"

"Just relax, my lord," Shannon murmured, glancing uncomfortably at Wallis and Mather and selecting another hypospray. "Just a little longer. Try to remember. Did he say anything else?"

"No. He just—died—there, in my arms—and there was nothing I could do. And there was blood everywhere, and—please, no more! I don't want to remember any more. No more, please!"

"All right. There's no more. You've done just fine." The hypo hissed as she triggered it against his neck again. "Go to sleep now. Relax and go to sleep."

Meticulously, then, and without turning off the recorder or looking at Wallis and Mather, who were exchanging puzzled glances, Shannon pulled another instrument down to point at Elderton, focusing an aiming light squarely between his eyes. After adjusting a timer, she keyed the machine with her thumbprint. The light pulsed blue for several seconds, emitting a low-pitched, throbbing hum, then cycled off. She would not look at either of her observers as she pushed the instrument back into place and removed the cartridge from the recorder.

"Go ahead and lecture me, Doctor Hamilton," she said, laying the cartridge on a counter behind her and leaning against the edge to look at them at last. "You, at least, must know what I just did."

Wallis nodded. "I have to say I'm surprised, however. I wouldn't have expected you to mind-wipe a witness in a murder case."

"*And* totally without his consent—I know," Shannon replied. "Still, it was necessary. Of course, mind-wipe is really a misnomer, as I'm sure you know. When he wakes up in a few hours, secure in his berth, he'll be able to remember, if he really tries. It will all seem like a dream, though, without the gory details and without the emotional involvement of the actual occurrence. The memory isn't really lost, of course—any competent psychotechnician could easily retrieve it—but it's submerged and veiled in less threatening symbolism. We'll do the same for his wife. It's company policy, not mine."

"Company policy, to tamper with a free citizen's memory?" Mather said in a low voice.

Shannon sighed. "Commodore, the Gruening Line doesn't like adverse publicity. Incidents such as this could be damaging to the company's reputation. Now, I may not agree with company policy, but I work for Gruening, and I owe them for my professional training. That's why I'm here, after graduating at the head of my medical class, instead of serving a plushy residency on one of the major research satellites. Besides, the procedure isn't illegal. It's often done if the attending physician feels that a traumatic memory might be damaging to the patient's health."

"Or to the physician's health," Mather said.

"Or to her job," Shannon agreed. "That's another reason the recording was made. It constitutes a legal record of Elderton's statement, and it gets all of us off the hook, if the situation should be questioned later on."

Without waiting for further comment, Shannon pushed a call button and then left as an orderly and a med tech entered with a floater. She took the record of Elderton's statement with her. After the technician had taken several samples from the bloodstains on Elderton's hand and clothing and a sample from Elderton himself, he and the orderly shifted the unconscious man onto the floater and took him out.

Wallis and Mather followed in time to see Shannon coming out of Deller's treatment room, now with two cartridges in her hand, solemn and thoughtful as she watched Deller guide another floater out to follow the first, deeper into the back reaches of the medical facility. Before they could decide whether to approach her again, however, the outer door to the reception area drew aside to admit another floater—this one covered—escorted by a tense-looking med tech and a security officer.

No one said a word as Shannon directed the floater past her office and into one of the surgeries, she, herself, lowering it to the table—though the security man gave Mather and Wallis an odd look when they followed into the room and remained as Shannon switched on lights above the table. And as Shannon pulled back the covering from the body, both the technician and the security man watched Wallis and Mather for their reaction.

Wallis gasped. Mather stifled an oath. Shannon's face went white as her gaze swept the body.

But it was not the body itself, or even the victim's manner of dying, that had caused their varying reactions. The apparent cause of death was massive trauma to the throat—the obvious source of the blood reddening the entire front of the body, as Elderton had described—but the wound was no worse than many that all three of them had seen before. It was the victim's right hand that riveted their attention, the entire arm badly slashed and bloodied, several of the lacerations exposing tendon and bone.

And clutched in the dead man's fingers was a tuft of long, blue hairs.

CHAPTER

5

For an endless instant, no one spoke. The blue hairs said all. The horrible wounds on the rest of the body reinforced the growing conclusion that no one had yet dared voice. A stunned Shannon glanced at Mather in surprise as the big man abruptly roused himself and headed toward the door.

"Commodore, just where do you think you're going?"

Shannon's voice was strained, and Mather turned to glance at her and all of them as he paused by the intercom just inside the door and punched the call button. The screen lit immediately with the bright Gruening Line logo.

"ComNet," said a pleasant voice.

"ComNet, this is Commodore Seton, in Medical Section. Please connect me with the duty officer in my cargo hold, priority status one."

"Stand by."

Shannon stared at him aghast as he glanced at her again.

"I know what you must be thinking, Doctor," Mather said carefully, "and frankly, I can't say I blame you. We'll soon see whether your suspicions are justified."

"But, isn't it obvious to you what's happened?"

"I know what it *looks* like happened. ComNet, are

you having some problem getting through?"

Even as he spoke, the speaker chimed and the Gruening logo dissolved to the gaunt face of a Ranger named Webb.

"Webb here."

Drawing a deep breath, Mather glanced at Wallis, at Shannon and the body between them, at the med tech waiting uneasily behind them, and at the security guard, who looked as if he might just draw the needler on his hip.

"Mister Webb, is everything all right there in the hold?"

"Well, sir, I was just about to call you." Webb's drawl sounded strained. "There are two men here from ship's security, demanding to see the cats. They seem to think the critters got out and killed someone during the night."

"Is that possible?" Mather demanded. "And have you let them see the cats?"

"No to both questions, sir. I wasn't about to let them in with weapons, and they wouldn't disarm before coming in. The cats are fine, though. They're still making a lot of noise, of course, but—what's going on, sir?"

"I'll explain when I get there," Mather replied, glancing at the others again. "In the meantime, I want you and Wing or somebody to go over the security tapes, working backward from right now. Look for anything, *anything* out of the ordinary. Have you got that?"

"Well, yes, sir, but—what about the security men?"

"They'll just have to wait until I get there. I'm on my way."

As he slapped off the intercom and headed for the door again, Shannon started after him.

"But—wait a minute! Are you trying to say that your cats *aren't* responsible? That's ridiculous. Any idiot—"

"Any idiot can jump to conclusions based on circumstantial evidence, Doctor," Mather said, stopping her with a glance. "Why don't you get started on the autopsy, while I go and do what *I* do best? Wallis, give her a hand. And *you*—" He turned on the anxious security guard with a finger pointed like a pistol. "If you intend to come with me, don't even think about pulling a weapon or trying to arrest me. I have the authority to place this ship under martial law, if I have to, and I'll place *you* under arrest if you interfere."

"He'd do it, too," Wallis told the man, who hesitated to follow the retreating Mather. "But go ahead after him," she went on. "He knows you have a job to do. Just don't try to keep him from doing his."

Shannon, still agape at the entire exchange, dismissed the med tech with a gesture and tried to collect her wits.

"What does he mean, *circumstantial evidence?*" she blurted when the door had closed behind the technician. "And who's the idiot?" She gestured angrily at the mutilated body. "Look at the man, Doctor Hamilton!"

Wallis let out a slow sigh. "I know. And I did. I admit that it looks fairly clear-cut. But you and I are scientists. Let's look at the facts. If the cats really are responsible, I want to know as much as you do."

"The facts speak for themselves, Doctor."

"But, these aren't the only facts," Wallis argued. "Look, will you humor me for a few minutes? Let's think about this."

With a look of extreme cynicism, Shannon set the medical sensors to scanning for data and pulled a disposable lab gown from a shelf, tossing another to Wallis before putting hers on.

"Go ahead. I'm listening."

"All right. Let's suppose—just suppose—that we've never heard of Lehr cats."

"I wish *I* hadn't," Shannon muttered under her breath as she pulled on surgical gloves.

"I know. Just suppose. We're provincial doctors. We've never been off-planet, we've never heard of Lehr cats, we've never seen them—we have no idea that such creatures might exist."

"Oh, they exist, all right," Shannon said, rolling a cart with surgical instruments closer. "Just ask Gustav Fabrial."

Wallis ignored the younger physician's comment as she, too, gloved and resumed her inspection of the body.

"Now," she continued, "this man, this Fabrial, is brought in dead, and you, as chief medical officer, are asked to perform the autopsy and form a hypothesis as to cause of death. Remember, you've never heard of a Lehr cat. Fabrial could have been the victim of anyone or anything." She gestured toward Shannon with a probe. "Now, who killed Fabrial?"

Shannon, cutting away the dead man's jacket with a pair of surgical scissors, only shook her head. "This is pointless."

"No, don't quit on me already. Who killed Fabrial? What was the physical cause of death?"

Shannon gave a stubborn smile. "All right, just offhand, I'd say he died of shock, contingent upon massive loss of blood induced by trauma. . . ."

"Good. Go on."

"He has multiple lacerations of the chest and forearms"—she looked shrewdly at Wallis—"perhaps from claws—"

"We don't know that yet."

"Very well, then, Doctor—not *necessarily* claws, then. Let's say multiple parallel lacerations, approximately six to ten centimeters apart, in groups of four to five." She threw down her scissors. "Oh, come *on*, Doctor! From *claws!* What else could make wounds like that?"

Wallis bowed her head and worried her lower lip briefly with her teeth.

"All right, I'll accept that for now, if you insist. Go on."

"And multiple throat lacerations, especially along the lateral aspects," Shannon continued sourly. "From *teeth,* Doctor Hamilton! *Long* teeth, *sharp* teeth—*fangs,* if you will!"

Wallis leaned both hands against the edge of the table and nodded slowly. "I know. And long blue hairs clenched in his fist, presumably from the murderer. Ergo, something with long blue hair, fangs, and claws killed Fabrial. And that something could only have been a Lehr cat. I have to admit, it looks bad."

Shannon's jaw dropped and she stared at her colleague dumbly for a few seconds. "You mean," she finally managed to reply, "you're still not convinced? You still maintain that your cats didn't do it?"

"Do you want me to assert that I think the cats broke through plasteel, a force lock, and the regular door of the hold, evaded regular ship's security on three decks, and then killed Fabrial and got back without anyone being the wiser?" Wallis countered.

"The screamers-in-the-night can do thus," said a familiar voice.

They turned to see Muon and Bana standing in the doorway, swathed in their fur-lined robes and shaking with cold and dread.

"I know that the demons were responsible," Muon continued, walking farther into the room and staring expressionlessly at the bloody body on the table. "Did I not tell you that the demons would devour us all? And now it has begun."

The cats were screaming even worse than the night before when Mather reached Deck Six and headed toward their hold. Four confused ship's security guards came to attention as he approached: two Mather recognized from the night before, and two he had never seen.

"Commodore Seton, just what *is* going on?" one of the familiar guards demanded as Mather pushed his way between them and thumbed the intercom button on the panel outside the door. "When Burton and Lewis, here, came and asked to see the cats a little while ago, your Rangers chucked us all out. Burton says someone was murdered by one of the cats."

"We don't know that yet," Mather said tersely, "and my men were just following their orders." He glanced back at the door as the upper half transluced. Behind it, Perelli came to attention as he saw Mather. He had a heavy-duty stun carbine slung over his shoulder at the ready and was wearing a strange headset arrangement that completely covered his ears.

"Ah, Commodore Seton, am I glad to see you."

Two more Rangers with headsets backed up the first as the outer door sphinctered open just far enough for Mather to duck into the security lock, but their stun carbines discouraged the remaining security men from trying to follow. Unlike a needler, whose darts could kill if too many struck a victim, a stun weapon would disable a living target with five to ten minutes of excruciating, paralyzing pain but leave no lasting effect or damage beyond sore muscles for a few days, making it an ideal defensive weapon for use aboard a spacecraft—and one with which the civilian-trained security guards had no desire to contend.

"What's happened, Perelli?" Mather asked, as the Ranger took a fourth headset off a hook on the wall and handed it to him, and the other two took over at the door monitor. "Did ship's security give you any trouble? And what is this thing?"

"It helps filter out the cats' screaming, sir," Perelli replied. "Wing put the first one together last night, after you left, and engineering made up several more for us. They don't help a lot, but they're better than nothing. And you don't really think those security guys wanted to mess with *us*, do you, sir?" he added with a grin. "They obviously don't know what they're talking about, if they think the cats got past *us*."

"I hope not," Mather murmured, glancing beyond Perelli at the cat cages and their vocal occupants. "Where *is* Wing?"

"Reviewing the tapes, sir, just as you ordered. And I'd really advise using the headset, sir."

With a nod, Mather put the device over his ears and turned it on. He concluded, as he began moving closer to the cages, that any benefit to be derived from the device was as much psychological as anything else. He slipped it off and let it hang loosely around his neck as he continued around the cages, for he wanted no interference with natural perceptions.

To all outward appearances, however, nothing had changed since the night before. The cages were still joined end to end, the four units forming a long, plasteel-meshed run in which the animals were pacing restlessly. As Mather passed one end, the female they called Matilda stopped to glare at him; she raised one velvet-sheathed forepaw as if to strike at him through the mesh, her tail lashing hard against the side of the cage. But he ignored her.

He was looking, first, for physical evidence: for blood, for missing chunks of fur, for any sign of an altercation—but there was none. Visual inspection revealed nothing at all untoward about the cats' appearance. However, desultory readings with a pocket scanner did seem to indicate some registration of pain. He flipped on the big cage scanners and checked those, too.

Now, that *was* unusual. *Something* was wrong. Granted, no one really knew very much about Lehr cats, and Mather himself claimed no particular medical expertise, but no seemingly healthy creature ought to be radiating that kind of pain without some accompanying injury or illness.

But there was more to the wrongness than that. It

had nothing to do with anything he could see, but Mather was increasingly aware that something was not quite right about the area itself—the cages, or perhaps even the hold.

Puzzled, he tried extending his senses slightly, to see whether he could detect anything psychically unusual. Something was out there to be read, but he could not seem to zero in on it. The sheer decibel level in the hold made it hard to concentrate. He slipped the headset back over his ears, but that only seemed to make matters worse, so far as his sketchily reliable psi abilities were concerned.

Very well. He shut down mentally and sighed. He was simply going to have to do this the hard way.

Casually he glanced over his shoulder at the Rangers. Perelli was busy logging something in his shift report, his two partners were watching the security guards still waiting outside, and the rest must be ensconced with Wing and Webb in the security room. He could see the dark green lump of someone lying in one of the hammocks the Rangers had strung at one end of the room so they could sleep during off-duty hours without leaving the premises. If Mather was careful, he should have things over and done before anyone was the wiser.

Slowly he made his way around the cages again, this time studying the room, rather than the cats, until he found a place he liked, where he could stand in the window of a stanchion without being closely observed, from either the door or the office. He pulled the headset around his neck again—he would simply have to put up with the auditory distraction until he could block it out—then leaned his shoulders and back against the bulkhead and let his head tip back, locking his knees to brace himself against the bulkhead. His hands fell loosely to his sides as he cleared his mind and took the three deep breaths that would—he hoped—trigger deep psi sensitivity. It would have been easier with the right medication to ease the transition, but he had done it cold before. (He had also come up blind, under the best of circumstances.) He never knew for certain whether it would work, but this time it did.

Slowly the sounds of the cats' screaming, the tiny vibrations of the ship, and even the pressure and chill of the bulkhead at his back began to fade from awareness. He let his eyes drift shut as he turned all his attention inward. After several moments of mental quieting, he gradually began to see though his mind's eyes.

He did not like what he saw. He was aware of the cats pacing in their cage, each of them radiating fear and the pain the scanners had detected earlier. In fact, he could distinguish among the cats in a way he had never been able to do before—not that he had ever tried to read an animal's mind. The level of pain varied from cat to cat, with the larger of the two females being most distressed by the sensation.

But the cats' discomfiture was not the sum total of pain around him. As Mather pushed his awareness farther to include other life forms in the hold, he was startled to realize that the pain extended to himself and the Rangers as well—though theirs was not nearly as intense as the cats' and registered only as mild but persistent headaches.

More than a little curious at that, and able to block his own pain now that he had become aware of it, Mather broadened his sensitivity to read the inanimate structure of the hold itself, sweeping his attention over the cages, the equipment, even the bulkheads, searching for something, anything out of the ordinary that might account for the pain he was reading from both cats and men.

He missed it the first time around. He almost missed it the second. But just before he was about to try a third sweep, he detected a blur of psychic noise to his right that grated like a fingernail on stone.

Slowly he slit his eyes open, visually inspecting the suspect bulkhead and integrating optical input with psychic. Another stanchion rose directly across from him, similar to the one whose shadow camouflaged him. The psychic static he had finally brought into focus seemed to be coming from that direction.

Still psychically open, Mather roused his body and forced it to move cautiously toward the place in question, bracing one hand against the bulkheads at his right, blocking the screams of the cats at his left, each careful step a conscious act. Bending to peer behind the bulk of the stanchion, he hesitated only briefly before extending his hand tentatively toward a flat, featureless gray box the size of his open palm; it clung to the back of the metal support. Though he did not touch it, he knew instantly that somehow the box was the source of the pain he had been reading.

With a blink, he was back in normal consciousness, the cats' screams reverberating at his back. He took a deep breath as he straightened and glanced toward the door and the security station. Most of the Rangers were still engrossed in their own duties and probably had not even noticed his silence or his stealth, but Perelli was watching him curiously.

"Perelli, would you come here, please?"

Perelli said something to the two Rangers at the door, then came on the run. Mather took out his pocket medscanner and made an adjustment as the man approached; then he dropped down on his hunkers to point behind the stanchion with bland detachment.

"Ever seen that before?"

Perelli looked, then gestured for one of the other Rangers by the door and shook his head as the other man came and gave a similarly negative response.

"And you're sure that no one has been around the cats?" Mather insisted, running his scanner close above the box's gray crackle finish and studying the readouts.

"Only authorized personnel, sir," Perelli replied, puzzled. "Webb and Wing are still going over the tapes, but—you don't think it's a bomb, do you, sir?"

"No. Nor does it appear to be booby-trapped to prevent what I'm about to do."

He handed the scanner to Perelli, then touched the box gingerly with a fingertip before using both hands to slide it sideways and pry loose the limpet seal holding it in place. The device was featureless but for two slightly sunken screw heads on the underside, both faintly glowing red.

"Well, well," Mather muttered to himself, reaching into an inner jacket pocket for a flat, narrow case as the two Rangers looked on with interest.

Balancing the case on one knee, he extracted a slender, nonmetallic probe, the blade of which he fitted delicately to the right-hand screw and gave a minute turn to the left.

The result was far more dramatic than he had expected. As the screw moved, the cats immediately stopped screaming; but the watching Rangers gasped and clutched at their heads in pain so intense that they could not even cry out. Casey, Perelli's partner, even fell to his knees.

Quickly Mather turned the screw in the opposite direction, relieving the Rangers and momentarily enraging the cats again—and then, nothing. The screw stopped glowing, the cats stopped screaming, and the Rangers could finally blurt out a few dazed words of inquiry as to what had happened.

Ignoring their questions for just a moment longer, Mather tightened down the other screw until it, too, ceased glowing—fortunately, without further ill effect on those around him. He did not bother to speculate as to why he had not been affected, but it was fortunate he had not—for, judging by the Rangers' reactions, he doubted he could have functioned coherently enough to neutralize the device if he had been.

Wing and a shaken-looking Webb came running from the adjoining security room. They were followed by the Rangers who had been sleeping and Perelli's other partner from the door. Casey's voice finally began to cut through Mather's concentration.

"Commodore! Commodore Seton! What did you do?"

"What's going on, Commodore?" Wing echoed. "We were running the last of the tapes, and I thought the top of my head was going to come off!"

"Mine, too," said Casey. "I've never felt anything like that in my life! What was it, sir?"

Mather replaced his probe in its case and got ponderously to his feet, controlling the tendency of his knees to go a little wobbly in after-reaction. "Apparently, someone has left us a not-so-friendly gift," he said, hefting the box in his hand as he slipped the instrument case back inside his jacket. "As nearly as I can tell without further analysis, it's a psychic irritator of some sort, designed to focus random psychotronic energy and then disperse it on specific frequencies. In this case, it was tuned to enrage the cats and to hover just at the edge of human awareness—which would account for the cats' behavior and for the headaches and general irritability experienced by almost everyone who's had to work near the cats for any length of time since we came aboard. Call it a psychic itch, if that's a good image for you."

"But, where did it come from, sir?" asked Peterson, Perelli's second partner. "No one's been in here, except our people and ship's security, since we brought the cats aboard."

"The tapes confirm that, Wing?"

"Yes, sir. There's been absolutely no unauthorized entry."

"I see." Mather thought for a moment. Then: "Mister Webb, how clear a view did you actually have of this area on the tapes?"

Webb blinked and glanced at Wing, at the other Rangers, and back at Mather. "Are you asking if I think one of us could have planted the device, sir?"

"I'm asking you to eliminate that possibility for me," Mather said. "Can you go back through the tapes and see who, if anyone, had the opportunity to place such a device? I'm going to have to give Captain Lutobo some kind of report, after all, even if it's a negative one."

"We'll see to it sir," Webb said. "Is there anything else?"

Mather pursed his lips in thought, then glanced at the cats, now sitting or lying peacefully in their cages. One of the males was grooming a huge blue paw with studied nonchalance. The other male and his mate were observing the activities of the humans with bored indifference. The fourth cat had opted for a nap, and occasional snorts of contentment came from her end of the cage.

All eyes turned to follow Mather's line of attention, then returned to him questioningly. Mather's lips compressed in a grim line as he hefted the device in his hand. "As a matter of fact, there is something else that you can do. Wing, do you remember those force nets that we didn't use on Il Nuadi? I think it's time we broke those out and set up a new perimeter."

"Aye, sir, I can do that," Wing said with a nod. He looked puzzled. "But—is it true, what security said—that someone was murdered, and the evidence points to our cats?"

Mather sighed, glancing back at the cats reflectively. "That's the way security is reading the evidence," he conceded, "though there *has* to be another explanation. Doctor Hamilton is working on the autopsy with the ship's surgeon right now. Since I'm going to have to answer to Captain Lutobo far sooner than I'd like, I don't suppose anyone wishes to change his statement as to unusual occurrences here in the hold since last night?"

No one did. There was some nervous shuffling of feet, a cough or two, but each man continued to look directly at Mather without evasion. Mather smiled grimly, nodding acknowledgment of his faith in their competence.

"Thank you, gentlemen. That's the response I expected, but you understand why I had to ask. Mister Fredricks, I'll ask you and Neville to help Wing with the new perimeter setup, since you're both fresh. Peterson, you go on the tapes with Webb. Casey will have to man the door lock alone for now."

"Very good, sir."

"And Perelli," Mather continued as the others began dispersing to attend to their new assignments, "perhaps you can help me with something else. I want to take our gadget up to engineering and run some tests before I have to confront the captain. Who's their best electronics expert? Who helped build these earmuffs?"

As he pulled the headset from around his neck and handed it to Perelli, the Ranger shook his head.

"We worked with a Wes Brinson, sir. But I can't guarantee he's ever seen anything like this."

"I'd be surprised if he had." Mather smiled. "Frankly, I'll settle for an open mind and some cooperation."

He whistled a grim little tune under his breath as he left the hold and headed for the crew lift, fielding the questions of the waiting security men with a polite but firm "No comment" and picking up his escort again, in the process. The rest stayed to keep watch on the cats.

In Shivaun Shannon's surgery, meanwhile, the situation had deteriorated badly. Wallis's and her confrontation with the Aludrans quickly escalated to the point that Shannon was ready to call security to escort the aliens from the room, except that Captain Lutobo arrived—and *he* called the guards.

Within three minutes the aliens were gone, Lutobo

had viewed the body of the victim, and an abashed chief of security was trying in vain to explain what his men had been doing instead of protecting the ship's passengers. Lutobo was not inclined toward charity this morning.

"I find it truly incomprehensible that my entire staff could be this incompetent, Mister Courtenay." Lutobo was raging, and Shannon wished she could disappear through the floor. "A Lehr cat is not a small animal. I want to know how a creature that large could have made its way from the cargo level to Deck Three, and back, without anyone seeing it."

"We're looking for additional witnesses, Captain," Courtenay began, "but I only have so many men."

"For all the witnesses you've found, it doesn't appear it makes any difference *how* many men you have!" Lutobo retorted. "And Doctor Shannon, according to your testimony, the victim was still alive when Lord Elderton found him. From the damage done to the body, how long could Fabrial have survived, between the attack and his death? I can't imagine that even a Lehr cat could move *that* fast, in that kind of situation, and not have *someone* see it. Doesn't *anyone* have any answers?"

Shannon toyed with a power probe she had picked up from beside the now covered body of Fabrial, and Courtenay shifted uneasily from one foot to the other, not daring to drop his attitude of attention. Wallis had tried to make herself as unobtrusive as possible behind the draped body, for she had no more answers than Shannon or Courtenay, but her reprieve was short-lived.

"Well, Doctor Hamilton? I haven't heard *you* offering any brilliant explanations. And where is Commodore Seton?"

"I believe he's gone to check on the cats, Captain. We're aware how the situation must appear. I expect word from him at any moment."

"You say that as if there were some doubt of who's to blame," Lutobo retorted, moving to the intercom and punching the call button. "ComNet?"

"ComNet here."

"This is the Captain. I want you to locate Commodore Seton. He should be in the cargo hold where his damned cats are berthed."

"Stand by, please, Captain."

As the tally light beside the Gruening logo went from red to amber, the captain glanced at Wallis again.

"Come, now, Doctor. Speechless? I seem to recall being reassured by your people, several times, that this could never happen. I suppose it does make a difference when one has seen the mangled body of a victim, however. Even the most calloused—"

At the sound of a chime, the tally light went to red again and the image of a uniformed crewman appeared on the screen. The man was half turned away from the video pickup, but the permanent legend across the bottom of the screen identified the location as Engineering Section. As the crewman moved aside, Mather Seton stepped into frame.

"I thought you'd be with your Lehr cats, Commodore," Lutobo said icily, not waiting for Mather to speak first. "Why are you in Engin—what the devil is that?"

Mather, a look of resigned patience on his face, had held up a gray, metallic box with several wires trailing from it.

"I found it in the hold with the cats, Captain. *We* didn't place it here. Regarding the cats, I did not find any sign of blood, a fight, or tampering with the cages. Nor, according to your own security scanners and the testimonies of your and my men, has anything happened in the hold in the past twelve hours that could be construed as unusual in any way—which the exit of one of the cats certainly would be. Furthermore, *your* people tell me they've never seen this thing before, or even anything like it. I have my Rangers rechecking the security tapes now, just to see who even had the opportunity to plant it."

The captain glanced at Wallis and Shannon, both now standing to one side of him, then stared suspiciously at the object in Mather's hand.

"You still haven't answered my question, Seton. What is that?"

"Apparently, it's a psychic irritator," Mather replied. "It's a very sophisticated device, just to make a few Lehr cats feisty. It transmits psychotronic energy on a fairly narrow band. In this case, it was set on a frequency that would be irritating to the cats—and to humanoids, to varying degrees—but that could not be specifically detected otherwise, unless one knew precisely what to look for. Incidentally, this tends to confirm that the cats *do* scream telepathically, Wallis, though I'll still want to check that aspect more specifically, when we have the time.

"But even though the screaming may have had some effect on those within the cats' broadcast range—probably a few hundred meters, at most—I suspect that we'll find the bulk of the irritation—to the cats, the crew, and probably the Aludrans—was due to this transmitter."

"The Aludrans?" Lutobo said. "But, I just had them—Are you trying to tell me that they may also have been affected by that device?"

Mather cocked his head thoughtfully. "That's possible. It's just occurred to me that their cabins are on Level Five, right above the cargo deck—maybe even right above our hold. That could certainly explain last night. I thought at the time that Muon's reaction was a little excessive to be entirely self-induced. Wally, does that sound plausible to you?"

"Well, they *are* slightly telepathic already, so it makes sense that they'd be more susceptible to that kind of transmission," Wallis said. "And with Muon being a seer . . ."

Lutobo rubbed a hand across his jaw and frowned. "Well, could the Aludrans have—damn it, you two! You're getting me away from the point. The Aludrans didn't kill Fabrial! I don't see how the cats could have done it, either, but that's the only evidence we have to go on."

"Then who put that device in the hold, Captain?" Mather asked. "And why?"

"Well, it certainly wasn't the *Aludrans!*" Lutobo replied. "We all know they're afraid of the cats. They certainly wouldn't want to do anything to stir them up."

Shannon folded her arms across her chest in speculation. "But remember what Doctor Torrell said about cat legends at dinner last night, Captain. We know that the Aludrans see the cats of their own mythical tradition as demons. Maybe their own discomfort was worth it, to make the cats miserable."

"Doctor, you're beginning to sound like those two!" Lutobo snapped, gesturing toward Wallis and the electronic image of Mather. "The next thing I know, one of you will be trying to tell me that the cats aren't involved in this at all."

"Your own technology suggests their innocence, Captain," Mather said.

Lutobo's jaw tightened and he said nothing for several seconds. Then he carefully clapsed his hands behind his back and looked directly at Mather's image.

"I can't account for that just now, Commodore. I do know one thing, however. I want the guard doubled around those cats."

"I've already stepped up security, Captain. From now until we reach Tersel, I intend to allow no one besides my Rangers, Wallis, and myself inside the cats' hold. I'm also having additional restraining devices installed around the cages, just to reassure you that the cats cannot possibly be involved in what happened."

"Yes, well," the captain said lamely. "I—ah—also intend to confine the Aludrans to their quarters until we reach Tersel. And if I could detain certain other people"—he glanced pointedly at Wallis, then glared into the viewscreen—"you can be sure that I would. As it is, I sincerely hope that both of you will stay out of my way and out of the affairs of my ship. Is that clear, Doctor, Commodore?"

Mather's bland expression betrayed none of his undoubted annoyance.

"I understand perfectly, Captain. If you don't mind, I wish to run some additional tests on this device, here in engineering. After that, if it is your wish, I shall withdraw as much as possible."

"Just make sure nothing else happens, Commodore!" Lutobo said, before he punched the button to break the circuit.

As the screen went to black, the captain cast one last, disapproving glance at the two physicians, then turned on his heel and stalked out of the surgery. Shannon, with an apologetic shrug of her shoulders, picked up a scalpel and began pulling back the drapes on the body of Fabrial.

"Doctor Hamilton, if you wish to stay for the remainder of this autopsy, I won't ask you to leave," she said quietly, not looking up. "This is my surgery, and I determine who is qualified to practice medicine aboard this ship."

"I wouldn't want you to get in trouble with your captain," Wallis said carefully.

Shannon gave her a wry, sidelong glance and tiny smile. "He didn't order you out of here. He simply expressed the hope that you would stay out of his way. I don't see him around, do you?"

Wallis could hardly argue that point. With a faint grin, she moved to the other side of the table and pulled an overhead light closer, losing herself for the next little while in the *buzz* of force probes, the *whirr* of suction devices, and the always fascinating exploration of the marvel that was a human body.

CHAPTER 6

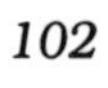

Shannon and Wallis finished the post mortem an hour later. Their findings confirmed Shannon's original opinion of the cause of death, but they still could not agree on the agent. Shannon grudgingly admitted she was less than convinced that the cats were to blame, despite the physical evidence surrounding the deceased; but there she faltered in an alternate hypothesis, as did Wallis.

"Well, it *was* Lehr cat fur we found in his hand, after all," Shannon said, frowning over the printout of their report.

"Yes, but is it from one of *our* cats?" Wallis replied. "I know, you can't tell me that until I get you samples to match against the evidence—and I'll do that a little later. But there's *got* to be another explanation. Did Fabrial have enemies? Do we know of anyone who might have wanted to see him dead?"

"I don't know," Shannon said. "I could ask the same question about the cats. We know the Aludrans hate them. Could they also have some reason to hate Fabrial? Is there *any* chance that one of them somehow killed Fabrial and then deliberately tried to make it look like a cat was responsible?"

"An Aludran? Almost certainly not," Wallis said.

"Violence is completely at odds with their philosophy. That doesn't mean that someone else couldn't have tried to frame the cats, though."

"But *why?*" Shannon sighed. "Dammit, Wallis, maybe the cats *did* somehow manage to get out and hunt! Torrell says that almost every culture has myths about supernatural cats. Maybe they walk through walls!"

The two racked their brains. They sat in Shannon's office for over an hour after orderlies had come to take Fabrial's body away to cold storage and tried to establish some possible motive for his murder, even if they could not assign suspects to those motivations. In desperation, they pulled Gustav Fabrial's files and set up a computer run to correlate his background against that of everyone else on the ship who had known or had contact with him. They went over their medical findings again and again.

"Try this," Shannon said, as they sipped hot tea in her office. "You're fairly sure the cats are telepathic screamers. Is it possible that telepathy is not their only psychic talent?"

"What did you have in mind?"

"I don't know. Maybe some kind of memory-erase? To a certain extent, we can do that with machines. Maybe the cats can do it naturally."

"Or"—Wallis raised an eyebrow thoughtfully—"maybe some people did it with machines, to cover their tracks. Who has access to yours, besides yourself?"

"Just Deller. We have two machines, but no one else is authorized to use them. And it takes a thumbprint to key them. Also, there's an automatic record made each time either one is used; falsifying it would be very difficult, if not impossible."

"It isn't impossible," Wallis said quietly, "believe me. However, I'd think it *is* impossible to have all seven of our Rangers up here, plus your security guards, without someone noticing such a mass troop movement and without at least one of them remembering something odd. Are the machines portable?"

Shannon shook her head. "Not readily. What you see above the tables is only part of the apparatus. The rest is built into the wall."

Wallis nodded thoughtfully. "That's fairly standard. Let's get back to the cats, then. Unless they're a whole lot more sophisticated than we've been led to believe, I don't see how they could change or erase the perceptions of trained observers without being detected. The gaps in continuity would stand out like supernovas."

"How about mass hallucinations, then?" Shannon asked. "What if only one cat gets out at a time—don't ask me how—and the others somehow create the impression that he's still there. No gaps, that way."

"True," Wallis conceded. "And a hunter who can make his prey think he's where he's not—that could be very useful." She shook her head and sighed. "But Imperial Rangers and trained security specialists are not the same as game animals, Shivaun. I think my men would know, even if yours didn't. Besides, nothing like that happened on B-Gem."

Shannon had to agree. For several seconds neither woman spoke, each lost in thought, until finally Wallis looked up and cocked her head to the side. "You know, I just had another idea. It's farfetched, and it's going to sound as if I'm conceding that the cats might be responsible for Fabrial's murder, but there are a couple of people aboard that we might talk to, who know a lot more about Lehr cats than Mather and I do. Vander Torrell is one of them. You heard him expounding on the lost race of Il Nuadi last night at dinner."

"One of the more boorish men it's been my misfortune to meet," Shannon observed with a grimace. "I don't suppose I should say that about a passenger, but nothing in my contract says I have to like them all. Come to think of it, he didn't seem to care much for you and Commodore Seton, either."

Wallis shrugged. "There's some cause, I suppose. Mather and I exerted quite a lot of pressure, trying to persuade him to join our expedition. He won't let us forget that it didn't work. I was hoping you might talk to him."

"Me?" Shannon rolled her eyes. "The things I do in the line of duty. Who's our other expert?"

Wallis smiled across at her unperturbed. "Believe me, you've got the better end of the bargain. I thought I'd pay a call on Lorcas Reynal. He boarded at B-Gem, too, but I don't think you've met him yet. He keeps pretty much to himself. He was born on Il Nuadi, as he prefers to call it, and he was a member of our expedition, albeit a less than enthusiastic one. He didn't think we should capture the cats, and he especially didn't want to see them taken off-planet."

"Then why did he help catch them?"

Wallis grinned. "Filthy lucre. Our fee would have been very hard to turn down—and he didn't. He's something of a cultural anthropologist—mostly self-educated, but respected on his own planet. I think he's using his ill-gotten gains to finance a sabbatical on Wezen I, where your friend Torrell did his work. That's why he's aboard. But once the cats were captured and he'd been paid, he made it perfectly clear that he wanted nothing further to do with us. Still, he might be able to tell us something."

"Aren't 'able' and 'willing' two different matters, in this case?" Shannon asked.

"Probably. But at least I ought to try—and I've got a better chance than Mather would of learning something. The two of them had a running battle—verbal, fortunately—almost from the first day we arrived on B-Gem. A few of our younger Rangers seemed to get along with him a little better, but even that was a strained truce, at times."

"Then why did you keep him on?"

"He knew how to track Lehr cats. Men like that are rare."

Shannon mulled that for a moment, then swiveled toward her console and punched up a medical record. The name at the top was Lorcas Reynal. "I think I know where to find Torrell, this time of day," Shannon said, skimming down the readout. "You'll probably find Reynal in his cabin—number thirty-nine, Deck Three. I see he's not a well man—but I expect you knew that. He asked for a sterile atmosphere in his cabin, which we gave him. He also wears a contagion force field most of the time. His record says he's extremely susceptible to outside infection off his own planet."

"I think he's a hypochondriac more than anything else," Wallis said, getting to her feet, "besides being a master of insults in several different languages."

"Well, if you think there's going to be any problem, I can send someone from security with you, but they're all a little busy right now," Shannon said.

Wallis shook her head. "No need. I'll pick up a Ranger on the way and meet you back here when we're finished."

At Reynal's cabin, Wallis buzzed four times before getting a response. She had begun to think Reynal was out after all, but it was his familiar, unpleasant face that came up abruptly on the door viewer. He did not appear at all pleased, and Wallis suddenly was very glad she had not come alone.

"Good morning, Mister Reynal. Or perhaps I should say good afternoon, since it's past lunchtime. May we come in for a moment?"

Reynal eyed both of them suspiciously, then thumbed the door control and stood aside as the door slid back. He gestured reluctantly for Wallis and Wing to enter. The room was chilly, the lights very low. As Wing took it upon himself to bring up the lights, Wallis was reminded again how unpleasant-looking Reynal was. Tall and long-limbed, almost painfully thin, with dull, mud-colored eyes in a pasty, hairless face, he seemed almost a caricature of a man, even though he was of human stock.

"Say what you have to say, Doctor, and then please leave," Reynal said. "I thought I made it clear before we left Il Nuadi that I have nothing further to say to you."

"Believe me, the feeling is mutual," Wallis said, "except that I need some additional information about the Lehr cats. There was some trouble earlier this morning, as you may have heard. Some questions have been raised."

Reynal shifted his cold eyes from Wallis to Wing, then back to Wallis. "Did I not warn you that the animals were unpredictable, Doctor, and should not be taken off Il Nuadi? I take no responsibility for their behavior."

"No one said that it was your responsibility, Mister Reynal," Wallis replied. "However, we learned this morning, to our very great surprise, that the cats scream telepathically as well as vocally. We wonder whether they might have other psychic accomplishments you haven't told us about—like the ability to teleport out of their cages or something. If you could—"

"I *could* do many things, if I wished, Doctor," Reynal said stonily. "However, I do not wish. My responsibility for the creatures, and to you, ended when the terms of my contract were fulfilled. I am not required to remind myself constantly that I sold my integrity for money."

"You were paid handsomely, Reynal," Wing said.

"Paid in Imperial credits—yes," Reynal snapped. "But eventually, it is I who shall have to pay with the coin of my soul, for having betrayed the Shining Ones. I shall not betray them again."

"Reynal, they're animals," Wallis said. "Clever animals, perhaps—maybe more clever than we know—but they're not gods. And one of them may have killed someone on this ship."

Reynal half turned away. "That is of no concern to me."

"Now, see here, Reynal—" Wing began.

"I do not need to *see* anywhere, Lieutenant," Reynal interrupted coldly. "You are the intruder here, not I. Now, if you will excuse me, I was on my way out. Unless, of course, you plan to detain me illegally."

With a perplexed sigh, Wallis moved toward the door, tapping Wing on the elbow as she passed. "Never mind, Wing. Mister Reynal is under no obligation to assist us further, if he doesn't want to. As he has so succinctly pointed out, he has honored his contract already. My apologies for having disturbed you, Mister Reynal."

Nor did Shannon have much better luck. She found Vander Torrell winning at Four-Card Deltikan in the ship's casino, but the historian was understandably reluctant to abandon his game. After several hands in which he began to lose, however, Torrell sourly dealt himself out and joined Shannon at the table where she had been waiting and watching him. He drained one Tejat brandy and ordered a second before he would look at her.

"Now that you've thoroughly destroyed my winning streak, Doctor, what can I do for you? I'm not at all accustomed to having my game interrupted."

"I'm sorry to inconvenience you, Doctor Torrell. I was fascinated by something you said at dinner last night."

Torrell glanced at her as if really seeing her for the first time behind the maroon uniform. "Oh, and what thing was that, Doctor?"

"Something you said about the Lehr cats and their relationship with the lost race of Il Nuadi. I wondered if—"

"Ah, wait, Doctor. Don't tell me. Let me guess," he

said unctuously. "The persistent Commodore Seton has sent you to pump me for information, hasn't he?"

"Commodore Seton knows nothing about this, Doctor Torrell," she said. That much, at least, was true. "But the Lehr cats are of special interest to me just now. I hoped you might be able to help me."

"Ah, yes, I heard about the little problem with the cats this morning. Naturally, you *would* have medical interest, wouldn't you? Ah, such an unfortunate occurrence."

"Unfortunate enough for you to tell me more about Lehr cats?" Shannon countered.

Torrell smiled and covered her hand with his on the table top, leaning forward conspiratorily when she did not pull away.

"Well, perhaps we could discuss it over drinks. What would you like to know, dear lady?"

And at the murder site, his mission concluded with the engineering section, Mather had been pursuing his own lines of investigation. It was always a pleasure to watch professionals doing their jobs well, and the forensic specialist of the security team, an elderly man named Jones, was definitely a pro. Mather chatted with him for nearly half an hour, while the man gathered his samples and quietly questioned the guards who had been first at the scene. When Jones had left, Mather wandered closer to the murder site itself. One of the cleanup crew was rubbing at a particularly stubborn stain just where the body had lain. Casually, Mather crouched down beside the man.

"Looks like hard work," he remarked.

The man glanced at him amiably and continued scrubbing at the carpet. "Just this one spot, sir. I think Jonesie must've splashed some fixative here when he was taking his samples. Most of the blood washed right out, though—and there really wasn't that much of it, considering what happened. I guess the poor devil must have died from internal hemorrhaging."

"Oh?" Mather tried to keep an interested edge out of his voice. "It looked like a pretty bloody affair to me."

The man shrugged. "I've seen worse. Two runs back, we had a couple of drunks go at one another with force blades in the main salon, and you should've seen the mess. The place looked like a slaughterhouse by the time security could break it up, but they both lived to talk about it."

"What about this one?" Mather urged.

"Oh, not this guy. He was definitely dead. There wasn't that much blood, though. An easy cleanup job."

Mather glanced around him at the drying carpet, then back at the man. "How much blood *do* you think he lost?"

"How much?" The man stopped scrubbing and looked around him, then said, "Oh, half a liter or so, if that. When it's spread out, it can look like a lot more, but—half a liter, maybe. Certainly no more."

"I see." Mather slipped the man a sharply creased note. "Thanks very much. You've been very helpful."

Within minutes, he was approaching Medical Section. The reception area was deserted, but he could hear Wallis and Shannon laughing behind a door that was partially ajar. With a quick knock, he slid the door open enough to pass, then let it glide closed behind him. Wallis had her feet up on Shannon's desk, and Shannon was washing her hands at a scrub sink across the room. They both grinned at him as he settled into a chair opposite his wife.

"Shivaun was just telling me about her near-capture at the hands of the notorious Van-der Tor-rell," Wallis said, intoning the name with mock solemnity. "I sent her to see if she could get any more information out of him about Lehr cats, and he decided it was really an attempt to get to know him better."

"Ugh, what a slimy character!" Shannon said, drying her hands and chucking the towel into a waste chute. "I found out some interesting things, though. How about you? Did the lab come up with anything on your gray box yet?"

Mather shook his head. "Not much. The crackle finish didn't take prints very well. All they got were a few of mine, badly smudged. I doubt they'll have much better luck on the inside. All the components are either handmade or else they've had the manufacturers' marks removed. We may be able to restore some of the marks, but I doubt that will be much help, either. I've got them running function analyses of the circuits now."

"Well, you didn't really think they'd be able to tell us much anyway, did you?" Wallis asked.

"No. How about you two? Did you determine the cause of death?"

Shannon sat down behind her desk and picked up a stylus.

"Vascular collapse, caused by massive loss of blood. Of course, we could have told you that after the first look."

"And the wounds?" Mather persisted.

"Other than the throat wound, mostly superficial, really. Much worse-looking than they actually were, for the most part. No significant trauma to any major organ, and certainly none that should have been fatal—other than the throat, of course. He simply bled to death."

"I see. And how much blood would you say he lost, for it to be enough to kill him?"

"Oh, two or three liters, given his other injuries and the amount of blood left in the body. Maybe more—he was a good-sized man. Why do you ask?"

"Intriguing," Mather said, by way of reply. "Tell me, Doctor, you never actually saw the murder site, did you? Or photos?"

"Not yet. Why?"

"Because I just talked to one of your cleanup crew,

and he can only account for about half a liter of blood at the site. What do you suppose happened to the other two liters or so?"

Shannon stopped toying with her stylus and looked at him oddly. "What are you trying to imply? That's impossible."

"Not unless your autopsy findings are grossly inaccurate, which I doubt. Wally, does this suggest a pattern to you—what I've just told you?"

"About the missing blood?" She looked quizzically at Mather, her auburn head cocked to one side in horrified suspicion as she guessed where he was leading. "You're serious, aren't you? You really want me to say it?"

"I am deadly serious."

"Oh, my. Well, since we can't account for the missing blood at the murder site or in the victim's body, it sounds as if someone or something has either consumed or carried off the rest of the blood. If the cats are responsible, which isn't likely, it's obviously the former. If a human, probably the latter." She paused a beat.

"Mather Seton, you don't *really* want me to tell Shivaun she's got a vampire on her ship, do you?"

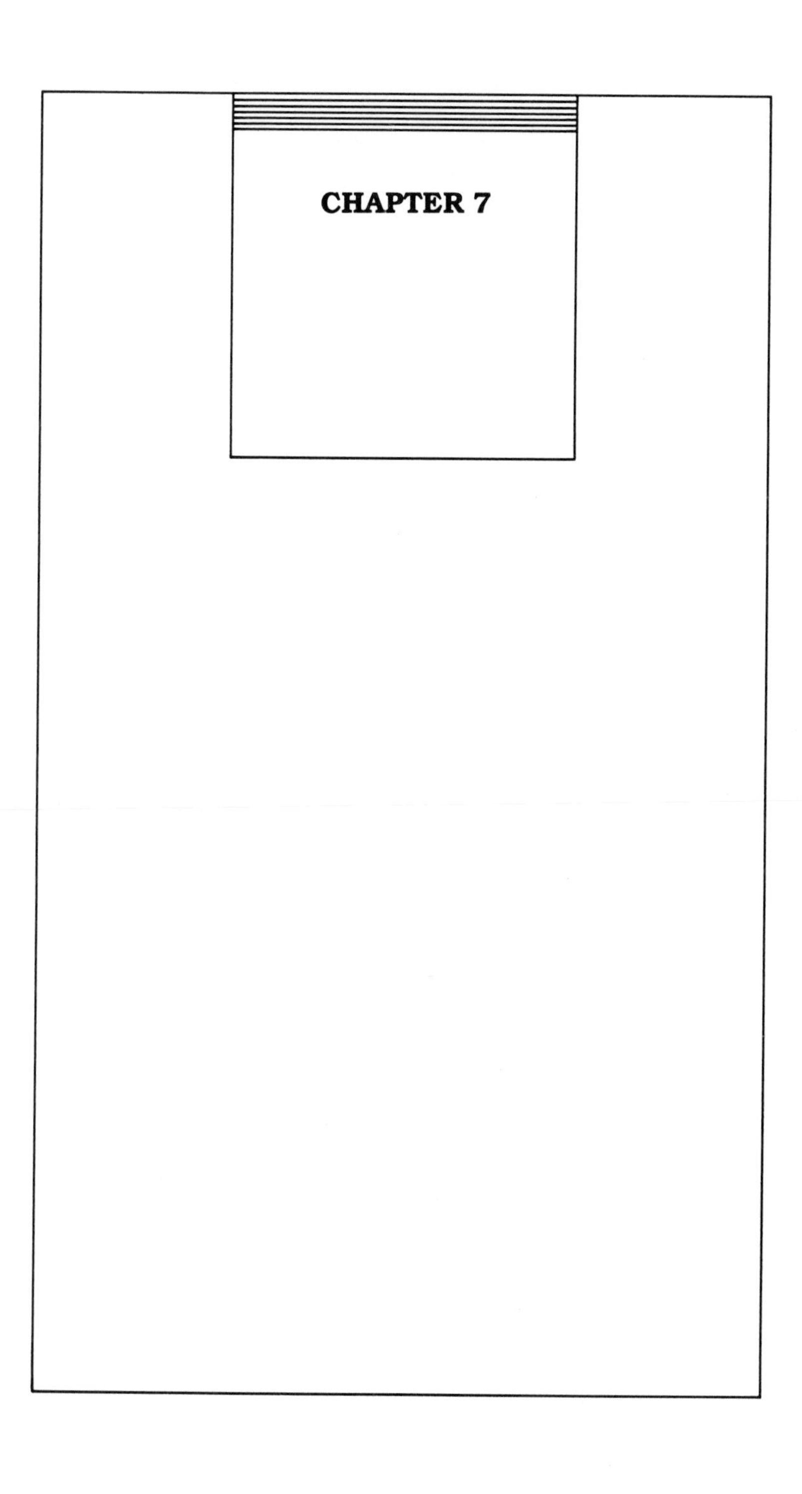

CHAPTER 7

"A vampire?"

Incredulously, Shannon looked back and forth between the two of them, expecting—and then hoping for—a sign of jesting that did not come.

"That—that isn't funny," she murmured, fighting back a nervous laugh as she set both hands very precisely on the desk top in front of them. "There are no such things as vampires. They're myths. They don't exist."

Mather rested his elbows on his chair arms and folded his hands, making a tower of his first two fingers. "Maybe not in the traditional sense," he agreed. "But it's curious that there's evidence of vampire legends in practically every race we've ever encountered, human or alien. The old Earth legends abound with tales of vampires and other related beasties, in otherwise widely divergent cultures. And as for alien races, why, the Aludrans have a version, and the Ainish, and the Warflemen of Procyon II. I could go on and on."

"Superstitious nonsense," Shannon stated flatly.

"Hmm, perhaps," Wallis joined in. "I suppose one could try to dismiss most legends as superstition or deliberate fiction. The only problem is that legends almost always have some basis in fact, if you look hard enough. And even discounting supernatural explanations, there are physiological and psychological bases for behavior patterns that simulate at least portions of activity we've come to associate with vampirism. Certain chemical deficiencies and imbalances in the body can lead to very bizarre behavior, as I'm sure you know. And psychotic individuals have been known to believe they were almost anything—and to act accordingly. Why not a vampire?"

Shannon hugged her arms across her chest as if suddenly chilled and hunched down in her chair. "This is ridiculous. You've almost got me believing you! There has to be a more plausible explanation."

Mather shrugged. "I'd certainly welcome one. But when we're dealing with a situation this bizarre, and no more logical explanation seems likely, then we need to consider bizarre possibilities. Now, either the cats are responsible, as our gross physical evidence indicates—except that we can't figure out how they did it—or else someone is trying to make it *look* like the cats did it, by carrying the blood away to make it appear that the cats drank it—which is not an altogether unexpected behavior for carnivores like the Lehr cats. Or he's consuming it himself and making it look like the cats did it."

"Or the murderer is carrying away the blood and *then* consuming it," Wallis added.

"*Or* he's flushing it down the toilet!" Shannon snapped.

"Also possible," Mather agreed. "And a true psycho might be doing it with no thought of implicating the cats at all. It could be just coincidence. But the blood has to go somewhere." He cocked his head at Shannon wistfully. "I think you'll have to admit that the basic vampire theory has merits in this case, Doctor—'vampire' covering the whole range of what we've been discussing, of course. At least it gives us another angle to consider."

Shannon glanced nervously at both of them again, her brow furrowed in concentration, then averted her eyes.

"Look, I think I understand what you're trying to do. You want to clear your cats, and I can't say I blame you. But this—theory of yours—I'm sorry, I just can't accept it."

"Well, it's as useful as all the other theories we've considered," Wallis said, "which is to say they all stink. Let's sleep on it, shall we? And don't we have another phase jump coming up soon?"

Wearily, Shannon glanced at the chronometer on her console and sighed. "Yes. I hadn't realized it was so late. You've got about twenty minutes. Commodore, if you still want to try that new suspension system, you can speak to Technician Gallinos, two doors down. She can set you up for it."

As she punched up a display on the console, obviously dismissing them, Mather murmured, "Thank you," and started to make an additional comment, but Wallis caught his eye and shook her head. Mather, with a sigh, got up and left the room, Wallis following behind him. When they had gone, Shannon turned to stare uneasily at the door for a long time, stirring only when the lights dimmed momentarily and the phase warning began to chime its five-minute signal.

She sat up at that, long enough to shake a tiny, rose-colored tablet from a dispenser in her desk drawer. Then she laid her head against the back of her chair and slipped the tablet under her tongue. She could feel it taking effect as the one-minute warning vibrated through the ship; she relaxed and let the medication do its work, wondering idly what it would be like to jump unmedicated—wondering how Wallis Hamilton managed it with no ill effects whatsoever. So absorbed was she in her speculation that the jump itself passed almost unnoticed.

She dozed afterward—she could not remember later

whether she had dreamed or not—but she awoke fretting about what the Setons had said regarding vampires, and the thought continued to plague her as she tried to finish the day's entries in her medical log. An orderly brought a tray with dinner, and she poked at the food for a while, but she was not hungry, despite the day's exhaustion. Major Barding floated in for his pain medication and was again in high spirits, once the drugs began to take effect. But Shannon sent him on his way far more brusquely than she had intended. Twice she started to request information from the library banks; twice canceled the request. Finally, when Deller came to relieve her, she cleared the board altogether and went back to her cabin to try to sleep.

But sleep would not come, despite all her efforts to drop off. Finally, feeling annoyed with herself and quite foolish, she got out of bed and padded over to the library terminal on her desk. The only illumination was the single tally light on the intercom unit beside the terminal. She stared at that for several minutes before finally reaching out to touch the query button.

The keyboard lit up and the display screen glowed a soft green, casting an eerie pallor on her face and hands. Slowly, and feeling even more foolish than before, she typed out her request.

Reference, vampires. General knowledge. Respond.

After what seemed to be minutes—unthinkable in a sophisticated device such as the library computer—the response began scrolling up the screen.

Vampire, from the Earth Slavic vampir. *A mythological being believed to arise from the dead at night to drink the blood of its victim. The phenomenon of vampirism appears in many cultures, both human and alien. (See mythologies of specific cultures for non-Earth traditions.)*

The best-known vampire in Earth mythology was Count Dracula, a fictional creation of 19th-century

British author Bram Stoker. (See Stoker, Bram. Dracula. *Menkar: The Literary Reprint Series, Society for the Preservation of Ancient Classics, A.I. 63.) However, there is evidence to suggest that Stoker based his character on actual folk superstitions prevalent long before in the area of Central Europe known then as Transylvania. Stoker's creation was a curious mixture of—*

Bored with the historical recounting, Shannon hit the cancel button and keyed the query again. This time, her question was more specific.

Reference, vampires. State characteristics of appearance and behavior. Respond.

Again, a seemingly endless pause before the information came up.

The unvarying characteristic of all vampires was the presence of elongated upper canine teeth, sometimes retractable. These the vampire would sink into his victim's neck over the jugular vein. He would then drain blood from his victim—whether by simply drinking it or by drawing it out directly through hollow passages in the teeth is not always clear. This could occur all at once, causing almost immediate death, or it could be stretched out in a series of attacks over a period of days or even weeks, until the victim eventually expired, the cause of death usually blamed on one or another of the wasting malaises common to that era of beginning medical knowledge. It was believed that a victim who died in this manner would also become a vampire, rising from his or her grave at night to drink blood and do the will of the master vampire. All vampires must return to a coffin of their native earth before sunrise, sunlight being fatal to their kind.

Her attention engaged in spite of herself, Shannon read on, fascinated by the breadth of the vampire concept and checking the information against what Mather and Wallis had told her.

Legendary sources indicate that vampires were able to transfix their victims with a hypnotic stare, often forming an obsessive bond that led the victim to aid the vampire in gaining access to his or her person. There are also indications that victims may have derived sensual pleasure from their liaisons with vampires, though this was rarely stated clearly in the repressive literature of contemporary authors. However, it should be noted that vampires generally (though not always) chose victims of the opposite sex, especially if the draining of blood was to be prolonged over a period of time. (See Von Calder, Gunther. Sexuality in the Legends of Old Earth. *Tersel: Journal of the Institute of Psychiatric Research, A.I. 82.)*

Vampires were believed to live forever, so long as their sources of fresh blood were not curtailed, and to confer immortality on those of their victims who became vampires. They could take the form of bats or sometimes other animals. Vampires also had the ability to turn into vapor and thus pass unseen through locked doors and walls. They were possessed of superhuman strength. Because they were believed to have no souls, it was thought that their reflections could not be seen in mirrors. They disliked garlic and garlic flowers, which acted as a repellent, and could not stand the touch of a cross or of silver. They could not cross running water or enter a house unless invited by—

"This is ridiculous!" Shannon whispered, hitting the cancel button again.

For a moment she sat staring at the faintly glowing screen. Then she tried one last query.

Reference, vampires. State methods for destroying. Respond.

The response came back immediately.

Vampires could be destroyed by: exposure to direct sunlight; branding with a cross, especially one made of silver; dousing with holy water; pounding of a wooden stake, preferably of ash, through the heart; burning. There is also some evidence that silver bullets—

In exasperation, Shannon hit the cancel button a final time and shook her head, all reason rebelling against what she had just read. It was sheer superstition. It had to be. And yet, something Wallis Hamilton had said kept flashing through her mind: that almost all legends have some basis in fact.

For several minutes she sat there in darkness, staring at the blank glow of the display screen as if it might impart some new wisdom that she could accept more readily. Instead, her imagination embellished what she had read and sent chill shivers down her spine. She finally turned off the console altogether and stalked back to bed, determined to put it all out of mind and go to sleep.

She did sleep this time, but she also dreamed—and woke angrily, more than once, to hazy recollections of silver crosses, garlic flowers—whatever *they* were!—and wooden stakes piercing hearts that did not beat.

Mather and Wallis also got some sleep eventually—though not before checking on the cats a final time. Wallis went directly there, to nurse the animals through any aftereffects from the phase shift, but Mather rode out the jump in one of the new suspensors, as Shannon had suggested.

"It did cancel out the usual discomforts of jumping," he informed Wallis afterward, when he had joined her in the hold, "but I lost consciousness for a few seconds. I could do without that."

"But you weren't nauseous or dizzy?" Wallis asked. "Darling, that's wonderful! I wonder if it would help our furry friends. This jump was a lot harder on them than the last time."

She gestured toward the cats, who were all slumped flat in the bottom of the cage, hardly able to pick up their heads, much less scream.

"Well, first you'd have to get them into the harness," Mather quipped. "Seriously, though, I'm afraid the thing is still very experimental. It *did* mean one less jump *I* had to suffer through, however. And if Lutobo is still speaking to me by morning, I plan to run the navigation coordinates to see if we can't refine his figures and eliminate another one. We might make up some of his lost time, too."

"Well, it might improve his temper," Wallis agreed. "Do you think the suspensors are worth trying again?"

Mather grinned. "Well, not for that jump, of course. And I don't know that they'd ever work out for military use. It's one thing for a civilian to pass out for a few minutes and avoid the usual after-grogginess from medication, but that wouldn't do at all in a battle situation."

"Well, you don't have to worry about battle situations anymore, darling," Wallis murmured, patting his arm with affection. "If you want to use the suspensors, you go right ahead."

"Woman, if you keep patronizing me about that, I'll banish you from my bed and board!" Mather muttered, though he smiled as he said it. "It isn't *my* fault that you got the right genes to make you immune to jump sickness."

Wallis grinned. "Poor baby. Are you satisfied with security, so we can go get some sleep?"

"I don't see what else we can do," he replied. "Mister Neville, the shift is yours."

"Aye, sir. I've got a few more things I want to install, so there can't be *any* question."

"Fine. We'll see you in the morning."

But though their sleep was not marred by nightmares the way Shannon's was, nor were they permitted to rest as long as they would have liked. Very early, the harsh rasp of the door buzzer jarred them from sleep. Mather, honed to the expectation of possible trouble by long years' experience, was awake instantly. He saw Wallis roll over and peer at him sleepily as he eased out of bed and glided silently to the door speaker. He glanced at the chronometer beside the speaker and yawned before thumbing the button. "Seton."

"Commodore, this is Courtenay, chief of security. I'm sorry to have to bother you so early, but the captain wants to see you and Doctor Hamilton in his office immediately."

Mather felt every muscle in his body tense and had to force himself to relax by conscious will. He laid an arm around Wallis's shoulder as she came to stand silently beside him.

"I gather that the captain's request has the force of an order, as far as you're concerned, Mister Courtenay," Mather said carefully. "Am I to assume that the captain considers us to be under arrest?"

There was an awkward pause. Then: "Sir, I can't say what's in the captain's mind about that. I'm afraid you'll have to take it up with him directly."

"I see." Mather glanced down at Wallis and signaled for her to begin dressing, then turned back to the door grille. "Can you tell me specifically why the captain wants to see us, Mister Courtenay?"

"I'd—ah—rather not discuss it out here in the corridor, sir. And I don't mean to rush you, but I do have my orders."

"All right, we'll be right with you."

Breaking the link with Courtenay, Mather moved across the room to the regular intercom and hit the switch.

"ComNet, this is Seton. Connect me with the duty officer in my hold."

"Stand by, please."

He began pulling on a pair of trousers as he waited for a response. Wallis tossed a tunic on the back of the chair nearby and continued with her own dressing.

"Wing here."

Mather secured the waistband on his trousers and hit the switch for visual circuits.

"Give me a status report, Wing. Is everything all right down there?"

Wing's face on the tiny screen had been bland, emotionless, when it first appeared. Now the young man raised one dark eyebrow, his manner becoming more guarded. "Is there some reason to suspect that everything isn't, sir?"

"You've had no trouble, then?" Mather insisted. "Nothing has tripped any of the alarms, and nothing has happened that you know of?"

"I would have called you, if it had, sir."

Mather nodded and pulled on a shirt over his head,

uncertain what to make of that news, and began yanking on boots.

"All right, Wing, just stand by until I can get down there—and don't let anyone near those cats! I don't even want you to lower the shields to see if everything is all right inside. Wait until I get there. Then there can be no question of any of you being blamed."

"Yes, sir. By the way, regarding any of us being blamed, all of us except Mister Perelli had the opportunity to place that device you found yesterday. The tapes show the spot at a bad angle, though. It's impossible to tell whether anyone actually did plant something since we've been in here."

Mather nodded. "Thanks, Wing. Maybe that will help to soothe the captain. We're on our way to his office under escort. I'll see you as soon as we can get away."

With a sigh, he broke off the connection and shrugged into the harness of his needler holster, checking the weapon before fitting it into place. Wallis had finished dressing and was checking the contents of her medical kit. Mather, with a worried glance in her direction, picked up a gray fatigue jacket and slipped it on as he crossed back to the door to thumb the door lock.

Courtenay was waiting outside, four of his security men drawn up at attention behind him, weapons conspicuous on their hips. Mather made no attempt to conceal his own weapon as he adjusted his lapels.

"Well, Mister Courtenay?"

"Commodore Seton," Courtenay acknowledged with a slightly sickly grin. "I hope we're not going to have to shoot it out with you."

"Not if I can help it. Won't you come in for a moment, Mister Courtenay? Gentlemen, we'll be with you shortly."

He had drawn Courtenay in almost before the man realized what was happening, and as the door closed behind him, the security chief swallowed and glanced around the room uneasily. Wallis, too, was slipping a needler into her med kit.

"I'm really sorry about this, Commodore. I—ah—Maybe you should know what's happened, before you go charging in to see the captain. There have been two more victims."

"Two!" Wallis said, looking up.

"Can you give us any details?" Mather asked.

Courtenay nodded uncomfortably. "I probably shouldn't be telling you this, Commodore, but my men will be blamed, too, because some of them were on duty outside the hold where your cats are. The first victim was one of our people—an engineer's mate named Phillips, up on Deck Two. He'd been dead a couple of hours when they found him—his throat ripped out like the last victim, his chest and arms badly slashed. There were—bloody cat paw prints on the carpet around him. And a—a tuft of Lehr cat fur in one hand and a bloodstained force-blade in the other."

"Cat blood or human, on the blade?" Mather demanded.

"I don't know that, sir."

"I see," Mather said quietly. "And the other victim?"

"One of—the Aludrans," Courtenay murmured. "The one called Ta'ai, Muon's mate. Apparently *she* was found right after her attacker left. She—had just stopped breathing, but a steward and one of my men were able to keep her ventilated until a medical team could get there and take over. She's been in surgery for nearly an hour now, but she's really critical. Doctor Shannon's been pulling blood from some of the other Aludrans to keep her going at all."

Wallis shook her head and sighed, then closed up her medical kit and slung it over her shoulder with a determined expression.

"Mister Courtenay, I hope you don't try to stop me, but I'm going up to Medical Section to see if I can help out. Mather can answer to the captain for both of us."

"I agree," Mather said, resting both hands on his hips just a little defiantly. "Courtenay, are you going to try to stop her?"

Courtenay shook his head. "Not me, sir. And I'm certainly not going to try to disarm you. *You* can explain it to the captain."

"I'll do that," Mather replied as they moved toward the door. "By the way, I've already checked with my people in the hold, and Lieutenant Wing reports nothing out of the ordinary. I've given him orders not to do anything or to admit anyone until I can get there myself, so if I were you, I wouldn't try any forcible entry that the captain might suggest before he has all the facts. Do you understand my meaning?"

"Yes, sir." Courtenay opened the door. "There's no problem, gentlemen," he added, as his men alerted. "Commodore Seton is coming with us. Doctor Hamilton is needed in Medical Section."

Five minutes later, all of them except Wallis were standing before another door on the command level of the ship as Courtenay buzzed for admission, then thumbed the door control. A tense Lutobo sat behind a large plasteel and leatherine desk, the dark polished surface reflecting his even darker mood. He said nothing as Mather came into the room, only signaling with a curt hand gesture that Courtenay should leave them alone. There were no chairs on Mather's side of the desk, so he approached to within arm's reach of the desk and stopped.

"Where is your wife, Commodore?" the captain said quietly.

Mather gazed back mildly, letting no inkling of his knowledge show on his face.

"Where a physician *should* be, Captain. She's gone to assist your medical staff. We were told that there'd been a serious medical emergency."

"Then you doubtless know what happened and have already constructed some suitably glib explanation," Lutobo said. "Go ahead, Commodore. I shall be fascinated to hear how you plan to wiggle out of this one."

"I'm afraid I can't oblige you, Captain," Mather returned evenly. "Your Mister Courtenay was very sketchy on details. Unless you give me something more concrete to work with, I'm afraid I can't do much to help you. We *are* working for the same end purpose, however."

"Are we?" Lutobo's eyes narrowed at that, as if trying to ascertain whether Mather was toying with him, then sat back in his chair. "Very well, Commodore. Here are some concrete facts. Two more people have been attacked aboard my ship, one of them fatally. The deceased was one of my engineers. He had a bloody force-blade in one hand, blue fur in the other, and bloody paw prints around his body. The other victim is still alive, but only because of the fast thinking of two of my crew. She was found in roughly the same condition as the other two victims, except that she wasn't quite dead yet. Apparently there's some slight chance that she might regain consciousness long enough to describe her attacker. I wonder what she'll say?"

"So do I, Captain, since I've already checked with my people in the hold, and—"

"I don't *care* who you've checked with, dammit, Seton!" Lutobo bellowed, pounding one fist on the desk as he lurched forward in his chair. "At this point, I don't even care whether your cats are the culprits or not. I can't allow this to continue. I've lost a passenger and a member of my crew already, and we're probably going to lose that second passenger. That's three lives, Seton! What am I going to tell my company?"

"Is that all you can think of? Your company?" Mather snapped. "Be reasonable, Captain. We're up against something outside both our experience. *I* don't understand it, *you* don't understand it, and no one *else* understands it—except, perhaps, whoever is actually doing these things—but we're never *going* to understand it if you keep jumping to conclusions and making wild accusations. Now, I just tried to tell you that I called the hold before leaving my cabin, and I was assured that everything is still secure. Your own security people confirm that no one has passed through that door."

"That isn't possible!" Lutobo said. "There were *paw prints* this time, dammit! Maybe they're teleporting—*I* don't know. But I won't have it. I want you to get rid of the cats."

"You what?"

"You heard me. I want the cats destroyed. You can have Doctor Hamilton put them to sleep, or I can have my security men blast them, or we can jettison them in space—I don't care how it's done, as long as it's done quickly. But I want them gone. I want them off my ship!"

"Lutobo, you didn't hear a word I said about the importance of those cats, did you?" Mather replied. "If they don't reach Tersel alive, I don't care to be around to answer for the consequences."

"That can be arranged, too!"

"*Can* it, then?" Mather said, leaning both hands on the edge of the desk to stare down at Lutobo. The movement opened his jacket so that the butt of the needler under his left arm was partially exposed.

"How dare you bring a weapon into this office?" Lutobo whispered, suddenly afraid. "Courtenay?"

But before he could push the button to call for help, Mather was leaning across to block the button, his wide hand pinning Lutobo's smaller, darker one.

"Mister Courtenay is more intelligent than to try disarming an Imperial agent, Captain. So, I would have thought, are you." He released the hand and straightened menacingly. "I hadn't thought it necessary, but perhaps I should remind you *again* who you're dealing with. Wallis and I receive our orders directly from the Imperial High Command. We are accountable to Prince Cedric himself. Now, it will take you about two hours to verify that and to confirm, for your own edification, just how slight are the limitations on our authority.

"While you're checking on that—and I have no doubt that you will—I intend to go to the hold and inspect the Lehr cats again—and to remain there with them until we reach Tersel, if necessary, to ensure that they come to no harm. If I should discover that the cats are, indeed, responsible for the attacks aboard this ship, then I will personally take appropriate measures, regardless of the animals' value. But in the meantime, I will brook no interference in the performance of my duties, either by you or by any member of your staff. Have I made myself perfectly clear?"

Lutobo, sitting stiffly upright in his chair, was almost white with suppressed rage by the time Mather had finished, but he was still sufficiently in control to realize that the agent probably would not dare to bluff under such circumstances. With icy calm, he stood and leaned forward with both hands on his desk, so that there was only a meter or so of shiny leatherine between them. His dark eyes shone like polished stone in his impassive face.

"I understand you perfectly, Commodore." His words were crisp, precise, cold with anger. "And now I want *you* to understand something. I intend to communicate with your superiors again, as you have suggested. And I intend to secure whatever authority it takes to ensure that your Lehr cats are destroyed and that you are broken in rank and ruined for this. You have your two hours, Commodore. But after that, we shall see whether your Imperial Command will allow you to abuse your authority to the endangerment of private citizens. The Gruening Line is not to be trifled with, Seton. Is *that* clear?"

"Perfectly," Mather said. "And now, by your leave, Captain"—he made a brisk, formal bow and clicked his heels precisely—"I'll continue about my business. You know where to find me."

He stopped at the new murder site on the way, but there was little there that he had not seen before. The bulk of the bloodstained carpet had been cleaned by the time he got there, and maintenance personnel were replacing a section where a guard said the paw prints had been. The piece had already gone to the laboratory for further examination and preservation until forensic chemists on Tersel could run detailed tests.

"Was it the victim's blood?" Mather asked a technician.

The man shrugged. "Well, I don't *think* it was cat blood, if that's what you're really asking, Commodore. As to whether it was the *victim's* blood, I couldn't say until I've seen the lab results."

"What about the force-blade?"

"That's gone to the lab, too." The man cocked his head at Mather. "Be honest with me, Commodore. Do you think we've got some kind of maniac loose on the ship, rather than the cats doing all of this?"

Mather only shrugged. "I'll let you know when I've formed an opinion."

Ship's Security was still in evidence outside the door to the hold when Mather got there, and the Rangers had installed even more stringent security measures during the night. After Mather had put his palm to the ident scanner that now activated the outer door, he stepped into the door lock and felt the brief tingle of sensors scanning his body for weapons, pausing on his needler. Then, just before the inner door slid aside, he was caught briefly in a tangle field that jangled every nerve ending in his body. Closing his eyes, he ceased all movement and forced himself to relax immediately, not even breathing as the energy tendrills wound around him; he waited while the Ranger on the other end scrutinized him and then deactivated the field. It was Webb.

"Sorry for the inconvenience, Commodore," Webb said, holstering his own weapon as he approached his superior. "You're the first to try out our new security system. I didn't hurt you, did I?"

Flexing his muscles experimentally, Mather shook his head. "No, you did fine. Next time, though, tell me when I'm going to walk into a tangle field."

"Sorry, sir."

Mather glanced toward the area of the cats' enclosure as Wing and three more Rangers came out of the security station toward him. Still in the little room, Peterson and Casey swiveled toward him, Peterson keeping one eye on the outside scanners.

In the center of the room, everything appeared to be as he had left it the night before. Electronic baffles cut off whatever sound might have been coming from inside the cats' cage, and the force nets around the cage area reduced the interior to a blurred, not-black glimmer that almost hurt the eyes to look at directly. Everything appeared to be all right—but suddenly Mather had the premonition that he did not want to see what lay beyond.

"Sir, can you tell us what's happened?" Neville

asked as he and the others clustered around.

Mather brought his attention back to them reluctantly, unable to shake the waves of foreboding that were assailing him continually now.

"There have been two more attacks during the night, gentlemen—one of them fatal."

"Well, it can't have been the cats, then," Perelli murmured.

"Aye, we were watching every indicator, every alarm," Fredericks said. "There was *nothing* out of the ordinary."

Wing shifted from one foot to the other. "You said that only one attack was fatal, sir. What about the other?"

"The other victim is still alive—or was, when last I heard. It was one of the Aludrans—a female named Ta'ai. Wallis has gone to assist."

"Then maybe this Ta'ai can tell us what attacked her," Perelli said. "It just can't have been the cats, sir. There's no way they could have gotten out without us knowing."

"I know." Mather sighed, clapping the man on the shoulder in reassurance as he moved a few steps closer to the first of the defenses around the cages.

"All right, Mister Peterson, let's see inside, shall we?"

Peterson ran his tongue across dry lips and turned back to his control console, setting recorders and backup circuits in operation and rechecking all systems one last time.

"Ready when you are, sir."

"Let's take 'em down, then."

There was the low *whirr* of the additional recorders and sensors cycling in, the *snick* of a needler safety being thumbed aside by one of the Rangers, the tension-amplified *snap* of the power switches being thrown. As the nets flickered out of existence, the mournful howling of three Lehr cats rose eerily in the hold. The fourth cat, who was the reason for their howling, would never howl again. His end of the cage was practically awash with blood.

"What the—"

Faster than a man his size had a right to move, Mather was beside the cage, peering in at the slaughtered Lehr cat and automatically activating the big cage scanners. The dead cat's mate, the smaller of the two females, stood her ground, her wails turning to snarling defiance as Mather tried to look closer. The Rangers did not move, too shocked and stunned even to murmur among themselves as to how the thing could have happened.

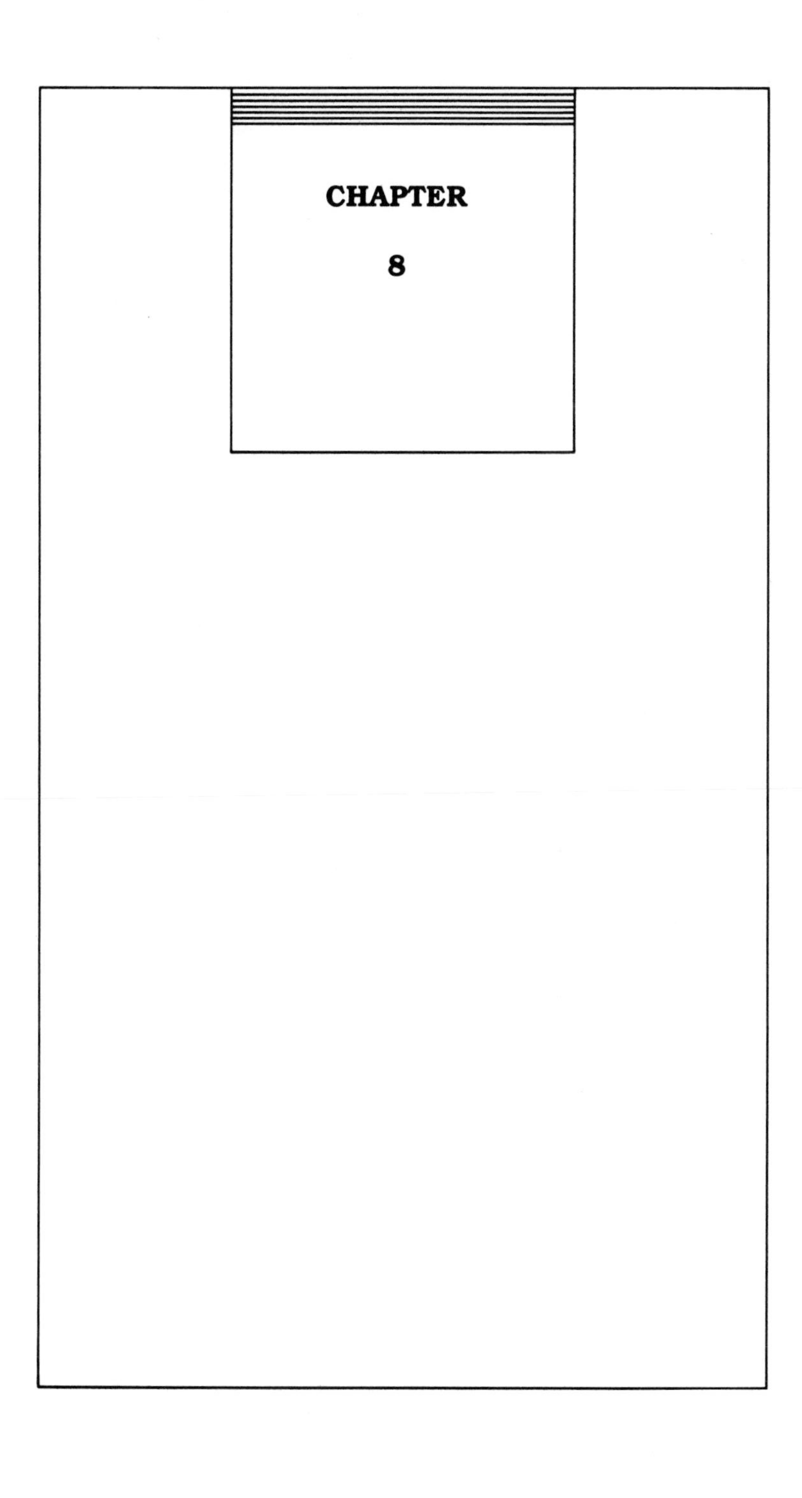

CHAPTER

8

KATHERINE KURTZ

"I'm sorry, Doctor, but both doctors probably will be occupied for at least another hour," a nurse told Wallis when she entered the outer reception room in Medical Section and asked to see Shannon. "Please excuse me. I have to get back."

The nurse had come out only to dispense a headache remedy to an adolescent boy, who turned anxiously to Wallis as the woman disappeared back into the innards of the medical complex.

"She called you *doctor*," the boy said, almost accusingly. "Are you a medical doctor?"

Wallis gave the boy a reassuring smile. "Yes, but I'm not part of the crew—just a passenger like you."

"Well, do *you* know what's going on?" the boy insisted. "People are getting pretty scared. Somebody said that there are some big blue cats down in the hold and that one got out during the night and killed someone."

"Oh? Who told you that?" Wallis asked. "It can't have been anyone very responsible, to go spreading such rumors."

"Then it isn't true?" the boy replied. "Well, *that's* a relief! They *are* handling some kind of medical emergency in there, though. I think it has to do with one of those aliens."

"Really?"

"Hmmm." The boy nodded as he drank down whatever the nurse had brought him for his headache. "Right after I got here, one of the security guards brought in one of those aliens that bundle up all the time—with the feathers on top of their heads."

"An Aludran," Wallis supplied.

"Yeah, I guess so. He looked awfully shaky. They took him inside, and it was ten minutes or so before anybody came out to see what I needed." The boy grimaced and rubbed at his temples. "I think I'll try a nap, to get rid of this headache. Maybe it'll be gone by dinnertime."

"I'm sure it will," Wallis said politely.

But when the boy had gone, and a quick glance outside revealed no one coming, Wallis went cautiously to Shannon's office door and touched the latch plate. To her surprise, the door slid back immediately. Heartened, she slipped inside and closed it behind her, heading immediately for the master console on Shannon's desk.

The controls were clearly labeled. Running her finger down the row of monitor switches, Wallis tried surgery first—empty, except for an orderly cleaning up—then looked in briefly on one of the treatment rooms, where Shannon and an assistant were performing an autopsy, presumably on the murdered engineer. After that, she punched up surgical recovery. Deller's back blocked most of her view of the bandage-swathed patient he tended, but the erratic life readings Wallis called up on another monitor identified the patient as Aludran—an Aludran very close to death. A crimson-robed Muon sat close by, his feather-crested head bowed over a bandaged hand that trailed tubes and wires, so the patient could only be the unfortunate Ta'ai.

Sighing helplessly, Wallis shook her head and flicked quickly through the half dozen infirmary rooms, glancing only in passing at other patients sleeping or resting, a few of them attended by a tense-looking nurse or orderly. Then she stopped to look more closely as another alien crest caught her eye. It was Ta'ai's brother, the quick, articulate Bana, sitting dejectedly on the edge of the bed where the technicians had left him after drawing his blood for Ta'ai. He was shivering, despite the thermal blanket he had pulled around himself against the cold of the ship's normal environment, but his own discomfort seemed to affect him very little. His eyes were fixed unwaveringly on the view screen a few meters across the room—the monitor in Ta'ai's recovery room—and occasionally he swayed weakly and shuddered. Once, his slender hand reached out as if to hold the motionless image on the screen before him, but the very act betrayed his knowledge of its futility. Only a miracle could save Ta'ai now, and miracles seemed to be in short supply.

Wallis watched for several seconds, sensing the despair that the little alien must be feeling, then noted the location of the room she was viewing and switched off her console. Less than a minute later, she was entering the room. Bana turned around as she came in, recognition flickering in the pained yellow eyes.

"Why have you come? Have you not done enough?"

"I'm sorry about Ta'ai," Wallis murmured, moving around to sit on the end of the bed near Bana. "I know that you hold us responsible because we brought the cats aboard the *Valkyrie*, but—Bana, I don't know how to say this without its sounding as if I'm just trying to defend the cats, but Mather—Commodore Seton—and I aren't convinced that the cats are to blame."

"Not to blame?" Bana interrupted hotly. "How can cats not be to blame? You saw body of first passenger killed, Doctor. You see Ta'ai, dying there on screen. How can you say cats be not to blame?"

Wallis exhaled heavily. "I can't prove it yet, Bana. But I *can* tell you that Commodore Seton found an electronic device near the cats, after the first man was killed. It was putting out a psychotronic—a mental 'sound'—that made the cats angry and afraid—and also everybody guarding them: the Rangers, the crewmen. And it may have been what upset Muon so much the night before."

"Electronic device?" Bana said blankly. "Machine?"

"That's right, a machine," Wallis agreed, trying to shift her terminology to a vocabulary that Bana could understand. "Maybe the cats didn't scare Muon at all. Maybe the machine scared Muon, but he thought it was the cats. Maybe someone put the machine there to make the cats angry and afraid and then killed the people, so it would look as if the cats killed them."

"Why someone want to do that?" Bana asked. "Besides, we know cats kill people on ship. Ship's officers find fur and cat tracks. Muon see death in worship trance. Now you say maybe cats not kill?"

Wallis shook her head. "I can't explain what Muon 'saw,' Bana. I do know what was found. But the cats *can't* have been out of the hold. We've got a lot of sophisticated equipment down there, which would have told us if they had. It doesn't lie. Besides, our cats are different from the ones you know and fear. Maybe blue cats don't act the same as green ones."

Bana bowed his head for a moment, then looked up wearily at the screen. "And maybe it not matter what color cats are, Doctor. Ta'ai, my *czina*, my sister, is dying, and they—will not let me be with her."

His voice broke at that, and he turned his head away and would not look at her. Thoughtfully, Wallis glanced up at the screen again—at Ta'ai connected to her life-sustaining machines, at the solemn-faced Deller monitoring the function of those machines, at Muon hunched beside Ta'ai and holding her hand.

"Why don't you come with me, Bana?" Wallis said,

standing to gently lay a hand on Bana's blanketed shoulder. "Much as I'd like to undo what's happened, I can't—but I think I *can* get you in to be with your *czina*."

Minutes later, she was back in Shannon's office and watching the surgical recovery room again. Deller had left, but Bana now sat on Ta'ai's other side, his very presence apparently strengthening Muon, at least—though Ta'ai's life readings grew weaker with each passing minute.

Satisfied—for there was nothing more she could do for Bana or for Ta'ai—Wallis changed the scene again until she relocated Shannon. The younger physician, the autopsy completed, was stripping off soiled surgical gloves and gown while she listened to a concerned-looking Deller. He spoke too low for the microphones to pick up what he said, but Shannon's face fell at his words, and she stood silently for several seconds after he left. Then, as her assistant began gathering up the surgical instruments they had used, Shannon reached wearily above the table and removed a data cassette—and headed for the door. Wallis heard a door sigh open and closed in the outer office, and quickly turned off the console as footsteps approached.

"What are you doing here?" Shannon asked dully as she entered and tossed the data cassette onto the console. She pulled off a blue surgical cap and shook out her short curly hair, then sank down in a chair opposite Wallis and closed her eyes, leaning her head against the chair back.

"I thought I might be able to help," Wallis said, watching the younger woman carefully. "I guess it's been pretty bad, hasn't it? And not enough sleep to deal with it well, either, I'll bet. We shouldn't have hit you with that vampire business last night. How much sleep *did* you get?"

Shannon shrugged but did not open her eyes. "Who knows? Two hours? Three? Deller called me to surgery just before six. It's nearly ten now, and already I've been through an extensive surgery and an autopsy, on top of what happened yesterday. My work isn't half over, either. There'll be another autopsy before the day is out. Ta'ai isn't going to make it."

"I know. I took the liberty of monitoring her while I was waiting for you. I suppose Deller told you I made him let Bana in to be with her. I hope you don't mind."

Shannon opened her eyes look at Wallis, then shook her head, though she made no effort to rouse from her comfortable position. "Of course not. He should have been there all along. In all the confusion, somebody obviously forgot to move him. We pulled quite a lot of blood from him when he first came in, hoping it might buy her a little more time, but the poor fellow could only give so much. She was pumping it out almost as fast as we could pump it in."

"I know. It won't be much longer." Wallis sighed and leaned over the desk to punch up Ta'ai's readings again. "Damn, look at that. She's started to go flat already."

Shannon grimaced, then sat forward far enough to insert her data cassette and order a correlation run between this one and the previous day's report. She glanced at Wallis again as she sat back and waited for the readout.

"I don't think I'm cut out to be a company doctor, Wallis," she said, rubbing a hand over her eyes. "Do you know what the captain had the audacity to remind me, when we were floating Ta'ai into surgery? That the murder of a passenger aboard a Gruening ship can do terrible things to the company's reputation. Not a word about Ta'ai. He was worried about the company's image."

"Well, I suppose that's part of his job," Wallis ventured. "He doesn't strike me as a hard-hearted man. Rigid, perhaps, but—"

Shannon sighed explosively and sat forward to

watch the readout begin crawling up the screen.

"Oh, I don't suppose I should really blame him," she said. "Don't let on that you know, but he's marking time until he can retire to a planetside assignment. He's developed a heart condition that—"

She broke off and sighed again as she continued to read the data, shaking her head as she tapped the screen with a fingernail. "Wallis, look at this report. You're going to have to face facts. Throats torn out, chests and arms slashed to ribbons, the bodies nearly drained of blood—and each one, Ta'ai included, had a tuft of blue cat hair in his or her fist. It's almost as if the beasts left a calling card!"

Wallis stood up for a better angle on the screen. "Yes, almost a little too perfect, don't you think?"

Sighing wearily, Shannon shook her head. "Come on, Doctor. I know you want to believe that the cats didn't do it, but we've been over this before. The blue fur is definitely Lehr cat fur. And what else could rip those bodies like that? Phillips's neck was snapped like a twig."

"I know what it *looks* like," Wallis answered, continuing to scan over the readout. "I still want to run a comparison of the fur found on the bodies with samples from our cats."

Shannon looked at her in disbelief, then sat back and exhaled violently, chasing a stylus around the desk top with one forefinger.

"When someone can get into the hold to *get* those samples, I'll be happy to do that, Doctor! And when I do, are you next going to tell me that, sure, the victims were killed by a Lehr cat, only it wasn't one of *your* Lehr cats? I wonder if you'd care to speculate as to where a fifth cat could be hiding aboard the *Valkyrie*, or how it would have gotten here!"

"All right, I agree, it's farfetched," Wallis said. "When none of the logical explanations fits, though, one has to try the illogical ones." She scanned over the next few lines in the report, then glanced across at Shannon again. "I understand that there were cat tracks on the floor near Phillips's body and that he had a bloody force-blade in his hand. Cat blood?"

"I'm still waiting for the lab work on that," Shannon replied sullenly. "But frankly, that's the least of my worries just now. We've got nearly eleven hundred passengers aboard this ship, and eight hundred crew, and every one of them is getting jumpy. The word has gotten out, and a lot of them can't sleep—or don't want to—and there were a couple more witnesses who found or saw this morning's victims before we could secure the scenes. They're sedated now, and I'll have to do memory wipes on them before too many more hours pass, but—damn it, Wallis, I can't wipe out the memories of everyone aboard this ship!"

"I don't envy you your job," Wallis said lamely. "If there were something more I could do, you know I would." She shrugged helplessly, and Shannon sighed and managed a wan smile.

"Look, I'm not blaming you. I guess I'm not even really blaming your cats, for certain—though you have to admit that the evidence looks pretty damning. At this point, I'm almost tired and desperate enough to even believe your vampire hypothesis, if you could produce a likely suspect." She grinned wearily. "You see what measures I'll stoop to, to get this situation off my back?"

"You're exhausted. You don't know what you're saying," Wallis said with a smile.

Shannon almost laughed as she agreed. "I'll say. I'm exhausted. My staff is exhausted. Not counting Deller and me, I've only got twenty people, and nearly half of those are orderlies. Deller was on call last night, so he's in even worse shape than I am, but he's got to last at least as long as Ta'ai. But the regular functions of medical service don't stop just because there's a crisis, you know."

"That's true. And if you don't get some rest while you can, *you're* going to need medical service. Why don't you lie down and have a nap? I'll cover for you while you sleep."

"Thanks, but I can't let you do that," Shannon said with a yawn, weaving to her feet to lean against the desk. "It's my responsibility. I've got to wait for that blood workup, and then someone will have to—"

"Someone *else* can handle things for a few hours," Wallis insisted, pulling the younger woman out from behind the desk and closer to the couch along the wall. "Sit down. I'm indirectly responsible for your situation. The least you can do is let me help."

"Wallis, I can't—really," Shannon protested weakly.

"Oh, yes, you can."

Wallis passed one hand close in front of Shannon's eyes, catching her attention, and snapped her fingers. "Relax and let go, Shivaun. Look at my hand and let your mind go blank for a little while. Watch the end of my finger. As it comes closer to your forehead, your eyelids are getting heavier and heavier—and when it touches, you will go to *sleep*."

And as her finger touched Shannon between the eyes, her other hand moved from its supportive position on the younger woman's shoulder to a spot just between the shoulder blades, which she pressed. The combination of suggestion, fatigue, and a pressure point that Wallis had learned years before from a monk of Tel Taurig was more than Shannon could resist. As she started to slump, relaxing in sleep, Wallis eased her back to lie down on the couch and pulled a thermal blanket loosely around her.

Then she went to the desk console and tapped out a request for information, keying with the access code she had seen Shannon use. Almost immediately, the readout began clicking up the screen.

Blood specimen taken from force-blade in hand of victim Phillips: homo sapiens, type B-positive. Fur-

ther breakdown of variants still in progress, due to small quantity of sample.

Blood specimen taken from victim Phillips: homo sapiens, type O-positive, accounting for all samples thus far analyzed from paw prints and other blood seepage at scene. Further analysis and comparisons progressing.

"And no mention of cat blood," Wallis muttered to herself, straightening from the console to glance briefly at the sleeping Shannon.

So. That knowledge alone was a gem of great worth, for it meant that Phillips's attacker almost certainly had not been one of the cats—not with type B-positive blood on the blade. Nor was it Phillips's own blood. And *homo sapiens* blood of whatever type excluded the alien Aludrans from the reckoning—though Wallis had never suspected them of such physical violence, anyway.

Which meant that Phillips's attacker almost certainly was a human with type B-positive blood—which, since close to ten percent of a given human population could be expected to fall into that general blood grouping, narrowed any potential list of suspects to only around two hundred of the *Valkyrie*'s nearly two thousand passengers and crew. Unless the computer could refine its parameters further, which seemed less and less likely as a readout was not forthcoming, that was still a lot of suspects, even putting the crew right at the bottom of the list.

Impatient, Wallis asked for a status check, only to confirm that the computer was having difficulty reading more than a very gross profile of the B-positive blood sample. The scant quantity of the specimen from the blade seemed to be part of the problem, but some other factor was also at work—almost as if the secondary blood characteristics were being screened by some unusual chemical bonding.

She decided not to wait in Shannon's office any

longer, though. After directing the computer to kick out separate lists of passengers and crew who fit the suspect profile—however gross that might turn out to be, given the incomplete profile it had to match against medical records—and to print out in the hold's security office as well as in Shannon's, Wallis left a progress report for Shannon to find when she awoke, and left for the hold. She wondered how her new information would fit with what Mather had found.

Other than his initial discovery of the butchered cat, however, Mather had learned very little. After partitioning off that end of the cage—which enraged the remaining cats and set off a new chorus of screaming—Mather set the big cage scanners to record the most obvious trauma to the dead cat's body. But he suspected that Wallis would need to do a proper post mortem to learn any real details of what had happened.

So he concentrated on *how* it had happened, questioning his Rangers and running yet another check of all their security equipment while he waited for Wallis to show up.

But he turned up no discrepancies. The tapes showed no break in service, from the time the phase nets were set the night before, until Mather himself had ordered them shut down and found the dead cat. All equipment seemed to be functioning perfectly, with no reason to suspect that it had not always done so. And independent interviews of all his men by himself and Perelli, his interrogation expert, failed to disclose any variance in individual reports of the night's events. By all outward evidence, *nothing* unusual had occurred in the security hold.

Except that the Lehr cat they called Rudolph lay slaughtered in a pool of his own blood at the end of a plasteel cage, his companions' voices lifted in mournful howls as the humans who had brought them there tried to discover the cause of his death.

Thus it was that Wallis found her husband crouching in front of the dead cat's cage and running tests with a portable scanner balanced on one knee. She glanced at his readings as she laid both hands on his shoulders and leaned down to kiss the top of his head.

"What do you want to bet that at least some of the blood in that cage is humanoid, type B-positive?"

"Mmmm?" Mather blinked, emerging only partially from his perplexed study of the dials on his scanner.

"That's right—though some of it is A-positive. Most of it is cat blood, of course." He blinked again, then turned enough to actually look up at her. "You don't even seem surprised. And how did you know that there would be B-positive?"

"There was B-positive blood on the dead engineer's force blade—and no cat blood anywhere. I wish you hadn't found A-positive, though. It means we must have *two* suspects instead of one. The engineer was type O."

"Wonderful," Mather muttered. "Now *nothing* connects."

"Yes, it does—it *has* to. We just don't have the connections figured out yet," Wallis said, kneeling down beside him. "Do you want me to take over here for a while? You look as if you could use a few minutes to unwind and try for a fresh approach."

With a grunt of agreement, Mather handed the scanner to Wallis and stood up stiffly to stretch.

"It just doesn't make any sense," he said. "I know there has to be *some* rational explanation, but damned if I can find it. About the only thing I know for certain right now is that old Rudolph didn't commit suicide. Nor did his mate rip him to shreds."

The mate in question, the cantankerous Matilda, let out a particularly grating screech, as if to underline his statement.

But merely pacing and looking at the remaining cats from other visual angles did not bring the inspiration Mather hoped for. In a very short time, he found himself standing silently in front of the slain Rudolph's cage again. Wallis had opened the end of the cage to examine the body more closely and collect more blood samples, and the other cats had finally stopped their howling, except for an occasional mournful cry from Matilda.

"Anything new?" Mather said quietly.

Wallis half turned in his direction. "Yes, as a matter of fact. Tell me, did you find any discrepancies among the men?"

Chilled, Mather crouched down beside her.

"No. Why? Do you think it was an inside job?"

"I hope not," Wallis replied, "but if our security arrangements are as good as we've been saying all along, we certainly have to consider that possibility. I *can* tell you that old Rudolph here didn't die of his wounds, however." She held out a tiny needler dart, its tufted drug receptacle clear and empty. "It's the same manufacturer we use, Mather—which is not to say that someone else couldn't have bought from the same source. This is the only one I found, but from the level of tranquilizer in his bloodstream, I'd say he took five or six of these before his killer settled down to cut him up. Somebody didn't want to take any chances. His breathing would have been paralyzed very quickly, and he must have suffocated."

"A low-load needler, eh? The poor critter didn't have a chance."

"Well, at least he got in a few swipes at his killer or killers," Wallis said. "You were absolutely right about the blood, too. There are traces of B- and A-positive blood on his claws and in the cage—which tends to confirm that our prime suspect is probably the same person who tangled with Phillips's knife. We should have a printout of B-positive suspects any time."

Sighing, Mather glanced at the three remaining cats, who had massed just on the other side of the separating partition and were watching him intently.

"I sure wish you guys could talk," he said softly, a little surprised to see them so quiet. "Or—*can* you?" he added, after a beat. "Wally, I've just gotten an idea. Do you suppose you could get everybody out of here for a few minutes? I'll want the force nets back in place, too. And have Perelli go get Doctor Shannon, just in case we have more trouble with this than I think we're going to have. This is a long shot, but I think it's worth a try, under the circumstances."

Wallis considered it more than a long shot, but she was not about to argue. After dispatching Pirelli as requested, she had Webb round up the remaining Rangers in the security room and cut in the shields. The not-black shimmer of the Margall force field made everything beyond it blur disconcertingly, and she blinked and shook her head to clear her vision as she turned back to the cages. Mather had already lured an oddly docile Matilda into the section of the cage nearest her dead mate and shut her off from the other pair, who seemed not to mind. Wallis turned on the cage scanner overhead, then began rummaging in her medical kit for a hypospray as Mather calmly drew his needler and shot Matilda.

As the dart struck, the big cat spat and hissed, licked furiously at the spot, then reeled drunkenly against the side of the cage and peered out at them with wide, startled eyes.

"Give her a minute or two," Wallis said, glancing at the scanner readouts and handing a loaded hypospray to Mather. "This shouldn't hurt her, but it's one thing you don't want to rush."

Holstering his weapon, Mather sat down heavily on the floor beside the cage, watching as Matilda's big, night-seeing pupils contracted to merest slits and the animal's legs collapsed, letting her down with a whoof. Cautiously, Mather reached the hypospray toward the cat's nearer forepaw, where the fur was shorter and thinner, and triggered it. Matilda hissed back at it, but her head was already weaving as it sank slowly to rest on the wide, hairy paws. As Wallis scanned the cat again, Mather reset the hypo and unsnapped the cuff of his left sleeve.

"You're sure you want to go through with this?" Wallis asked, turning the scanner on him and reaching to check his hypo setting before he could set it to his wrist.

"I'm sure I want to find out what happened," Mather countered with a wry little smile. "Our fuzzy friend, here, saw everything."

Briefly, he reached over to stroke the blue fur pooching through the mesh of the cage, then glanced at the setting of the hypo one more time before triggering it against his inner wrist. He winced at the cold that immediately began spreading up his arm from the injection site, but he managed a ghost of a smile as he handed the hypo back to Wallis.

"Don't worry. You know the drug isn't going to hurt me in such a low dose; and if I start to get into trouble otherwise, I promise to come right back."

"Sure," Wallis murmured, readying another hypo, just in case, "as long as you know you're risking your life to save a cat."

But Mather had ceased to pay attention to her. Easing himself back to lean against the side of the cage, his shoulders resting against the mesh and the soft blue fur, he stretched out his right arm toward Matilda's head, hooking two fingers through the mesh to burrow in the fur of one great forepaw. His eyelids fluttered and then closed as he laid his head back against the mesh of the cage.

By the time Wallis had scanned him again, verifying a steady pulse with her hand on his free left wrist, Mather was no longer aware of what was going on around him. He sensed only the odd play of light and shadow against his closed eyelids as the Margall field fluctuated and shimmered; the pleasant, musky smell of cat in his nostrils; the softness of fur beneath his fingers.

And then, the touch of a totally alien mind.

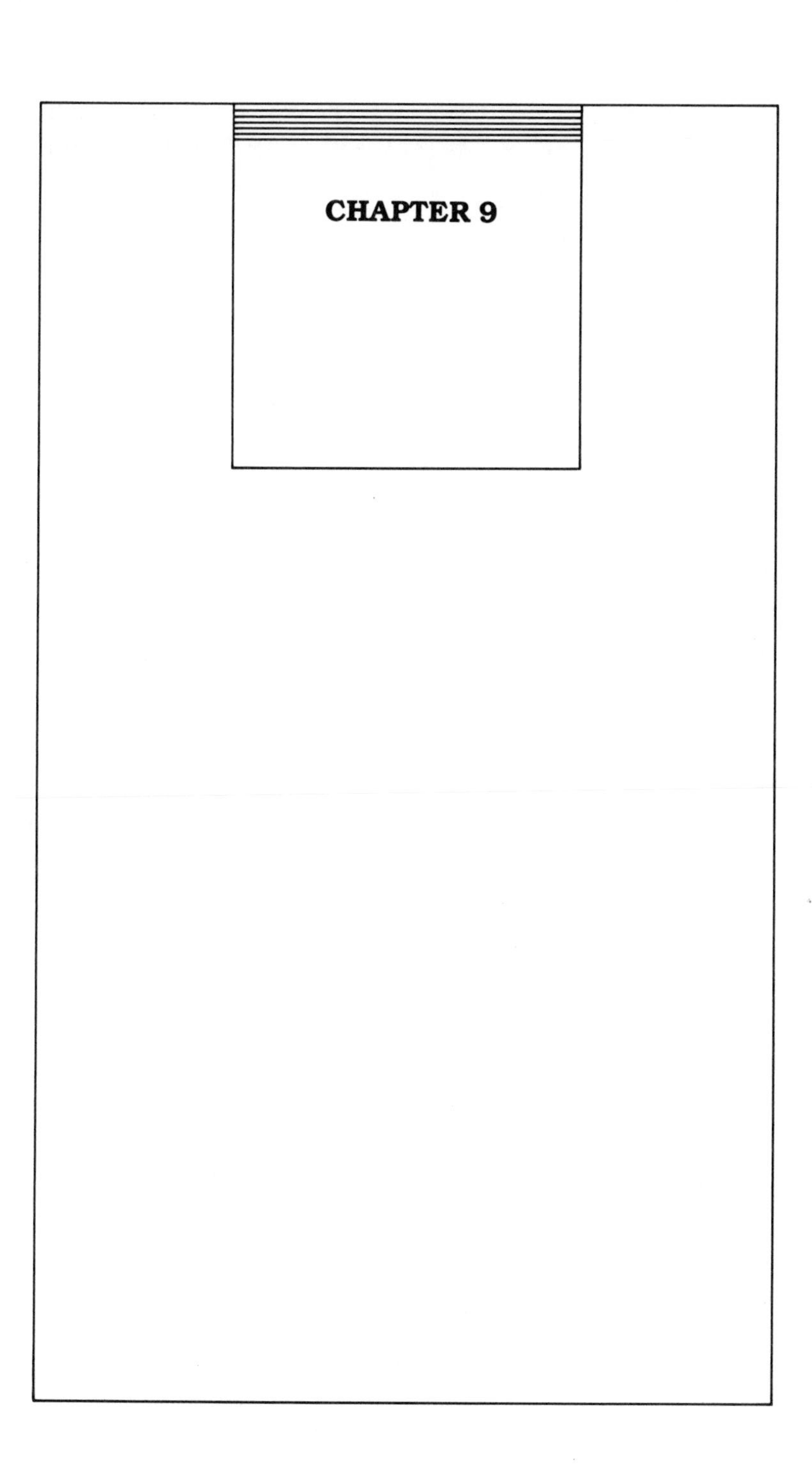

CHAPTER 9

The contact was different from any Mather had ever attempted before. Lehr cats, though the most cunning of hunters and stealthy of carnivores, were relatively uncomplicated beasts. Despite the fact that their brains were geared for lightning reflexes, killer instincts, and fine-honed sensory awareness, their reasoning ability had always been thought limited—and this one was sluggish from the drugs that Mather had risked to bring her to this state.

That distracted Mather at first. For a heart-sinking few seconds he feared that the feline mind was too alien, the channels too convoluted for him to enter and still retain his own identity. But then he was inside the big cat's mental processes—he could hardly call it thinking, especially with the drugs—remembering with fear and hatred the man-thing that had come and slain her mate.

It was cold-bloodedly done, and he wished fervently that the cat's ability to distinguish between individual humans were more acute—because he watched only through the eyes of her uncomprehending perception as the annoyingly flickering shields disappeared, and not one but two man-shapes approached the cages. He felt her wariness, then surprise and fear as something like a cloud hissed at her from one man-shape's paw—and the other one shot her mate with one of the stinging things she remembered from her capture.

He bit at the dart and tried to tear it from his fur, but the drug worked quickly—and something was draining *her* strength as well. She could not seem to make her legs obey her. She saw her mate staggering, weaving drunkenly, then collapsing as more darts struck his side, and she tried to call to him. He was panting now, lying flat on his side, his tufted tail lashing more and more weakly, and her hunting mates were sprawling helplessly in the cage behind her.

Then one of the man-shapes was emerging from the cloud and circling the end of the cage nearest her mate, opening the mesh, and raising something that shone in the odd light.

She tried to force her heavy body to respond, to drag herself upright and rend the hated enemy limb from limb, but she was as weak and helpless as a new cub. She saw the flash of metal, then the bright fountain of blood, as the man-shape savaged her mate—who fought bravely, for as long as he could.

But soon she could lift her own head no longer and felt her own awareness draining away, her vision going dim, as the drug continued to work.

When next she could stir, her mate lay motionless in a congealing pool of his own blood, not even breathing, his soft fur matted and streaked with red. She had nosed at him desperately, raking her tongue across his face in a futile attempt to rouse him, but he was as still as the fleetbeasts they had used to hunt together. Her howl of anguish had soon been joined by those of her hunting mates, as they sang their grief to an unhearing and uncaring universe.

Mather shuddered at the poignancy of that raw emotion, staying with it a few seconds longer to let the full impact sink into his mind, then withdrew, opening his eyes carefully to turn and gaze at the creature whose memory he had just shared. The big cat slept more easily now, as if sharing the horror had somehow brought a measure of comfort to her simple mind. Perhaps she had sensed Mather's outrage as well. Softly Mather stroked the giant paw where it lay beneath his fingers, finally turning to glance at Wallis. His wife was sitting patiently and waiting, a strangely fragile smile on her lips.

"Some of it spilled over, didn't it?" Mather murmured, letting his head lie back against the cage once more. "Did you see what happened?"

"Not really. But think I felt a little of her loss," Wallis answered softly. "They mate for life, don't they?"

With a drowsy smile, Mather held out his hand to her and pressed her palm to his lips, retaining her hand in his as he leaned back once more.

"Unfortunately, this confirms that our intrepid killer definitely was not working alone," he said, his eyes not yet focusing as he coaxed his recall to more conscious levels. "Matilda saw *two* man-things, and one of them had a knife. Whoever they were, one of them gassed the cats and then the other one needled her mate and cut him up while he was dying. It's pretty obvious now that someone is trying very hard to frame the cats—why, I have no idea."

"That does tell us *how* they managed to do it, though," Wallis said. "If they gassed the cats, they probably gassed the Rangers, too. Hey, easy!" she added, rummaging in her medkit for a stimcap as Mather started to get shakily to his feet. "Here, break this under your nose and breathe deeply. You're not quite out from under the hypo yet."

"Yeah, I know."

Bracing himself against the side of the cage, Mather snapped the plastic capsule between his thumb and fingers and cupped his hand over his nose. The brief whiff of vapor was pungent, but it cleared his head. Nodding his thanks as he finished standing up, he handed the empty back to Wallis. "Thanks, that's better. Now, where were we? You're saying they gassed the Rangers? Wouldn't someone remember?"

Wallis shook her head. "Not necessarily. I'll have to run some tests to determine exactly what was used, but there are several definite possibilities. Properly administered, the men would never even know they'd been out."

"Well, that's just dandy," Mather muttered under his breath. "Who would know how to do that? *I* don't."

"No, but *I* do. And unfortunately, it's quite possible that any of our Rangers might. It isn't difficult—just rather specialized."

"So you're saying that it really *could* have been an inside job?"

"It could have been. The killer's accomplice could have been one of our men, at least. But it's equally possible that the gas could have been introduced from outside the hold. I'd rather not get bogged down in suspicion of our own people right now—especially since more than half of them, including ourselves have A-positive blood."

Mather shook his head and sighed again, glancing at the bright-black shimmer of the shields still around them. "Would the gas show up in blood samples, after this long? And if so, would a drug screening clear our men, if they all had it in their systems?"

Wallis shook her head. "It would probably show up, but unfortunately our culprit probably would've been smart enough to gas himself, too, after he'd reset all the security systems. You're asking all the questions I've already asked myself, Mather." She threw the inside switch to lower the shields. "I only wish I had some answers for you."

With the shields gone, a red light could be seen flashing insistently above the lock system in front of the outer door. Four Rangers waited there with stunners at the ready.

"Incidentally," Wallis added, "the captain arrived just after you went under, and he's madder than a Sirian swamp stalker. Do you want to let him in?"

Mather snorted. "Not particularly, though I suppose I'm going to have to. If I don't, he's likely to burn the door off, or some other fool thing. Anything else I should know?"

Wallis grinned. "At least a dozen things, I'm sure, but no one knows them yet to tell you. While you talk to him, I'll be in the office, checking on those printouts. Shall I have them reactivate the shields, so he doesn't hit the cats if he comes in shooting?"

"You can be *so* encouraging," Mather muttered, moving closer to the lock. But he signaled Webb to reengage the shields before giving Casey the sign to admit Lutobo.

"Now, see here, Seton—" The captain was the first one through the door, a needler strapped conspicuously to his right hip, his dark face a mask of smouldering resentment. Four armed security guards followed him, but they kept their hands carefully away from their own weapons when they saw the Rangers' stunners. Last came Perelli and Shannon, the latter more than a little cowed by the captain's black mood. Mather decided immediately that the best defense was going to be a strong offense.

"Seton, I want some answers, and I want them *now!*" Lutobo began.

"Yes, Captain, I'm sure you do," Mather interjected smoothly. "But before I give you any, I'd like to know about your communication with the Imperial authorities. I trust that our respective positions and authorities have been defined to your satisfaction?"

Lutobo's expression hardened at that, but he broke off what he had been about to say and took a deep breath, visibly forcing his temper back in check.

"Commodore Seton, if you were the emperor's own cousin, it would still be my responsibility to safeguard the lives of the passengers and crew entrusted to me. If you cannot allow me to take what I feel are the appropriate preventive measures to ensure their safety, and you refuse to offer reasonable alternatives, then you almost force me to go against direct orders from your superiors."

"As long as we're permitted to continue our investigation and the cats aren't harmed, I won't interfere with any reasonable measures that you may wish to take, Captain," Mather said calmly.

"Investigation? You'd think there was some question as to what's been going on here!" Lutobo bellowed.

"And just what *has* been going on here, Captain?" Mather countered. "Because if *you* know, I wish you'd tell me!"

"Well—for God's sake, Seton, three people have died!"

"Three?" Wallis said, coming out of the security office to join them. "Then, Ta'ai—"

"She died half an hour ago," Shannon replied, speaking for the first time. "There was nothing else we could do for her."

"You see?" Lutobo said accusingly. "Three deaths, Seton. Where does it all end?"

"Not before we stop blaming the cats and start considering other alternatives, Captain," Mather said. "It now appears—and we do have evidence to this end—that there's been a massive frame-up shaping under our noses. Would you like to have a look at the body of the cat that was killed?"

He signaled Webb to deactivate the security net again, but Lutobo barely glanced at the cages that became visible.

"At least poor Phillips got in a few good blows before the cat mangled him," the captain muttered. "I understand that there was blood all over his force-blade."

Mather shook his head. "Phillips may have gotten in some good blows at his assailant, Captain, but that assailant was not a Lehr cat. The blood was humanoid, type B-positive."

"What?"

"There wasn't any cat blood anywhere in the area, either," Mather went on. "The tuft of cat fur in his other hand was the *only* link to our cats—and anyone could have put it there."

"What about the paw prints?"

"I can't explain those yet, but the blood itself was the engineer's, with a few drops of the same blood as on the blade—type B-positive."

"But—if someone besides a cat killed Phillips, how do you account for your butchered cat?" Lutobo asked, astounded.

"Will you let me finish, Captain? I said that there wasn't any cat blood in Phillips's vicinity. Furthermore, the blood we found on and around the dead cat here, other than its own, was humanoid blood. For the most part, it was the same type as on the force-blade."

Lutobo's jaw dropped a fraction, but he managed to cover most of his astonishment well. "You mean that someone killed Phillips to make it look as if a cat did it and then came down and killed the cat, too?"

"It's beginning to look that way," Mather agreed. "Someone with type B-positive blood, which is reasonably rare."

"Well, do you know whose it is?"

Mather shook his head. "Not yet, Captain, but we can tell you several people whose blood it *isn't.* It isn't Phillips's, and it isn't Ta'ai's or any other alien's."

"Then who—and how—and *why?*"

Mather shook his head again. "We only know a little of the 'how,' so far. As nearly as we can gather, whoever killed Phillips—getting himself wounded in the process—knew he would have to cover if it was going to continue to appear that the cats were responsible for the murders. I can't even speculate as to why he's doing this yet, or especially why he's doing it the way he is—

but that's another facet of the story. At any rate, he came here to the hold, managed to get past my Rangers and tamper with the recording devices—we think he gassed them, but we haven't figured out exactly how he did *that,* either; we're working on it—and then he gassed and needled the cats, one of them fatally."

Lutobo, glancing past Mather at the bloody carcass, frowned. "I thought the cat was knifed."

"He was, but only after he was already dying from too many needler darts. Our fearless murderer climbed into the cage with the dying Lehr cat and started to butcher him, trying to make it look exactly as you thought it happened. Only he moved in too quickly, and the cat wasn't as helpless as it appeared. That's how humanoid blood got on the cat's claws and in the cage. In fact, there are two different humanoid blood groups unaccounted for, so our murderer must have had help."

"*Two* people involved," Lutobo breathed. "That's incredible. But *who?*"

"That shouldn't be too difficult to find out," Wallis replied. Our murderer and his accomplice, whoever they are, will have a few claw marks to show for their trouble. In fact, Mister B-Positive will also have one or more force-blade wounds, and those are rather difficult to hide. Doctor Shannon, you haven't had anyone come into Medical Section to be treated for lacerations or force-blade wounds today, have you?"

"Not that I know of," Shannon replied. "In light of what's been happening, I'm certain my staff would have notified me. I do have the list you requested of all passengers and crew with type B-positive blood, however. Assuming that it wasn't one of the crew or a child—and we do know that it's a male—that gives us about forty names."

She produced a printed list from inside her tunic and handed it to Wallis before going on. "I also discovered something odd when I tried to narrow down the list further. I wondered why I couldn't get past the very basic blood profile for a more precise match. He's taking some kind of drug that blocks the more subtle blood factors."

"You don't know what, specifically?" Wallis asked.

Shannon shook her head. "No one on our list is on record as taking anything that could do that, either. I correlated everyone's medical records on the entire ship."

"Well, what does *that* mean?" Lutobo asked.

"It means," said Wallis, comparing her list with Shannon's, "that one of the people on this list will have such a substance in his bloodstream now—so in a worst-case scenario, we can simply draw blood from all of them until we find our probable murderer."

"The *probable* murderer?" the captain muttered. "Wouldn't that be conclusive proof?"

"No, because more than one person could have taken such a drug. What *would* be conclusive proof is that our man also has at least one force-blade wound and probably several cat lacerations. He's likely to move a little carefully; the wounds may even be infected, Lehr cat claws being what they are. Our type A-positive accomplice is also likely to have a cat scratch or two, but he may be more difficult to spot, since he probably didn't get scratched as badly, judging by the amount of A-positive blood we found."

The captain's face had gone stony with suspicion as Wallis spoke, and now he glanced from her to Mather to Shannon and then back to Mather; he scowled as one of the Rangers brought Wallis another computer printout. "Seton, if this is some kind of clever cover-up or stall tactic—"

"And just *what* am I supposed to be covering up or stalling for, Captain?" Mather demanded, setting his fists on his hips. "Granted, the cats are very important to us. You checked with our superiors, and you know the scope of our authority, so you can imagine the value the Imperial government sets on the cats. But if you think, even for a minute, that I would deliberately jeopardize the lives of innocent people aboard this vessel, just to complete my mission successfully, then you are very much mistaken."

"Well—how do you plan to proceed, then?" Lutobo replied, a little taken aback at the newest turn of events.

Wallis, who had been scanning the second list with Shannon, raised an eyebrow as she glanced up at him. "As a matter of fact, Captain, Doctor Shannon and I talked with a man on each of these lists, only yesterday. They both have some knowledge of Lehr cats—and, therefore, a conceivable connection with what's been going on. Not that this necessarily makes them any more likely suspects than anyone else on the lists, but they're a good starting point."

"Who are they?"

"Vander Torrell, the historian who sat at your table the other night," Wallis said, "and a man called Reynal. He helped us track the cats on B-Gem."

"Who would have thought Torrell has good old A-positive blood?" Shannon murmured. "I thought it would be blue, to hear him talk. I guess we do have something in common, after all."

Lutobo glanced at her suspiciously. "Then you're on the list, too, Doctor."

"And so am I, and so is Mather," Wallis interjected, "along with a good third of the human population. However, it does leave Torrell right near the top of the list—though I'd guess that our B-positive suspect is the more dangerous of the two. I think I'd like to have blood samples from both Reynal and Torrell, for starters, to check for that odd drug—and see if either of them has any wounds he can't account for. It we come up cold, we'll start working our way down the rest of the lists."

"Well, I can have Doctor Shannon call them in to be

checked, if that's all it's going to take," Lutobo said.

"True," Wallis agreed, "but I'd rather do it myself, if you don't mind. I've had more training in this sort of thing than Doctor Shannon. I'll take along two Rangers as well. That way, if one one of these men *is* our murderer, we can deal with him. You're welcome to come along, though, Captain."

Lutobo still looked doubtful, but finally he snorted under his breath and folded his arms resolutely. "Very well, we'll try it your way for now, Doctor. Not that I'm totally convinced, you understand." He pointed at Mather. "I still don't trust those cats of yours—and I want to leave some of my own security here, *inside this hold,* while I go with Doctor Hamilton."

Mather spread his hands in a conciliatory gesture. "As long as they're outside the shields, as my men also will be, I consider that most equitable, Captain. In fact, I'll join you as soon as I've made a few final adjustments."

"Suit yourself," the captain muttered. "Mind you, though, if the cats do turn out to be involved in any way—"

"Captain—"

With a perplexed sigh, Mather glanced at Wallis and Shannon, at the cats, back at Lutobo, then briskly drew his needler and strode back to the cat cages, holding the weapon close along his thigh. The female whose mate had been slain was still asleep; the other pair sat quite still and looked at him suspiciously as he approached, the male occasionally letting out a low, warning growl.

Mather studied the pair for several seconds, recalling the price the animals had extracted even before the *Valkyrie*—the bearers injured and maimed during the capture, the two Rangers killed on B-Gem. Then he glanced down wistfully at the weapon in his hand and raised it, carefully squeezing off a needle into each animal's side. The cats looked startled; the female started to bite at the spot where the dart had struck; and then both of them staggered and collapsed to the floor of their cage. Behind him, Mather heard someone let out a low sigh.

Holstering his weapon, Mather reached up and turned on the scanners above the two groggy cats. He could hear the others approaching behind him as he watched the readings stabilize and the cats slipped into labored sleep. The touch on his arm was Wallis's as he turned to face the captain.

"Would you say that the cats are now incapable of voluntary action, Captain?" Mather asked.

Lutobo's dark eyes flicked over the cats briefly, then returned to Mather's face. "You're really certain they're innocent, aren't you?" he said gruffly. "So certain, you'd endanger them to make sure they can't be implicated any further."

"In the final analysis, we're talking about human lives, aren't we, Captain?"

Lutobo looked around uncomfortably—at Shannon and Wallis standing by, Wallis with hard copies of the blood lists in her hands; at Mather and his Rangers; at his own security men—then clasped his hands behind his back and rocked up and down a few times on the balls of his feet.

"Very well. Doctor Hamilton, I'd appreciate it if you'd allow me at least the semblance of command in this operation, but otherwise, I shall bow to your expertise, both medical and otherwise. And I'll insist that you get the cooperation you need. Doctor Shannon, I think it best if you return to Medical Section for now. We still have a shipful of passengers to care for."

"Yes, Captain."

"Courtenay, I'll ask you to come with us, please," he said to his security chief.

"Ay, sir."

"Take Wing and Casey for your Rangers," Mather said to Wallis, reasoning that if a Ranger *was* their second suspect and was one of the two he had chosen, at least the other might be able to neutralize him if he tried anything. "I'll join you at Reynal's cabin as soon as I've finished here. Don't take any foolish chances."

"Don't worry," she said with a laugh.

Wallis was not laughing by the time she and her party reached the crew lift. And when the lift stopped at Level Four, one deck short of where Reynal's cabin lay, the reaction of the couple waiting to board reminded her how formidable a band they must appear: she and her Rangers, Lutobo, and Courtenay. The couple decided not to board—she could hardly blame them—but just as the doors began to close, Wallis lurched toward the control panel and hit the door button, worming her way between the doors as soon as they had opened far enough.

"I saw Torrell," she murmured over her shoulder as she leaned out to peer to the right, then pointed toward a tall, retreating figure. "There he is. Let's take him right now, since he's here."

With a glance at the captain, who nodded, Casey and then Courtenay and Wing hurried after. Torrell looked surprised and a little annoyed as they, Wallis, and the captain converged on him.

"Is something wrong, Captain?" he asked. His manner was coldly appraising as he glanced among them.

"I hope not, Mister Torrell."

"It's *Doctor* Torrell—"

"Very well, *Doctor* Torrell," Lutobo said. "There's a steward's station just a few meters down the corridor, where we can have some privacy. I'd like you please to step inside with us to answer a few questions."

Torrell started to object, but he suddenly realized that he was now flanked by Courtenay and both Rangers, and that other nearby passengers were watching with increasing curiosity. No one laid a hand on him, but the implied threat was no less real for that. With a curt "Very well," Torrell moved with them without resistance to the door of the steward's station. Lutobo, on checking the room and finding it empty, stood aside and motioned for the others to enter. As soon as the door had closed behind them all, Torrell turned on Lutobo.

"I don't suppose you'd mind telling me what this is all about, Captain?"

"We're conducting an investigation, Doctor Torrell. Would you please remove your jacket and your shirt?"

"My what?"

As he realized that Lutobo was serious, Torrell went into a tirade. "I'll do no such thing! What is this, anyway? Star chamber proceedings? I warn you, Doctor Hamilton?" he barked, even more agitated when he saw that Wallis was removing an instrument from her medical kit. "If you think you can drug me and get away with it, you're dead wrong. You have no right—"

"As captain of this ship, I have all the right I need, Torrell," the captain said calmly, "and you won't be drugged unless that's what it takes for Doctor Hamilton to get a sample of your blood. Now, are you going to make this easy or difficult?"

Torrell looked as if he had been seriously considering making it difficult, but before he could open his mouth to tell them, Casey cleared his throat and snapped from parade rest to attention, slightly behind and to Torrell's right. The sound and movement froze Torrell in his place. He turned and looked hard at the impassive Casey, pivoted to glance at Wing and Courtenay, now flanking him, then turned back to Lutobo uncertain and definitely subdued.

"Captain, there had better be a very good reason for this," he said uneasily, unfastening his jacket and shirt and starting to remove both at once.

Before he could get free of either sleeve, Casey and Wing caught him deftly by his shirt- and jacket-tangled arms and held him long enough for Wallis to take her sample. Torrell went a little pale as she drew the blood, but he sensed it was best not to struggle or protest too much with a needle in his arm. His bravado returned when they released him, however, even his color coming back as he wriggled out of his jacket the rest of the way and then continued wrestling with his shirt. Wallis, as she stored the sample in her medical kit, decided that Torrell probably was *not* their killer—but in case he was, she had a strong knockout hypo waiting for him—for in these close quarters, there might not be time for needlers.

"I hope you're enjoying this, Doctor," Torrell said sarcastically, finally freeing one wrist from his shirt and shifting his attention to the other. "Usually, when I undress in front of a women, there's no other audience. Or maybe it's the *captain* who's enjoying it!" He pulled off the shirt the rest of the way and flung it at Lutobo, then stood defiantly, hands on his hips, glaring. "Are you satisfied, Captain? I'm going to hold you personally responsible for this outrage. You won't get away with it, you know."

Calmly, Lutobo handed the clothing to Courtenay to hold. "Neither threats nor insults will make this any easier, Doctor Torrell," Lutobo said. "Just do as you're told and turn around, please."

"Of course, Captain. Anything you say, Captain, sir!" Torrell turned around several times, making assorted mocking poses and postures as he did. Wallis looked closely at his arms and chest as he turned, but aside from a few obviously old and very minor scars—and several sets of parallel welts on his back, from a far more human kind of cat than those residing in the hold—there was no sign of a wound anywhere on his body.

"He seems to be clean, Captain," Wallis murmured, closing her kit on the hypo. "I don't think we need to see any more."

With a nod, Lutobo sighed for Courtenay to return

Torrell's clothing. The historian glanced at the captain with something akin to loathing as he thrust his arms back into his shirt.

"What, no total skin search, Lutobo?" he said with a sneer, shrugging the shirt into place and straightening the cuffs. "I'll have your job for this. Just watch me! I plan to take legal action as soon as we reach Tersel. You can bet your pension on it. I don't suppose you'd like to tell me now what you were looking for, to excuse this outrageous treatment?"

Lutobo remained impassive. "I apoligize for any inconvenience or embarrassment you may have suffered, Doctor Torrell. We have reason to believe that someone of your blood type was wounded by one of the Lehr cats early this morning, while trying to kill it. If my manner seemed somewhat precipitous, it's because three people have been murdered aboard this ship in the last thirty-six hours."

"And you thought that *I* might have committed those murders?"

"We thought you might be an accomplice," Wallis said. "You have the right blood type."

Torrell snatched his jacket from Courtenay and jammed it under his arm in a wad before wrenching the door open. "I'll see you in court, Doctor! And you, too, Captain! *All* of you!"

As he stalked down the corridor, Wallis sighed and glanced wistfully at Lutobo. "You know, you could have asked me to take him out, Captain," she said. "I had a hypo all ready. Then we could have sent him on to Shannon for a nice mind-wipe. I won't say it's strictly legal, but Mather and I would have backed you all the way."

Lutobo snorted, almost smiling.

"You're going to back me anyway, Doctor. Didn't you know? Any legal repercussions that may arise from this investigation will fall on the two of you. All that Imperial clout ought to be good for something besides bullying a starliner captain."

"It is," Wallis said, controlling her own smile. "Believe me, it is."

Meanwhile, on the deck just below, one of their killers stalked his next victim even as they spoke. Grim and purposeful, he lurked in the shadows near the entrance to the Fourth Level Gymnasium, watching until just the right quarry should come along. He was weakened from his interrupted attack on Phillips; further debilitated from the wounds sustained in the slaughter of the Lehr cat. But it was not long before his ideal victims emerged: two young boys, laughing and talking and paying scant attention to where they were going and who or what came near them.

They were not on guard. They were children, the older no more than nine standard years of age, neither of them schooled in reading the subtle signs of being *prey.* They did not notice the figure coming at them from a side passageway until it was too late.

It was almost too late when their attacker swooped out in front of them in a swirl of blue fur, golden eyes glowing with fanatic purpose in the shadow-folds of a hooded cloak. It was too late when hands reached out to seize both boys—the younger by the wrist, the older by the throat, a mere touch stunning all voluntary movement, dulling perception, numbing will. It was far too late as their captor drew the older victim closer in fatal embrace, murmuring alien words in a harsh, discordant tongue before sinking pointed teeth into a helpless, upturned throat.

Nor could the younger boy even try to escape—for all volition, all ability to react, had been obliterated by the merest touch of that hand that held him captive. Still quivering in that grasp, the younger boy could only watch his companion pale and die, not even able to flinch as their attacker dropped his lifeless first victim to the carpet and turned to draw the second into that same deadly embrace.

And only a few corridors away, Doctor Shivaun Shannon paused near the elevator to calm a trio of agitated passengers. The man was white-faced with tension, the two women babbling almost incoherently that they all surely would be murdered in their beds before the ship made her next port.

Shannon listened politely, dispensed reassurance and a tranquilizer capsule to each, and had just continued on toward her office when a woman's shrill scaream shattered the air.

"What was that?" one of the passengers asked with a gasp.

Shannon bolted for the source of the cry with only a muttered "Pardon me!" but a steward and a security guard reached the scene before she did. The guard even caught a glimpse of the presumed murderer fleeing around a far turn in the companionway. While the steward called for an emergency team and tried to give aid to the young victims and a hysterical woman who apparently had raised the alarm, the guard sprinted off in pursuit, only to skid to a confused halt as he nearly ran into a hulking figure in a dark cloak.

The figure reached out for him, though, and its touch paralyzed the guard, bringing him to his knees, head bowed to touch the figure's boots. Through his pain, the guard was dimly aware of the figure bending over him, but he could not summon the will or the strength to raise his head and look.

"You have seen no one. Do you understand?" whispered a voice at his left ear.

"I—I—" the guard managed to stammer. He could feel the speaker breathing close to his neck and caught the stench of blood on the other's breath.

"You will remember none of this," the whisper continued. "You tripped and fell, and that which you were pursuing eluded you. You remember nothing of what you saw."

Something cold touched the side of the guard's neck then, lingering briefly over the pulse point, and then fire radiated sharply outward from that point, quickly filling his head with such agony that he lost consciousness. When he came to, footsteps were pounding down the corridor around him and someone was pausing to ask if he was all right. He picked himself up dazedly, wondering what he could have tripped over to nearly knock himself out, and headed back toward the source of all the confusion in the vicinity.

Shannon and a steward were bending over a hysterically sobbing boy of seven or eight when the guard arrived. A whey-faced male passenger had covered the still body of a slightly older child with his jacket, and another tried to comfort the weeping woman who had found them. Two more from security came and tried to begin clearing the area of morbidly fascinated passengers. Deller arrived with a med tech and an emergency kit, briefly glanced at the still body under the jacket, then signaled the tech to begin seeing to the other passengers. He crouched beside Shannon and began running a scanner over the hysterical child in her arms.

"Miraculously enough, I think he's just shaken up," Shannon murmured, trying to rummage one-handed in the medkit while she continued to hold the child against her and rock him soothingly. "Let's give half a cc. of Suainol, all right? There, now, hon, you're going to be just fine. You're safe now. No one is going to hurt you. Just relax, sweetheart. It's all over now."

The boy did not flinch as Deller administered the drug; and gradually, under Shannon's ministrations and the gentle compulsion of the tranquilizer, his sobbing diminished and words began to become distinguishable.

"The b-b-boolim b-b-bit Laije!" the boy stammered, shuddering as the fright overcame him again. "I saw it!

It bit Laije on the neck and m-made him bleed, and there wasn't anything I could do!"

'The *boolim?"* Shannon asked.

"A boolim! A boolim!" the child shrieked. "It hurt Laije! It made him bleed, and then he wouldn't move!"

The last word was choked off by a hiccup and a bout of coughing, and Shannon exchanged a troubled glance with Deller as she rocked the child closer.

"What's a boolim?" Deller whispered.

Shrugging, Shannon turned her attention back to the child. "There, now, honey, it's not going to get you. Don't worry. Think back before the boolim. Forget about the boolim for now. Tell me what happened. Where were you going?"

"L-Laije and I w-were playing f-f-floatball in the gym," the boy said, his sobs subsiding a little as the drug became more insistent. "When we came out, we—we were just walking along—and all of a sudden th-the boolim grabbed us, and I couldn't get away, and neither could Laije. It had Laije by the neck. And then it came and—and—"

"What did the boolim look like?" Shannon asked, glancing aside momentarily as a guard knelt to listen. "It can't get you now, honey. Try to remember what it looked like."

The child swallowed, his voice becoming smaller. "It was big and black—"

"How big?" Shannon asked. "Bigger than me?"

One teary eye looked up at her, and then the boy nodded. "B-bigger. And it had big, black wings—I think—and there was blue inside the wings—and—and when it touched me, it hurt, and—and—I couldn't move, and neither could Laije. And then—and then—"

"Go on. What happened then?"

"Then it bit Laije! It had big yellow teeth, and—and there was blood on its mouth when it finally let him go—and he wasn't moving!"

"Did it come after you, then?" Shannon insisted.

The child yawned and nodded sleepily, his answers becoming automatic. "Uh-huh. The boolim grabbed me, and it was going to bite me, too. I could see its teeth, and Laije's blood—but then it ran away."

"It ran away," Shannon repeated, mystified. "It was going to bite you, but it ran away?"

The boy managed a sleepy nod. "Just like Laije," he murmured. "Only—it didn't. I think . . ."

"What do you think?" Shannon prodded, as the boy started to drift off to sleep.

"I think . . . it was . . . afraid. . . ."

"Afraid?" Shannon breathed, though only Deller and the kneeling guard heard the echoed word. "Del, what do you make of that?"

Deller shook his head. "It's a fantastic story. Do you think it's all true?"

"Well, I'm sure he thinks it is." Cradling the sleeping child close, as much in comfort to herself as to him, Shannon narrowed her eyes as if trying to recall something. "Del, do you have any idea what a boolim is?"

Deller shook his head. "Sorry, Shivaun. The boy is an Al Kaffan, though. I checked his ident tag while you were questioning him. It sounds like some fairy-tale reference. Maybe boolims are what Al Kaffan parents use to threaten their kids with if they don't behave themselves."

"I'll check that angle," Shannon agreed. "In the meantime, I want you to take our young friend back to the office for a thorough going-over. Locate the boy's parents and have them meet me in my office. Ditto for the dead boy's parents. I need to—"

She had started to pass the sleeping boy into Deller's arms as she spoke, but as she gathered him up, she froze in midsentence and midmovement to stare in shock at a length of stout, pale-metallic chain that had fallen across her hand from around the boy's neck. A jewel-studded ident tag dangled from it, and Shannon had the sudden, certain suspicion that neither the tag nor the chain was steel or any other base metal. All at once everything started to make sense—of a sort.

"Silver!" was all she whispered, as she finished giving the boy into Deller's keeping and rose to go and find Mather Seton.

CHAPTER

10

Silver. She could not help remembering what she had read concerning silver and vampires, and what the Setons had told her, but she was not about to risk Deller's ridicule by mentioning her suspicion to him. Removing the chain from around the boy's neck—at least the jeweled ident tab bore no cross—Shannon murmured a vague excuse about wanting to run the boy's medical records, then fled for the nearest lift as fast as she dared. She punched the call button and fidgeted as the indicator light crawled toward Deck Four.

The whole thing was incredible, too ludicrous for a trained scientist even to consider. She knew that things were not always what they seemed, that evidence could easily be misinterpreted, yet she could hardly ignore what apparently had happened. The boy's attacker seemed to have been frightened away by the silver chain in her hand. That might be coincidence, but tradition had always associated silver with the warding off of evil beings—such as vampires.

But surely there could be no such things as *real* vampires, and certainly not aboard a sophisticated starliner like the *Valkyrie*. And even if there were, it was ridiculous to suppose that such creatures would be repelled by such superstitiously recommended objects as crosses, or garlic—or silver.

Silver. The chain seemed to burn in her hand even as she thought about it, and she poured it back and forth between her two hands nervously as she waited for the lift.

Yet, if not the silver chain, then what had saved young Nikkos Vedarras? For that was his name, she saw from the ident tab. Why were there not *two* pale, bloodied bodies lying in the corridor behind her, instead of one? Was it possible that there really *was* a vampirelike being aboard the ship—with B-positive type blood that carried odd factors—and that it *did* fear silver?

The lift still had not arrived—it appeared to be permanently stuck at Deck Three—and in growing irritation, Shannon jammed her override token into the appropriate slot. The indicator began to move almost all at once, the doors soon opening on several surprised passengers.

"Sorry, ladies and gentlemen: medical emergency," she told them as she pushed aboard and pressed the button for the hold level, ignoring someone's muffled protest in the back as she priority-keyed that as well.

She would return to Seton first, she decided. She was not sure what to do with her new knowledge, now that she had it, but Mather Seton would know. Besides, Captain Lutobo and Wallis Hamilton probably were interrogating possible suspects even now. What if they should find the murderer and then themselves be attacked? They did not know to protect themselves with silver—if, indeed, that was a deterrent to the being they were seeking. And if he or it had the physical strength to rip the bodies of his victims as he had—

She darted between the opening doors as soon as the lift came to a stop and raced to the outer door of the hold to press her palm against the ident scanner. When the door sphinctered, she ducked through that, too, only to be caught for a breathless instant in a tangle field. Someone switched it off almost before she had time to feel its power, but she was breathless and still staggering a little as the Ranger named Peterson caught her under one elbow.

"Commodore Seton! Where are the captain and your wife?"

Mather, who had been conferring with one of the ship's security officers just inside the security room, looked up and then stood as he saw the expression on her face.

"What's happened?"

"Another murder and an attempted murder, two decks up." She leaned across the terminal to punch up a communications circuit. "ComNet, this is Shannon. Please locate the captain for me, as quickly as possible. He may be on Deck Two. This is an emergency. And Smitty," she added to the security man as she motioned for Mather to draw a little to the side, "keep on that until they find him, would you, please?"

At his nod of assent, she led Mather even farther from the console.

"You've discovered something," Mather guessed, raising an eyebrow in question as Shannon took his hand and put a mass of warmly glowing silver and jeweled ident tag into his palm. "What's this?"

Shannon drew a deep breath and let it out. "I think it's silver."

"And?"

"Don't you dare laugh. The latest victims were two children. The one who survived was wearing that around his neck. I think it's silver, and I think it's what saved him."

Mather's expression did not change, but his hand tightened minutely around the heap of chain and medallion before he opened it to scrape a thumbnail tentatively against one link.

"It *would* appear to be silver," he said impassively,

"though I'd have to test it to be sure. Were you able to get any description of the killer?"

"The boy called it a boolim, whatever that is," Shannon said impatiently. "Smitty, have you found him yet?"

The security man flipped another set of switches and shook his head. "He doesn't answer a standard page, Doctor. He must be inside one of the cabins."

"Doesn't he carry a personal communicator?" Mather asked.

"I've tried that, Commodore. Either he's turned it off or left it somewhere, which I doubt, or else it's being shielded inside a room. A lot of our passengers insist on extra security and privacy protection—and the rooms with controlled environments, such as some of our alien passengers require, would read the same way. If you could narrow down the possibilities, though, I can override some of them, for good cause."

"I assure you, this is a good cause," Mather said, hefting his handful of chain. "Try Lorcas Reynal's cabin, and then work through the other passengers on our B-positive blood list."

"Yes, sir."

As Smitty set to his work, Mather turned back to Shannon.

"You mentioned a boolim. Do you know what that is?"

Shannon shook her head.

"*Boolim* is a common Al Kaffan slang term." He glanced more closely at the ident tab. "Yes, I thought so. Young Nikkos is Al Kaffan. It's one of those curious parallels I was trying to tell you about the other night. In the general sense, it's akin to the old Earther 'boogieman,' but it has its specific roots in the Al Kaffan myth cycle as the *abul-aienim*, meaning *he who drinks blood by night*."

"In other words," Shannon answered weakly, "a vampire."

"If you will."

Mather had just turned to query the security man again when the man looked up.

"He isn't in any of those cabins, Commodore."

"He isn't?"

"I mean, he definitely isn't in all but one of them. I can't tell about number thirty-nine, on Deck Two. There's some kind of interf—"

"Thirty-nine is Reynal's cabin!" Shannon said with a gasp.

"There's interference? Is that what you were going to say?" Mather asked, leaning over the man's shoulder to adjust a control. "What do you mean, you can't tell?"

The man tapped out a set of commands, then set his finger under a small green tally light.

"Do you see that light? It's for cabin twenty-two, on Deck One—a Mister Carrington's cabin. The green means that no one is in there. A yellow light would mean that Carrington himself was present. If the captain were there, the light would show red, since that's who we're looking for. But when I reset for cabin thirty-nine, Deck Two"—he pushed another series of buttons, and the tally light went off—"I don't get anything at all. And it isn't a malfunction in the circuits, either. I checked that already. Doctor, could there be some kind of special life-support system in cabin thirty-nine that I don't know about?"

"Yes, there could!" Shannon said, snapping her fingers as she remembered. "He requested a sterile air circulation system and microbe-repellent force screen for the room. I think he also wears a personal microbe shield. Either one could be interfering with the locator signals."

"Is there any way to jam through a message?" Mather asked.

Smitty shook his head. "Afraid not, Commodore. Not without going up there and altering the systems that are causing the interference."

"Never mind." Mather gestured to one of the Rangers. "Get the rest of our people together, Perelli. Leave—ah—Fredricks here with the cats, and the rest of you go up to cabin thirty-nine, Level Two, and wait for us. Gather up as many of ship's security as you can along the way and arm with stunners as well as needlers. Do what you think necessary, if anything happens before we can join you, but otherwise, just stand by. Any questions?"

"No, sir."

"Meanwhile, Doctor Shannon and I are going to make a detour through Medical Section, on the way. I want to make sure this is silver." He flourished the chain in his hand. "And I want to pick up a few things. Doctor, I hope that your reagent shelf is well stocked, because I think I know how to stop our vampire."

And on Deck Two, Lutobo, Wallis, Courtenay, and the two Rangers were already in cabin thirty-nine, having finally opened the door with Courtenay's passkey when their buzzing and pounding brought no response. The room was dim inside, especially once the door closed behind them, and the five of them stood very quietly just inside the door until Wing could turn the lights up. Wallis's medical scanner had already told them that Reynal was not in.

"I wonder where he is," Wallis said, glancing around the rather austere cabin. Other than a decanter and glass on the table beside a chair, and a few personal toilet items behind the frosted plastic of a lavatory storage cabinet, the room showed few signs of occupancy. The captain followed Wallis's gaze and snorted.

"I don't want to even think about where he is, if he *is* the one who's responsible for what's been going on," he muttered, motioning for Courtenay to keep watch for Reynal's return on the door viewer. "What kind of man *is* this Reynal, anyway?"

As he gestured around the pristine cabin in disgust, pushing a chair into better alignment with one foot, Wallis put her scanner back in her medical satchel and went briskly to a set of wall storage units, opening a drawer and riffling through the contents.

"He doesn't get along well with people, Captain," she replied. "His forte is really archaeology—which is fortunate, since archaeologists mainly have to deal with dead people and things. He does know animals, though—and he was the best Lehr cat tracker we could find on B-Gem. Wing got along with him reasonably well, didn't you, Wing? At least he never seemed to deliberately pick fights with you."

Wing opened a closet door and browsed casually among the few garments hanging there. "We spoke a few times," he allowed. "Actually, I think he's really more of an anthropologist than an archaeologist. His people consider him one of the honored preservers of their lore. He told me some fascinating stories about the days before Il Nuadi was rediscovered: the Years of Light, they call it. He says that when the Empire found Il Nuadi again and began bringing it back into the mainstream of human civilization, they brought darkness and oblivion with them, just like the original settlers did. He says his race is dying out."

"What does he mean, 'his race'?" Wallis said, closing the last of the storage drawers to begin rifling the desk. "The present inhabitants of Il Nuadi are descended from human stock. The genetic pool may have shifted a little during four hundred years of isolation, but they're cross-fertile with almost any other human-originated race in the Empire—and that's the true test of species, after all."

"All I know is what he told me," Wing said with a shrug. "He says his people changed during the Years of Light, that they were becoming—godlike was the word I think he used. He says it was supposed to have been somehow tied in with the vanished native race of the planet. Reynal says—"

"Reynal is a very sick man," Wallis interrupted, lifting aside a folded piece of cloth to reveal a shallow box-lid containing dozens of small ampules of a clear, straw-colored fluid. Two hypospray units lay beside the box, along with a cleaning kit. Lifting out one of the little ampules, Wallis carefully turned its label to the light.

"Reparanol," she read. "That's a last-chance drug for inhibiting tissue rejection." She glanced at the captain and Wing. "This doesn't fit with what *I* know of his medical history, though. He may be just a hypochondriac, or he may have a real medical problem—he was always afraid he was going to catch some disease—but you don't take a drug like this, if immunity is already low—though this could cause it. I wonder if it could also mask the lesser blood factors. . . ."

As her voice trailed off speculatively, Lutobo picked up another of the ampules and examined it. "Is Reparanol valuable, Doctor? I mean, is it difficult to get or something?"

"If you mean, could he be smuggling it," Wallis said, "I shouldn't think so. It isn't a cheap drug, but it's easily obtainable by those who need it, even on B-Gem. It *is* under moderately rigid control, in that dosage is tricky—you have to have a specialist's prescription to get it—but I don't know why anyone would smuggle it. Besides, the presence of the hypos suggests that it's here to be used."

With a sigh, Lutobo put the ampule back where he had found it and began poking farther into the drawer. "All right, then, he's a sick man. And for some reason, he didn't want the exact reasons in his medical records. That's his right, I suppose, so long as he's prepared to take the risks involved, but—here! What's this?"

Pulling out a stack of ship's stationery, Lutobo pointed to several miniature power packs, no bigger than a man's thumbnail, then yanked the drawer out of the desk entirely and dumped its contents on the bunk. Far at the back had been half a dozen boxes of low-load needler darts, packed twenty to the box. One box was nearly empty.

"And no pistol," Wallis siad breathlessly, when they had spread out all the contents of the drawer. "These darts are from the same manufacturer as the one I took out of our dead cat, too."

"Then Reynal is our murderer," Lutobo murmured.

"It certainly looks that way."

Lutobo shook his head. "I have to confess, I almost wish the cats *had* been responsible for all of this, Doctor," he said a little sheepishly. "I doubt that Lehr cats are half as cunning as the human animal. This also means that Reynal probably has the weapon on him, too, doesn't it?"

"I'm afraid so, Captain."

"We'd better put out a search for him, then," Lutobo said, heading for the door where Courtenay had been keeping watch. "And Doctor Hamilton, I may just owe y—"

"Uh-oh, Captain, we aren't going to have to look for him," Courtenay said suddenly, stiffening at what he saw in the door viewer. "He just came around the corner, headed this way, and there are six or eight other passengers in the vicinity. Do you want to risk a shoot-out in the corridor, or shall we try to take him in here?"

"Hide and let him get inside!" Wing said, taking charge before Lutobo could answer and motioning with an already drawn needler for all of them to move. "Captain, get down behind the bed! Casey, behind the chair. Courtenay, hit the lights and then hide in the shower with Doctor Hamilton. *Move*, people!"

The two civilians obeyed immediately, instinctively recognizing Wing's more specialized training, and Wallis and Casey were not far behind. As the young Ranger lieutenant wormed his way into the tiny closet, needler at the ready as he eased the door shut, the captain ducked down on the hidden side of the bunk, sweeping the telltale debris from the drawer onto the floor and also drawing his weapon. Wallis, when Courtenay had doused the lights, drew the security chief into the bathroom with her, stumbling a little in the suddenly subdued light; she left the shower door just slightly ajar so she could see, one hand rummaging in her medical kit as quietly as possible for her knockout hypo.

Endless hours seemed to pass before she heard the cabin door sigh open and then closed, and the owner of heavy footsteps immediately wrenched open the bathroom door and staggered into the little room though he did not turn on the lights. Wallis tried not to breathe—and prayed that Courtenay would not, either—as a dark form half collapsed over the sink and began to gag, almost immediately vomiting up an enormous quantity of fluid.

She could feel Courtenay fighting his own gag reflex as the stench of blood inundated their enclosed cubicle, and she almost considered using the hypo in her hand on *him*. But then the figure at the sink—it *was* Reynal—was straightening and glancing into the dark mirror, staring incredulously at the reflection *behind* him, and she knew that she needed Courtenay very badly.

"Take him *now!*" she shouted, kicking the shower door open and shoving Courtenay ahead of her as she lunged with her hypo toward Reynal's bare wrist.

It connected with empty air; or rather, it hissed harmlessly against the microbe shield that, she immediately realized, was now a defense against far more than germs. Nor were Courtenay's needler darts any more effective. Reynal recoiled in momentary panic, though, seizing Courtenay in a grip that instantly incapacitated him and then glancing around wildly as Casey and the captain exploded from cover and came out firing, their darts also splatting harmlessly against the shields—except for several that hit the already helpless Courtenay.

Reynal howled at that, his golden eyes blazing and thin lips curled back in a triumphant sneer, and dropped Courtenay—but it was only to turn his attentions on the captain and Casey, the latter of whom dove back behind his chair to reload. As Reynal advanced on Lutobo, scorning the weapon that Lutobo emptied impotently against the shields and then threw at him, Wallis scrambled after and grabbed the decanter off the table he had just passed.

But as Reynal reached Lutobo and grabbed him, too, taking him to his knees with no more than a flick of his wrist, and Wallis drew back to fling the decanter at Reynal, hoping the impact of a larger, slower projectile might at least divert him, a familiar voice suddenly called her from behind. She whirled to see Wing emerging from the closet. An odd little smile played around his lips as he raised his needler.

But, that won't stop Reynal! she thought in that instant of confusion and disbelief, just before he swung the weapon to aim squarely at her, instead—and as she saw Casey sprawled motionless behind the chair.

"What are you doing?" she screamed.

"Put it down, Doctor," Wing said softly. "Don't you see that you can't hurt him?"

She could try, though. Whirling, she drew back again to throw the decanter, just as Reynal's hand clamped onto her shoulder at the collarbone and a jolt like a stun charge set every nerve ending screaming for relief.

"Do as he says, Doctor," Reynal whispered, though his voice seemed hollow and distant, as if filtered through layers of cotton wool.

She could hardly see for the pain, as her legs buckled under her. She tried to keep hold of the decanter—

one desperate possibility for a weapon to use against him—but she could feel it rolling from nerveless fingers as the pressure of Reynal's relentless grasp forced her to her knees, her arms dangling bonelessly at her sides and twitching uncontrollably as raw energy continued to rage through her body. While a calm, disjointed part of her managed to observe that Reynal's shielding device must be responsible, all instinct shrieked that she must surely pass out or even die if the pain did not cease.

It did cease very shortly, as Reynal suddenly gasped and released her, though she still could hardly see, much less move. It took her several seconds to realize that he had finally noticed the ampules and needler charges scattered on the floor behind the bed, some of the ampules smashed in the scuffle with Lutobo, who also lay twitching on the floor.

"How did this happen?" Reynal gasped, falling frantically to hands and knees to gather up the intact vials. "Why did you bring them here?"

He deposited a handful of ampules on the end of the bed, then groped for a hypospray.

"They know that the cats aren't responsible," Wing replied, his attention temporarily diverted from her as he watched Reynal.

Wallis could feel sensation returning—not fast enough!—but the effort of forcing order back to scrambled synapses was agonizing, and she wondered whether Wing would shoot her before she could make it to the intercom unit at the door and signal for help.

"I did everything you told me," Wing went on, "but somehow Seton found out how the cat was killed last night. He did something to the dead cat's mate."

"He knows us, then," Reynal said. "We are lost."

His hands shook slightly as he slipped an ampule into the hypo and sat down on the bed; he touched a control on what looked like a wrist chronometer before triggering the hypo against his inner arm. Wallis shuddered at his sigh of relief and gathered herself for a dash to the door as Wing moved a few steps farther from it—and close to Reynal.

"I—wouldn't say Seton actually *knows* us," Wing said quietly, shaking his head. "He doesn't even suspect me, or I wouldn't have been allowed to come with Doctor Hamilton and the captain. They were checking on you because they matched the blood types found on the engineer's knife, and also on the cat's claws. You were merely among the first on their list, probably because of—Not so fast, Doctor!" he snapped, suddenly noticing her movement and darting between her and the door—for she had only been able to manage a crawl rather than the planned dash.

As he planted a boot against her shoulder, shoving her helplessly onto her side, she heard Reynal chuckle. "Such a persistent woman," he said. "Her spirit is strong. She will make a most worthy sacrifice. Shoot her, Wing, and you shall share in the glory."

Wallis's stomach churned as she watched Wing smile and raise his weapon, but she kept doggedly trying to struggle to her hands and knees—for to fail was to die. She never saw the faint spark of Wing's needler as he pulled the trigger, but she heard its faint pop, and she felt the dart sting her shoulder. The impact made her body jerk at that close range, and she thought insanely of the bruise she would have if she survived.

Then she felt her balance going, her vision starting to swim, her ears beginning to ring. She did not lose consciousness as she sank back to the floor—the low-dose needler Wing had used was not sufficient to really knock her out—but she could not keep herself from falling.

Dimly she was aware of Wing bending over her, of something bulky being dragged closer. Then a dark, smothering softness was being drawn across her body. It was Reynal's cloak, full and black—the "wings" one of his victims had described—lined, she saw now, with soft, blue Lehr cat fur.

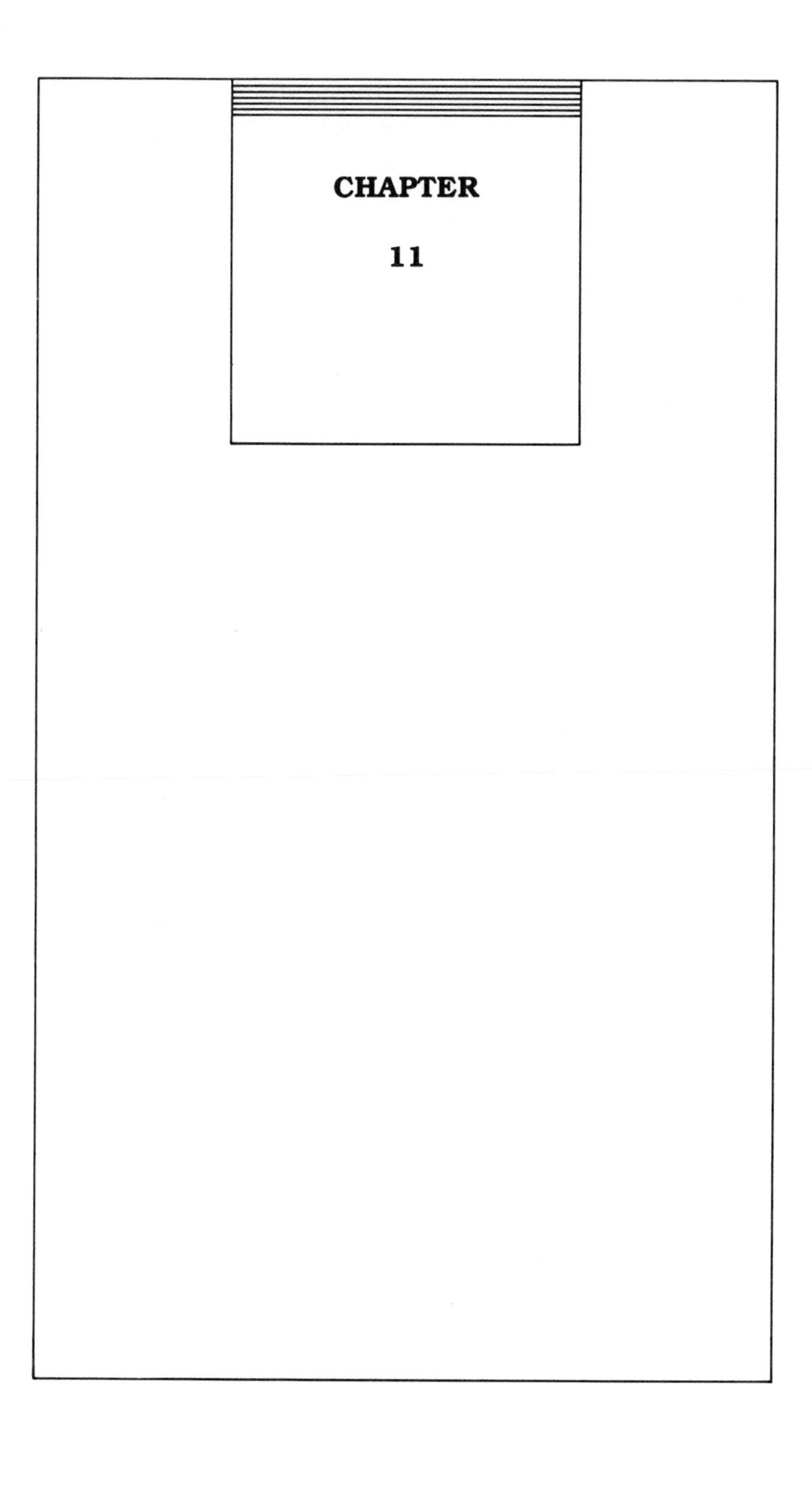

CHAPTER

11

Wallis tried to will her drug-clouded mind to recall everything she could about the man who now held her captive. And Wing—she still could hardly believe that the brilliant and career-conscious Wing, always so fastidious in his observation of military discipline, could have been won over so thoroughly to this madman's cause. It was *he* who must have gassed his comrades and let Reynal in to kill the Lehr cat.

"What are we going to do now?" Wing was saying, holstering his weapon and dropping to one knee beside the berth where Reynal now lay back, shoulders propped against the headboard and trembling in after-reaction from his injection.

"I am sorry to have dragged you farther into this, Wing," Reynal said softly. "Now the unbelievers will kill you, too, if they have their way. But at least the Coming Time will be sweet, if the Shining Ones are avenged. We have the final sacrifice in our power now."

"*We?*" Wing said quietly. "What, exactly, did you mean before, when you said you would share the glory?"

"That, if you wish it, I shall make you truly *their* servant," Reynal replied, closing his eyes dreamily. "You shall taste of *their* glory. Nor do I make this offer lightly,

Wing. You are not of my people, but you have been an earnest and loyal seeker. And after, I shall give you a clean death, if we cannot escape—though I have a plan for that, too."

"I hope so," Wing said quietly, "because I've betrayed my own people for you. Even if I should survive, I'm finished if anyone should find out."

"I shall give you a far more glorious vocation in *their* service," Reynal answered, stirring himself to sit up on the bed. "Nor was your sacrifice for me, but for *them.*"

He thumbed the ejector on the hypospray, sending the spent Reparanol ampule tumbling and twinkling toward Wallis in a high arc before it bounced on the carpet and came to rest a few feet from her paralyzed foot.

"Prepare Doctor Hamilton and the captain, and then come to me, *tsortse,*" Reynal said, "for I must prepare you as well, if you are to taste of the gods' ecstasy."

The click of his reloading the hypo was like a portent of doom as Wing went briefly to the door to do something to the lock. Wallis's stomach churned and knotted even more than it had before. It got worse when Wing returned and pulled the Lehr cat cloak over the armchair, fur side up, then lifted her to a half-sitting, half-reclining position between its arms, her head lolling helplessly against its back.

The chair faced toward the door, only the foot of the bed visible in her peripheral vision, so she could not really see Reynal, or what he did to Wing as soon as the young Ranger had sat down near the head of the bed. She did not want to believe that Wing had actually made the conscious decision to aid Reynal, but the hiss of the hypospray convinced her that he was, indeed, won over. She saw Wing's foot jerk as the drug hit him, and heard his stifled moan, and found herself almost hoping that Reynal had miscalculated and overdosed Wing. Death would be kinder, in the end, than what Mather would do to him when his betrayal was discovered.

"Rest a while now, *tsortse*, while the drug transforms you," she heard Reynal say.

Then he was suddenly standing over *her*, his pale, golden eyes staring down at her with a hunger that she had never thought to see outside a nightmare.

"You have been a great trial to me, Doctor," he said softly. "Nor have the Shining Ones been as cooperative as I might have wished, despite my best efforts, in their behalf, to avenge them. Even with their voices stilled by the drugs last night, they betrayed me—*me*, the servant of the gods, *their* servant! *This* was the thanks I got!"

He yanked back one sleeve to reveal a heavily bandaged arm, then pulled open the front of his shirt so she could see the long, angry welts splayed across part of his chest.

"Reminders of my carelessness," he said bitterly. "I should have waited for the darts to take effect more fully. Now the wounds fester, further reducing my effectiveness. This would never have happened, if you had not taken the Shining Ones from Il Nuadi!"

The sleeve was let fall, but he did not bother to refasten the shirt.

"However, I can forgive you that, Doctor, once reparation has been made. Tell me, are you curious at all, before you taste oblivion? Would it comfort you to learn how the rest of it was done?"

Wallis was far more interested in the *why* than the *how*, but she could not stop herself from watching as Reynal picked up a dark cloth bag from the floor near the door and put it on the small table close beside her chair. She had to force her eyes to focus closer as he removed a thick handful of loose blue fur, an embalmed Lehr cat paw, darkly bloodstained, and a close-fitting leather glove with steel blades set into the fingertips. The *how* became clear in an instant, even as Reynal began working the glove onto his left hand.

"Do you understand now, Doctor?" Reynal asked, flexing his fingers in the steel-studded leather. "Wing's little—ah—'improvement' to my microbe shield enabled me to stun my victims to helplessness before they knew what hit them, as well as protecting me from attack. Then, wearing my cloak of fur and with these aids for misleading even the 'experts,' is it any wonder that my hunters believed me to be a cat, especially when they knew the cats were aboard?" He clicked the claws delicately under her nose.

"Fur and claws, Doctor. And bloody paw prints. Clever, don't you think? I must modestly admit that the teeth were my own."

He drew back his lips at that, in a gaping caricature of a smile, and Wallis could see the bright, deadly fangs protruding from beneath his upper lip. She wondered why she had never noticed them before—then realized that in all the weeks she had worked with Reynal on the expedition, she had never seen him smile.

She swallowed, stiffening as he trailed one blood encrusted claw down the side of her neck in sinister caress. Whatever else he was planning was curtailed, however, at least for the moment, by the insistent shrill of the door buzzer.

With a mutter, Reynal reactivated his shield and closed his bare hand briefly across her upturned throat. His touch sent agony vibrating through all her nerve endings again, intensifying her paralysis, blinding and almost deafening her before he withdrew toward the door. Though Wallis knew she had no hope of moving, still she strained her vocal cords, hoping she might be able to make some warning sound, once Reynal opened the audio circuit. But it was futile.

"Yes, what is it?"

Outside, Shannon started at the low, calm voice. She had her override key in her hand and had been about to try overriding the door as well as the audio circuits, but now she paused and glanced aside at Mather. Beyond the Imperial agent, three security guards waited, with two Rangers just out of the door's visual field to her right.

"Mister Reynal, this is Doctor Shannon, ship's surgeon," she said, lowering her hand at Mather's headshake. "I'm trying to locate Captain Lutobo."

"Oh? And what makes you think he might be here, Doctor?"

"Because the ship's computers said he might be," Shannon replied. "I tried to page him a little while ago, but he didn't answer. I thought the special environment in your room might be interfering with his communicator."

"How curious. Well, he is not here, Doctor."

"What about Doctor Hamilton?" Shannon persisted, with a glance at Mather. "Have you see her?"

"Now, why would I wish to see *her?*" Reynal replied. "This really is becoming most tiresome, Doctor. Good day."

As the intercom went dead, Shannon positioned her override strip again, glancing at Mather and preparing to dart out of the way as the door withdrew. At his nod, she inserted it and pushed—but nothing happened. Shaking his head, Mather motioned her to join him, moving farther out of range as the guards eased in to fill his place. The normally mild hazel eyes were like stone. Suddenly, Shannon felt a little afraid of him.

"He's done something to the door," she whispered. "He shouldn't have been able to short out my override."

Mather nodded, looking past her at Reynal's door. "I'm not surprised. I already knew he was lying. Wallis is in there—I know she is—but there's something grossly wrong."

"You—*know* she's in there?" Shannon whispered.

Mather avoided her eyes. "I—ah—it's a talent I have for finding people. It isn't reliable for strangers or mere acquaintances, but—well, Wallis and I have been together for—many years. The indistinct blur I was reading means—to me—that she's been injured, or drugged, or—I don't know exactly *what* is wrong; just that something is *wrong.*" He looked at her at last. "The others must be in there, too—the captain, Wing and Casey, and—Courtenay, the security chief."

"That would make sense," Shannon agreed. "But could Reynal have taken all five of them? One or two, maybe, but—"

"It Reynal is responsible for what's been happening, I think we've completely underestimated what he may be able to do." Mather glanced back at the guards and Rangers. "I'm also afraid either Casey or Wing was his accomplice. I think they're both type A-positive. I wonder what's taking that door burner so long."

"Well, it isn't exactly standard issue on a civilian ship," Shannon muttered. "I don't see *your* men performing any miracles just now."

Mather gave her a tiny, bitter smile. "I'm sure they're doing their best," he conceded. "I just don't know how much time we've got. Wallis is still alive—I know that much—and I'm pretty sure the others are, too. But how long that will continue to be true, I couldn't begin to guess. I wouldn't want to rush Reynal into anything rash, but I don't think we dare delay very long."

Inside, meanwhile, Reynal and Wing had not been idle. The room was already strewn with tufts of blue Lehr cat fur.

"We shall try to make them think the cats have been here," Reynal was saying as he gathered up more of the scattered ampules, power packs, and needler charges in a satchel and checked the settings on both his hyposprays. He had also produced a highly illegal miniature stun pistol from a hiding place in the closet and stuck this in his waistband as he approached Wing.

"The evidence still points to the cats, even though no one understands how that could be possible. All that is really necessary to keep us in the clear is a reasonable doubt."

Wing, who had dragged the half-conscious captain to a sitting position against the foot of the bed, drew back as Reynal knelt and briefly laid his bare hand against the captain's throat again, his shields giving Lutobo another stunning jolt. Lutobo was still twitching as Reynal withdrew and turned the shields off; and Wing braced him as he sagged more heavily against the end of the bed, breathing a little erratically.

"Isn't it a little late to still be blaming the cats?" Wing asked. "Commodore Seton knows your blood type, and he's already connected that with the earlier deaths. Besides that, he needled them just before I left. He'll know they couldn't have come here."

"He knows *nothing* of the true powers of the Shining Ones," Reynal said, snapping off the top of a Reparinol ampule and handing it to Wing with a fanatic fervor in his eyes. "Drink that now. It will help you to assimilate the blood."

As Wing obeyed, grimacing as he sucked the ampule dry and pocketed the empty, Reynal went on.

"Good. Now breathe deeply to calm yourself while I tell you what must be done afterward, for I still must perform the culminating sacrifice, once we have finished with the captain. When all is completed, we must make it look as if the cats have been here on a rampage, with only the two of us surviving. We shall destroy the evidence of our true handiwork. And afterward, when all is in confusion, we shall escape in a shuttle ship. The fools will never understand the full truth. Hold him, now. I will prepare him for you, but he is yours. Even stunned, he will try to fight at first."

Wing's face showed no emotion as he locked down on both Lutobo's wrists. "*Seton* is no fool," he muttered.

With a derisive laugh, Reynal hooked a claw in the closure of Lutobo's tunic neck and ripped it open, forcing the proud neck back against the edge of the bed with his right hand while his left closed around the throat, a steel-gleaming, razor-tipped forefinger poised over the right jugular vein, just below the pulsepoint.

"Seton *is* a fool, *tsortse,*" he murmured, staring into Wing's eyes, "but you are none. And you shall join the numbers of the blessed. Taste of the sacrifice now, and become one with the gods!"

Wing flinched as Reynal opened their victim's jugular with a deft flick of one claw, and Wallis felt her stomach clench at Lutobo's faint, strangled whimper of terror as his eyes opened wide and startled and he dimly sensed what was happening. The captain tried to struggle as his first blood sprayed all over the front of Wing's uniform in crimson baptism, but he was no match for either of his captors, especially with strength and reflexes still sapped by Reynal's shields. Lifting the bloodied claw-hand in horrible benediction, Reynal murmured something in a language Wallis did not recognize and was answered by Wing—who did not even blink as Lutobo's blood continued to soak him.

Wallis did not want to watch as Reynal's clawhand pressed Wing's head against that pulsing source to drink, but she could not look away—any more than she could look away as Reynal bent to sink his teeth into the other jugular—though she did close her eyes, especially when Lutobo began to moan and his limbs began to twitch feebly.

Hours seemed to pass, though she knew, by counting her own heartbeat, that it had been only minutes. She opened her eyes again when she suddenly heard a faint choking sound and saw Wing and then Reynal drawing back from their victim. At first she thought that they had killed Lutobo outright, but then she saw his chest move—though, with blood continuing to stream steadily down both sides of his neck, she knew he could not last long. Wing coughed, pressing a bloody fist to his lips and doubling over briefly, then drew a deep breath and straightened on his knees to look at Reynal in awe, blood now smearing his face as well as his green Ranger coverall. Reynal, more fastidious in his supping, was only red around the mouth, though his golden eyes seemed to glow red as well as he glanced in Wallis's direction.

"Well done, *tsortse,*" he whispered to Wing, though he did not take his eyes from Wallis as he handed Wing one of the hyposprays. "Use this now, and try to hold the offering. I must set the stage for the others, before the culmination."

Wallis made herself breathe deeply, observing in numb fascination as Reynal rose and began upsetting furniture, slashing the upholstery and carpet with his clawed glove, and scattering more tufts of the loose blue Lehr cat fur around the room. She failed to notice whether Wing had dosed himself again as ordered, but soon he, too, was contributing to the chaos, dabbing the Lehr cat paw in a runnel of blood still seeping from the wounds on Lutobo's neck and making terrible, bloody footprints in Lutobo's vicinity.

Wallis felt a curious detachment as she watched all of this—knowing that her fate was likely to be the same as Lutobo's, dreading the moment when Reynal should finish his preparations and approach her. She wondered desperately where Mather was; whether Shannon had believed Reynal's glib denial of Lutobo's and her presence; whether she really was about to die.

Then Reynal suddenly was standing over her again. In her panic, she could not recall his having moved; he simply was *there,* his terrible golden eyes holding her from any physical resistance.

"Tell me, Doctor, does your great learning give you any comfort now?" he asked, gently lifting a loose strand of her hair and caressing its texture between his thumb and fingers. "Can all your scientific training and erudition save you from the glory that awaits you in these final moments?"

Wallis fought to swallow, her throat suddenly gone dry, and tried to speak, but no words would come out. The dart drug still working in her body kept her balanced just on the edge of lethargic indifference, and the further abuse her system had taken from his shields ensured that no physical resistance was going to be possible. She hoped Reynal would at least tell her why she had to die this way. And what would it be like?

"It will be an easy death, Doctor," Reynal whispered, almost as if he had read her thoughts—though she was fairly certain he had not. "In ancient times, before the Earthers came to Il Nuadi, the Old Ones walked the ways of the gods. The Shining Ones, whom you stupidly call Lehr cats, were the divine messengers of those gods—lesser gods, themselves—and the priests of the Old Ones took blood sacrifice for *them*, that *they* might carry the people's petitions heavenward.

"But the Earthers brought disease and a destruction of the old ways," he went on, his eyes hardening. "Their dying had only begun when the Earthers' wars cut off Il Nuadi from further contamination, but that start was enough. Soon all the Old Ones were gone; and for centuries, the gods received no sacrifices.

"But half a century ago, our wise men learned to emulate the ancient examples, Doctor. Joyously we revived the ancient sacrifices, that we might make atonement for what was done to the Old Ones and once more send the people's petitions to Them. And when one of the Shining Ones is taken from Il Nuadi, or is killed, sacrifice must be made. The drug Reparanol was the key; for with it, we can assimilate the blood of the sacrifice even as the Old Ones did. Now, once again may the sacrifice experience that awesome, awe-full ecstasy of union with the gods, as he or she sinks into blessed oblivion."

He leaned closer to her, his hands resting on the

chair arms to either side of her, and stared into her eyes. The stench of blood was on his breath.

"It is a sweet pain, Doctor Hamilton. Do not resist it. Your life shall be sealed to the gods. Accept this and rejoice."

And she *must* accept. She could not pull away or struggle. As he drew her up into his embrace, murmuring words of alien ritual that she did not understand, she closed her eyes and felt his steel-tipped fingers tilt her head to one side, his other hand slipping behind her back to support her neck and head.

Then she was aware of his lips brushing moistly over her throat, the hot shock of his tongue probing for the pulse point. She braced herself for his teeth but instead felt the subtler sting of one of his claws nicking the vein, just before his lips clamped down in a kiss of death.

She had not expected it to be so painless. She was able to count a full minute by her heartbeat before she felt consciousness begin to wane from loss of blood. Soon she would pass out, never knowing her own ending.

But further impressions of the experience were never to come. For just as empty despair began to overpower her, an explosion jarred the room, the sound filtering hollowly through her dazed senses, and Reynal was pulling away from her and leaping to his feet.

As the door disappeared in a flash of hot air and smoke, Rangers and security men suddenly began pouring into the room, their needlers sparking. But the darts flashed harmlessly around Reynal, for he had reactivated his shielding device at the first sign of trouble. Even stun bolts had no effect. Charred bits of plastic and surgisteel rained around him like hail, and the stun pistol he drew immediately began to take its toll of the men pouring into the room.

And Wing's assistance was of an even more insidious sort. Pretending to be one of Reynal's victims—

which was not difficult, given his bloodstained appearance—he had thrown himself on the floor when the guards began bursting through the door. From this position of feigned unconsciousness, he fired his needler from underneath his body whenever an opportunity presented itself, thus incapacitating at least three guards or Rangers whom Reynal's stunner had missed.

When Mather burst in at the tail of the attack, his needler sparking while he seemed to be evading every stun shot that Reynal tried, Wing broke his cover. Raising up on one elbow, he fired point-blank as Mather started to push past him to reach Wallis. He got off at least two more shots before Mather could deal with him.

But Mather was fast, despite his bulk. Seeing Wing's movement out of the corner of his eye, he dropped to the floor, rolled, and returned fire in one smooth movement. Nor did the gyrations mar his aim. Even as Wing was trying to squeeze off a fourth shot, he took five of Mather's darts in the chest in a close-grouped pattern that would have made any range master proud.

But at least one of Wing's darts had found its mark, too, and Mather could not ignore its effects for long. Cursing under his breath, he managed to roll onto his side and catch another glimpse of Wallis, sprawled limp and bloody in the chair where Reynal had left her.

But the drug dragged at his limbs, and his needler slipped from increasingly numb fingers. He could not seem to keep his eyes open. He felt the velvet crush of unconsciousness pressing closer and closer as his eyelids closed, but he fought to maintain at least a shred of awareness.

Across the room, as silence descended, Reynal began to laugh.

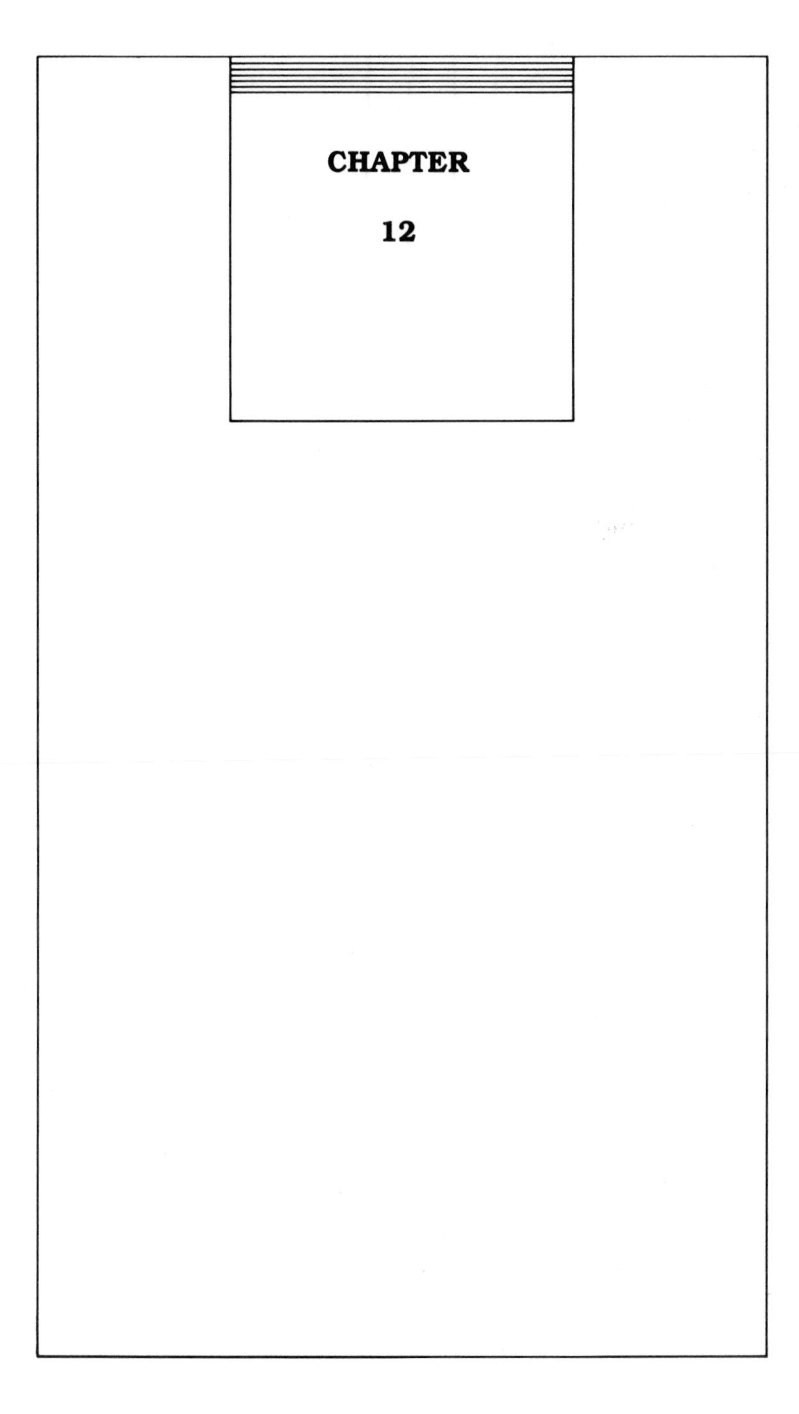

CHAPTER

12

The laughter saved Mather.

The sound was something he could hold onto—an anchor on consciousness, a beacon to help keep the growing twilight at bay. He wondered why he was still conscious at all, for he knew he had taken at least two of Wing's darts. In a supreme effort of will, he managed to open his eyes slightly and make a quick evaluation of what he could see without moving.

The prospect was not encouraging. Of the six security guards and three Rangers he had sent in after the door was blown, he could see two of his own men sunk in drugged slumber with Wing's darts in them and three more men twitching in after-reaction from Reynal's stunner. The sudden silence, as Reynal stopped laughing, suggested that everyone else was similarly incapacitated.

Nor was his own situation exactly encouraging. He had ended up on his right side, with his knees partially drawn against his chest in a fetal position and his right arm fully extended to the side, the useless needler still grasped loosely in his numb right hand. His left arm was curled close to his chest, one of Wing's darts just visible beneath the hand cupped near his heart, and a cautious further inspection suggested at least a partial reason he was still awake. Another dart was stuck in his left shoulder at an angle that made him suspect it had hit the needler harness under his jacket. That, plus the low dose of the darts the Rangers carried, plus his sheer bulk, must be what had saved him.

But he was not safe yet. As Reynal suddenly started to move, passing among the motionless bodies to disarm them, Mather closed his eyes, praying that Reynal had not noticed the movement—for he was as good as dead, if Reynal thought he was still conscious, and he might never get the chance to implement his plan.

He heard Reynal coming closer, but with the anchor of vision gone, he started to drift again. He managed not to slip away entirely, but it took all his remaining concentration. And he did drift a little; suddenly he was aware that someone was standing over him.

Mather continued to play dead. He knew who it had to be. Remembering what Reynal had done to Wallis, he had to fight an almost uncontrollable urge to roll violently away from that cold scrutiny, but he knew he dared not, no matter what else happened. He sensed Reynal bending closer—and then pain seemed to explode up his arm and race all through his body as the needler was plucked from his fingers.

Not that the needler could have done any good against Reynal's shields, anyway—for the shields were surely what Mather had just experienced, judging by what he had seen before he went down. It had not been as bad as taking a stun charge, for which he was grateful, but that was small comfort as he lay twitching, every nerve ending screaming. His limbs continued to twitch and jerk uncontrollably for several seconds after Reynal moved on toward the door.

Nor was there any way Mather could warn whoever remained outside. His Rangers all were out of commission except Fredricks, still down in the hold with the cats; the ship's security people would be all but useless against someone as ruthless as Reynal. For the next minute or two, as he listened to the whine of more stun bolts being discharged in the corridor outside, Mather could only concentrate on trying to make his abused nerveways reconnect properly again and trying to make his left hand work—for that was crucial, if he hoped to stop Reynal. When the sound of stun bolts finally ceased, his heart sank as he heard Reynal's voice.

"Come on in, Doctor, or I'll have to shoot you, too! I have a patient who requires your attention."

"You've—killed them!" He heard Shannon gasp.

"Only some of them, Doctor. Now come and see to Lieutenant Wing. Don't make me touch you, or it will be very unpleasant. And if Wing dies, I can promise that you shall follow him."

Mather still could do nothing yet, though feeling was starting to come back into his arms and legs. Cautiously he watched Reynal march Shannon past him to where Wing lay, Reynal covering her with his stunner and further menacing her with his clawed glove. Wing was hardly breathing and must be close to comatose, with five darts in him. Tense and obviously frightened, Shannon dropped to her knees and scanned Wing briefly, then removed the darts from his chest and began charging a hypospray. With Reynal engrossed in watching what she did, Mather sensed that this might be his last chance to take positive action.

His left hand was shielded from Reynal now, as would be anything Mather removed from his jacket—unless, of course, Reynal came back. Carefully Mather started to work. Every centimeter of gain hurt, but he finally managed to get the larger, wider-mouthed of the two plastic vials out of his jacket and into the shelter of his side and got the stopper out. But he had only begun to pull out the second vial when Reynal looked up from where he knelt by Wing and Shannon and glanced around the room again. As Reynal stood up, Mather palmed the small vial and closed his eyes to merest slits, praying that the man would not notice the larger vial nestled behind his cupped hand. (And why should he even think of Mather again, believing him to be incapacitated by Wing's darts and his own touch?)

But as Reynal's gaze swept the room again, moistening bloodstained lips with a bloody tongue, Mather suddenly knew why Reynal might approach. The knowledge chilled him, but not half so much as when he realized that Reynal's gaze had fixed itself elsewhere—on Wallis, still sprawled in the chair where he had dropped her. Her eyes were closed, and blood stained the right side of her neck and had run down that side of her clothing, but her breathing seemed steady. Reynal's expression changed from speculation to purpose as he began walking slowly toward her, and Mather had all he could do not to launch himself at the man.

He made himself think, instead. He had to have time! As far as he could tell, Wallis was not yet in any real danger from loss of blood—though there might be other complications that he could not anticipate. By any outward sign that Mather could perceive from where he lay, Reynal probably had not had time to do her any grave damage—though he apparently was preparing to resume where he had left off.

Not only did Mather need time to finish preparing his weapon, but he needed a chance to get to his feet so he could deliver it. If Reynal stopped him before he could get up, Reynal would kill him and then kill Wallis, anyway. Nor could Mather take another charge from Reynal's shields and expect to survive.

Feverishly he searched his mind for some delaying action, some diversion that might give him—and Wallis—the time they needed. His eyes lit on Shannon, still laboring over the unconscious Wing and nervously trying *not* to look at Reynal.

It was a very long shot, because he did not know Shannon well, but it was the only shot he had. He did not know whether he could pull it off, especially in his presently befogged condition, for only determination and his sheer bulk were enabling him to keep fighting the needler's drug as long as he had.

There was no way to know but to try. Closing his eyes briefly and betting everything on his sometimes unreliable psychic resources, he sought the state of altered consciousness from which he had empathized with the Lehr cat. To his relief, he felt himself shifting mental gears almost immediately and guessed that, in this instance, the needler's drug probably was helping him achieve the results he sought, rather than hindering.

Heartened, he reached out a tentative probe toward Shannon, aware that lack of physical contact was not going to help matters any, and tried to concentrate all his strength, all his heightened awareness, on a single act of *willing* Shannon to action. Reynal was within an easy arm's reach of Wallis now. He had turned off his shields and was settling on the chair arm beside her, bending across her body toward her bloody neck. Frantic, Mather launched his remaining strength into one emphatic command. He could almost feel Reynal's teeth sinking into his own neck as he *willed* Shannon to leap up and scream.

Suddenly he knew she had heard him—and even as he sensed her lungs filling with air, he was dumping the contents of his smaller vial into the larger one, swirling the mixture together in an opalescent haze. In that same instant, Shannon shrieked, *"Noooo!"* and sprang to her feet.

Reynal gasped and threw himself back from Wallis's chair, switching on his shields again—which was just what Mather wanted. Reynal started toward Shannon, murder in his eyes as he reached for her with the clawed glove, and in that instant Mather staggered to his feet to fling the contents of his larger vial directly at Reynal, splashing the milky liquid across his shields in a dazzling display of blue sparks, smoke, and an odor of wet seaweed.

For just an instant the shields held, the outer perimeter alive with blue flame and acrid greenish smoke, and Mather was afraid it wasn't going to work. He rummaged frantically in his pocket for the silver chain, ready to throw that, too—but then Reynal and the center of the room exploded in a sheet of white fire, and Mather was throwing himself at Wallis's chair, overturning it and her to shield her with his body, clapping his palm to the wound in her neck. Shannon recoiled against a bulkhead with the concussion, collapsing to her knees in a heap as the flames raged. The explosion brought more ship's crew bursting through the doorway, and they made valiant attempts to drag those nearest the door to safety.

But Reynal himself was afire, screaming hideously as the flames roared around him and singed the acoustical baffles in the ceiling. Fire-fighting equipment was summoned, but it was too late for Reynal by the time it arrived. By then, all that remained of him was a charred, smoldering hulk, vaguely humanoid in shape.

The stench of burnt flesh and hair hung heavy on the air, along with utter, disbelieving silence, until the ceiling ventilation system cut in and began to clear the smoke from the room. The sound released Mather, who raised his head and started to pick himself up from over Wallis's limp form. As he did so, Shannon also staggered to her feet and limped painfully to his side, there to support herself wobbily against the overturned chair and gaze with horror at what remained of Lorcas Reynal.

"What next? A stake through the heart?" she whispered, in a voice that only Mather could have heard.

Mather grinned and patted his free hand unsteadily against the toe of her boot in reassurance, then shifted

Wallis enough in his arms so that he could peek carefully under his hand at her wound.

"You'd better get the rest of your medical people up here as fast as you can, Doctor. As far as Wallis is concerned, I can handle basic first aid as well as the next man, but you'd better see to the captain, if we haven't already lost him."

"But is Wallis all right?" Shannon asked.

"She'll be fine with me until they get here. Go to Lutobo."

Still a little dazed, Shannon nodded and moved to Lutobo's side, where one of the newly arrived crew was already administering emergency first aid. Mather managed to find a pressure dressing in Wallis's medical kit and slapped that over her neck wound, then rummaged in the kit again until he found a familiar hypospray, which he charged and then triggered against his own wrist. As he felt the stimulant racing through his system, clearing his head and helping to counteract the effects of the needler dart he had taken, he took a few seconds to pull out the darts in his torso, shaking his head as he discovered another in the back of one thigh. He was running a pocket scanner over Wallis, trying to decide whether to give her a stimulant, too, when she opened her eyes and managed a weak smile.

"Hi, there," she whispered. "Will I live?"

"Afraid so," he answered with a grin. He glanced up and half turned as Deller and a medical team entered the room. "We need some oxygen over here right away, Deller—and an IV started, as soon as you can manage it. She's lost a lot of blood."

Deller came over immediately with a technician and equipment and bent to check Mather's scanner readings.

"Let's type and cross-match for a couple of units of whole blood, too," he ordered, as the technician knelt on Wallis's other side and started setting up. "Commodore, are you all right?"

Mather nodded. "Yes, and if type and cross-match are going to take too long, you can set up for a direct transfusion from me. We've exchanged blood before, so I know we're compatible."

"See to it, Jacy, while I check on some of the others," Deller said to the technician, moving on.

Mather helped break out the oxygen unit, but Wallis raised her hand long enough to give Mather's a slight squeeze, then she took the oxygen mask and held it to her face. After a few deep breaths, she looked up at Mather again.

"You might see if someone can manage a vasoconstrictor, too," she murmured. "I can tell that my pressure is 'way down."

The technician starting the IV gave Mather a nod, and Mather echoed it as he smoothed a lock of red hair from her face.

"It's being taken care of," he murmured. "How do you feel?"

"Woozy. What did you do to Reynal?"

Mather smiled a devilish grin. "You aren't going to believe me when I tell you."

"Try me. *You* didn't watch him and Wing drain Lutobo dry."

"No, but I thought I was going to have to watch him do it to you. Anyway, do you remember how we discussed the possibility that we were dealing with a vampire, and we talked about some of the classic defenses against same?"

Wallis took another deep breath of oxygen and waved off the technician to see to other patients.

"So you branded him with silver, exposed him to sunlight, and threw holy water on him, eh?" she murmured, her voice sounding hollow inside the mask. "You cultural anthropologists are all alike."

"Well, as I recall, it was you who pointed out to Doctor Shannon that most superstitions and legends have some basis in truth."

She took away the mask to stare at him incredulously. "Are you joking? You're not, are you? Mather Seton, if you tell me that the analytical, Academy-educated darling of the Imperial Service reverted to superstitious—

"Are you going to talk or are you going to listen?" Mather said simply.

Wallis studied him for a moment, taking another few breaths of oxygen, then thrust out a petulant lower lip. "I don't believe a word you're going to say, but go ahead. This should be very interesting."

"Oh, I assure you, it is. Now, we know that Reynal wore a microbe defense shield, right?"

"Well it was a little more than that, after Wing got through with it. You do know that he was the one working with Reynal, don't you?"

Mather snorted. "I should. I took a couple of his darts. In any case, despite what Wing did to the shield, it wasn't as perfect as they might have wished. I spotted a potential weakness before I even saw Reynal use it."

"What do you mean?"

"Well, you were busy doing other things, so you weren't aware of it, but there was another attack after you and the captain left the hold—two little boys down on Level Four." He skipped over her expression of dismay. "One of the boys was killed in the usual manner, though Reynal didn't stop to slash him up, for some reason; but Reynal let the other one go—rather suddenly, it appears. It seems the boy was wearing this chain and ident tag around his neck." He pulled it out of his pocket to show her. "Shannon found it when she was called to the scene to treat the surviving boy, and she brought it to me. It's very high-grade silver."

"Silver!" Wallis exclaimed, stifling a giggle. "Oh, Mather, does it have a cross on it?"

"No, but it's an excellent conductor," he replied, ignoring her jibe, "and Reynal's shields generated a high-voltage electrical field around him, rather like a walking stun bolt. He probably came close to shorting out his shields right then. That, plus the legends, was what gave me my idea."

"So you threw the chain at Reynal and his shields exploded?"

"Close, but not quite the whole story. There was too much danger of missing, and I suspected I'd only have one chance." He paused to give his arm to the technician who had returned to set up the direct transfusion. "I raided Doctor Shannon's reagent cabinet before we left Medical Section, after making sure that the chain really was silver. And what I brought with me was a small beaker of salt water—"

"Salt water? As in sodium chloride in water?"

"Sure. It's a good conductor, and supernatural beasties can't stand salt."

Wallis let her head fall back against the floor dispairingly and took another deep breath of oxygen. "Salt water," she finally murmured. "Doesn't holy water always have salt in it, too? I don't suppose you had it blessed?'

"Well, as a matter of fact—"

"I don't think I want to hear about it." Wallis shook her head. "So, you brought salt water and what?"

"Salt water and a strong silver nitrate solution. Can your brilliant biochemist's brain tell me what happened then?"

"My brilliant biochemist's brain has turned to mush," she said impatiently. "Are you going to tell me what happened or not?"

He took her free hand in his and brushed her fingertips across his lips, then smiled. "Silver nitrate plus sodium chloride, in an aqueous solution, gives a silver chloride precipitate—plus some other things that aren't important in the reaction at hand."

"But silver chloride isn't metallic silver. . . ."

"No, but when you pass an electrical current

through it, you get metallic silver and chlorine gas. And you'll have to admit that throwing silver chloride precipitate against Reynal's shields subjected it to one hell of an electrical current."

She closed her eyes wearily and nodded. "Metallic silver."

Mather nodded. "And chlorine gas—and holy water, none of which are well loved by creatures of the supernatural."

"But, Reynal wasn't super—"

"Hush." Mather laid a finger across her lips. "Of course he wasn't. But what does it hurt to take a few precautions, just in case?"

As she drifted off to sleep, he caught her slight smile and nod of agreement.

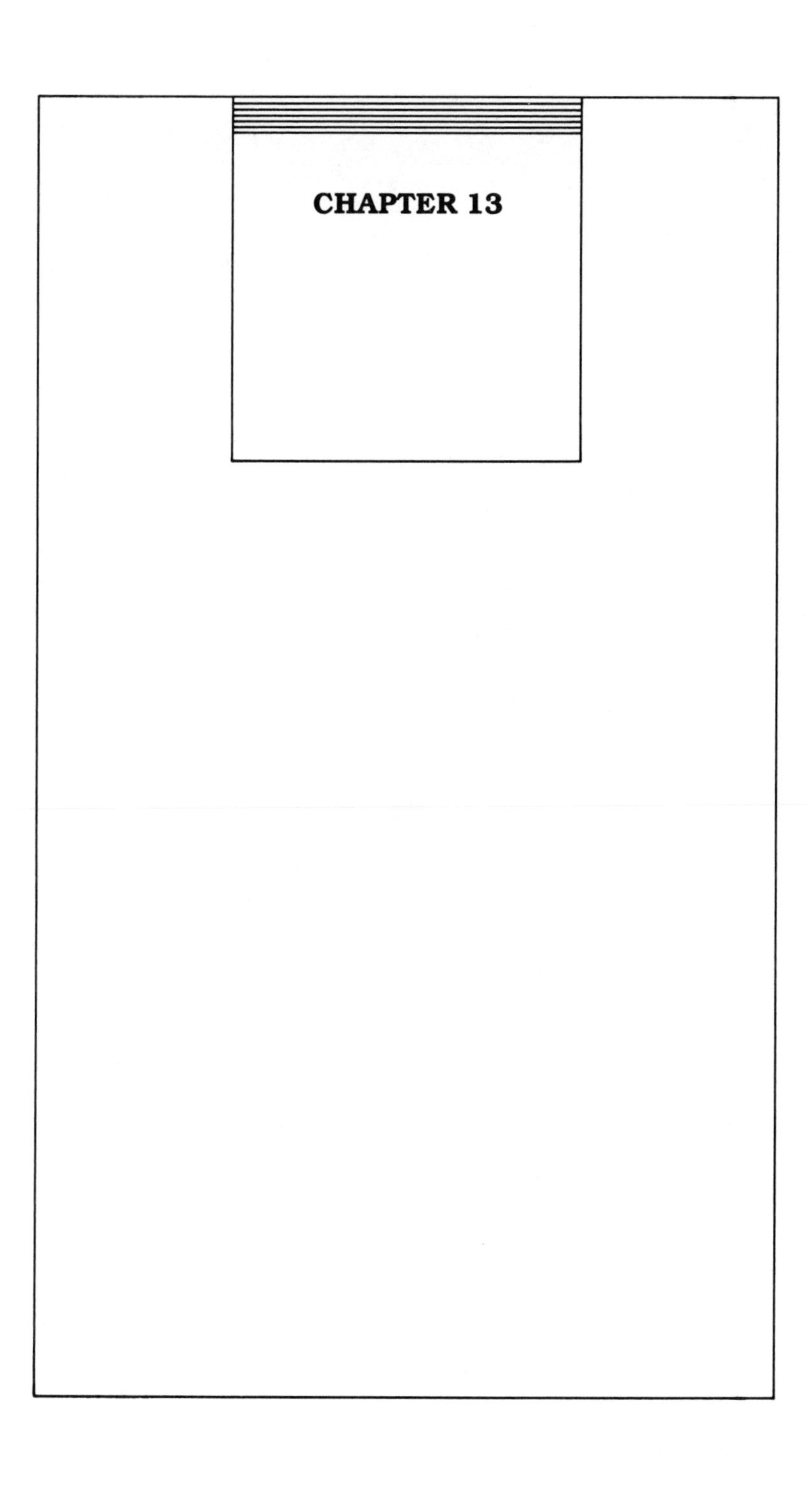

CHAPTER 13

KATHERINE KURTZ

Two days later—but a day earlier than had been anticipated, thanks to Mather Seton's recalculation of the necessary phase jumps—the Gruening Novaliner *Valkyrie* entered the Hyadum Primus system and made orbit around Tersel, the third planet, headquarters of the Second Imperial Fleet and capital of the Kafeor Empire. As soon as she had established orbit, her shuttles began ferrying passengers down to the planet's surface. Scheduled layover had been cut from twenty-four hours to twelve, but many were going planetside anyway, eager to set foot on solid ground again after the frightening events of the voyage. A few had elected to leave the ship altogether and wait for the next available transportation.

Nor was all the traffic one-way. A coroner's shuttle had been the first ship to dock with *Valkyrie*, followed closely by one carrying officials and legal counsel of the Gruening Line. But none of these would ever know the full extent of what had happened aboard the *Valkyrie* between Il Nuadi and Tersel.

The Imperial authorities knew—at least those to whom Mather and Wallis reported, and to the extent that even the two of them understood what had occurred. Wing's deception in particular was still a mystery. And since neither Wing nor Reynal had survived, the full story was likely never to be known. Once assured that Wallis, the captain, and the rest of the Rangers and crew would make full recoveries from their ordeal, Mather had spent the best part of a day composing his report: checking details with Shannon and the still-weak Wallis, interviewing crew members who had been at least partial witnesses, and just generally tying up what loose ends he could.

Now the Imperial cruiser *Shantar* was standing by as close as safety permitted, one of her shuttles maneuvering toward one of the *Valkyrie*'s receiving bays. The craft bore the markings of a member of the Imperial family aboard, and *he* was not likely to settle for the report alone.

"How upset do you think he's going to be, because we're only delivering three cats?" Wallis asked in a low voice.

She and Mather were watching the last of the docking maneuvers from an observation port in one of the crash doors that closed off the bay from the rest of the hanger. Other than a scarf that concealed the healing wounds on her neck, Wallis showed no signs of her recent ordeal—unlike Captain Lutobo, who was still recovering in sick bay. The *Valkyrie*'s first officer was supervising operations this morning; he and Shannon presently were trapped in nervous conversation with the Gruening folk who had come up from Tersel.

Mather shrugged and leaned both hands against the edge of the porthole. "All things considered, I suspect he'll be delighted to get even the three. I've already reminded him that we're lucky Reynal didn't decide to butcher them all. I'd be willing to bet that we see a proper team set up very quickly, too, to study the cats in their own environment. I shouldn't be surprised if even the obnoxious Doctor Torrell wants to be involved, once the dust settles."

"That depends on whether he still intends to sue us

for harrassment and general embarrassment," Wallis said with a chuckle. "He was a very unhappy man when the captain and I left him, and I noticed that he was aboard the first shuttle to head planetside."

"Maybe he'll get the project and a Lehr cat will eat him," Mather said with a smirk.

"Now, is that nice?"

"Of course not—but he'd deserve it, if only for sheer boorishness."

Wallis could hardly argue that point. Laughing in spite of herself, she looked down the row of shuttle bays, then glanced up at the passenger observation deck above them and nudged Mather. Two heavily swathed figures with feathered crests spread open both arms in greeting as he looked their way, and Mather made both of them a pronounced bow of acknowledgement, one hand touching his heart and then extending palm outward.

"I suppose the Aludrans will be glad to see us go," Wallis said after she, too, had saluted the two.

"They'll be glad to see the cats leave, at least," Mather agreed, "though they finally came around to admitting that Lehr cats are nothing like their green demon cats. I had a chance to talk a little with Muon and Bana while you were recuperating. It's fascinating how so many cultures seem to have cat mythologies. We were made tragically aware that vampire legends seem to run through almost every culture we've encountered, but no one has really developed a similar thematic treatment for feline myth cycles."

"It sounds like a good topic for *someone* to research," Wallis said, arching a reddish eyebrow.

Mather caught her meaning immediately and returned her grin. "Yeah, I know. Someone besides us. We only clear the way."

He glanced across the shuttle bay at the cargo loading area, where Lehr cats prowled in three shiny plasteel cages, only occasionally letting out a yowl. He tried not to look at the large, hermisealed capsule nestled with the rest of their equipment—the remains of the fourth cat, which Reynal had killed—and he wondered again whether they could have done anything differently, to have averted all the senseless slayings that had marred the expedition. In any case, that was all academic, now.

What was not academic, however, was the need to square things with the Gruening officials before the Imperial shuttle docked. Those worthies were in the next bay, at the foot of the ramp extending from a shuttle bearing the markings of Health and Immigration. A fussy-looking coroner's deputy stood a little apart from them, sourly inspecting the outside fittings of five plasteel caskets while a clerk checked off items on a sheaf of clipboarded forms. (A sixth casket, Ta'ai's, had been launched into Tersel's sun, according to Aludran ceremony and custom, immediately after *Valkyrie* emerged into normal space.)

Cargo handlers came to take the first casket aboard the shuttle, snapping on anti-grav lifters and slowly guiding the container up the loading ramp. The coroner shook his head and went to rejoin the others at the foot of the ramp; he scowled even more as he noticed Mather and Wallis watching him.

"Now's our chance," Wallis muttered under her breath. "I hope you're in top form today."

"Why, my dear, you know I am *always* in top form," Mather murmured from between clenched teeth. "Why don't you wait here for HRH, while I have a word with civilian officialdom?"

He headed toward them with an outward air of nonchalance, but he could not honestly say that the group inspired optimism. One of the older men, bearing an advocate's badge stitched to his sleeve, was engaged in animated and angry discussion with a younger man wearing the planetside livery of the Gruening Line. Doctor Shannon and Arthur Bowman, the *Valkyrie*'s first officer, were listening gravely to both sides of the argument, Bowman occasionally attempting to make some comment and getting cut off.

As the coroner noticed Mather approaching, he muttered something under his breath to the attorney, and the argument became even more vocal. Discussion seemed to revolve around the general topic of lawsuits, liability, and varied legal action contemplated against Gruening, the crew of the *Valkyrie*, and all other persons possibly accountable.

"Good morning, Mister Bowman, Doctor Shannon, gentlemen," Mather said heartily. "I hope I'm not intruding." He shook Bowman's hand, then Shannon's, and nodded to the others in the group, taking perverse delight in the knowledge that he was, indeed, intruding. "I want to thank you again for the excellent cooperation we received in getting our cargo here safely. In fact, your entire staff is to be commended, Mister Bowman."

The Gruening official looked startled, if relieved, the advocate outraged, the coroner dubious. Shannon and Bowman merely looked grateful for the rescue. It was the coroner who first found the presence of mind to speak.

"You must be the Commodore Seton who is responsible for this sorry state of affairs—in which case, I hardly think that commendations are in order. I have five bodies to account for here, and another has already been disposed of under very irregular circumstances."

"The Aludrans didn't think it was irregular, Coroner," Mather said easily.

"Now, see here, Commodore!" the Gruening man interjected. "It seems to me that you're taking this matter altogether too lightly. I can assure you that my company considers six deaths excessive for a five-day journey."

"So do I," Mather replied, "and I take full responsibility for two of those deaths, as you'll see when you examine the official reports. It was not my intention to kill either one of them, but I assure you, it was necessary. As for the others, I share in your dismay, for it is, indeed, a great tragedy that innocent people should have perished. But I can in no way fault the performance of the officers and crew of the *Valkyrie*. Under the circumstances, I doubt that experienced officers of an Imperial ship of the line could have handled the situation more expeditiously. Certainly the Imperial Rangers under my direct command were able to do no better in the situation. I repeat"—he turned back to the coroner—"the crew and staff of the *Valkyrie* are to be commended."

"We'll see whether a court of inquiry agrees, Commodore," the advocate said, drawing himself up disdainfully.

"Indeed, we shall."

Mather made a crisp, formal bow, resisting the impulse to click his heels, then turned to Shannon and Bowman and shook their hands once more.

"Again, thank you, Doctor, Mister Bowman. And please give my regards to Captain Lutobo when he's able to receive visitors. Doctor Hamilton and I are most pleased that he's going to make a full recovery."

"I'll tell him of your concern, Commodore," Shannon replied.

"Thank you."

With that, Mather made a short bow in the direction of the other three men, then turned on his heel and strode the short distance across the deck and into the next bay to rejoin Wallis. The ramp of *Shantar*'s shuttle was just telescoping down, and Mather's Rangers waited expectantly as several naval ratings came down the ramp first.

"Just who the devil *is* this Mather Seton, anyway?" the advocate muttered under his breath.

Just then, a tall, silver-haired man in the white uniform of a full fleet admiral appeared at the top of the ramp, accompanied by an aide. The Rangers and ratings snapped to attention momentarily, then returned to work at the man's signal. Mather and Wallis, too, drew themselves up respectfully as the man descended the ramp, but it was obvious from the man's jovial expression that protocol was not to be strictly observed. His booming laugh carried all the way across the deck to the watching civilians as he first shook Mather's hand and pounded him enthusiastically on the back, then drew Wallis to him in an exuberant bear hug.

The Gruening contingent watched in incredulous silence as the three conferred a moment. Then the admiral glanced in their direction and spoke briefly to Wallis, who grinned and turned to approach them. The advocate shifted uneasily as Wallis walked right up to Shannon.

"Pardon me, gentlemen, but His Royal Highness Admiral the Prince Cedric would like Doctor Shannon to be presented to him. Would you come with me, please, Doctor?"

"Prince Cedric?" Shannon whispered, awed.

"The emperor's brother?" The Gruening man gasped.

Wallis raised one eyebrow and swept them all with a bemused gaze. "Why, yes, I thought you knew. We work for him. Shivaun, shall we go? We shouldn't keep His Royal Highness waiting."

With a nervous shrug and a half grin in the direction of Bowman, Shannon followed Wallis across the hangar floor. The Rangers were floating the Lehr cats up the ramp on their anti-grav sleds, one at a time, and the animals showed every indication of almost enjoying the experience. Prince Cedric surveyed each aspect of the operation with great interest, listening avidly to Mather's commentary, and grinned ear-to-ear when he leaned closer to one of the passing cages and its occupant favored him with a great yawn and a basso purr that could be heard clear in the next bay.

"What a marvelous creature, Seton!" the prince was saying. "My brother shan't want to give away any of them."

"Sir, I have the honor to present Doctor Shivaun Shannon," Wallis said, guiding Shannon slightly ahead of her as they approached. "Shivaun, this is Prince Cedric, our boss."

Shannon almost gasped at the liberty Wallis seemed to have taken, but the prince, whose profile matched those of his brother on all the coins and credit notes, turned to smile and shake her hand.

"I'm very pleased to meet you, Doctor. Mather's report spoke of you in the most glowing of terms."

"His—report, sir?" Shannon managed to whisper as she straightened from her bow.

Mather smiled and put an arm around her shoulder. "If you were naval personnel, you would have been 'mentioned in dispatches.' As it is, I suspect there will be some sort of civilian commendation. And because I had to make Lutobo abort his record run to Tersel, His Royal Highness has already arranged that all the crew of *Valkyrie* will get the equivalent of the bonus pay you missed out on."

"*And* an Imperial bonus, for having completed the mission successfully," Cedric added. "It may also interest you to learn that the Kwia-t'ai ship is standing by, and the ambassador has been informed of the cats' safe arrival."

"Well, only three, sir," Shannon murmured.

The prince shrugged. "I know that couldn't be helped, Doctor. The full situation has been explained to the ambassador. He also understands."

"The point is," Mather said, "we succeeded in the main—and you're partially responsible for that success."

Shannon swallowed, not really knowing what to say, but the need to comment was eliminated by the prince.

"Please accept my personal thanks, Doctor, as well as that of my brother, for a job well done. You may well have helped keep us out of a war—which is not at all as farfetched as it might sound, believe me. Your part in all of this will not be forgotten."

The prince's aide, lurking in the background, cleared his throat discreetly, and Cedric glanced behind him, where the last cat cage was just disappearing inside the ship.

"Ah, I see that duty calls. Doctor Shannon, it's been a pleasure meeting you," he said, taking her hand again briefly. "And now, your part of this mission being completed, you must permit me to return aboard and complete mine. Mather, Wallis, whenever you're ready."

At their nod, the prince inclined his head slightly, then went clambering up the ramp after the last of the cat cages. The naval ratings and Rangers continued loading the last of the other gear, but it was obvious their job was nearly done.

"That means we'd better get aboard, too, or he'll leave us," Mather said, giving Shannon's shoulders another affectionate squeeze. "He can be a very hard taskmaster. Let us know if the bureaucrats give you any further trouble."

He winked at her and gestured toward the bureaucrats in question as he started up the ramp. Shannon, with a dazed little smile, turned and took the hand that Wallis offered, grinning wider as the older woman pulled her closer in a quick embrace.

"You're one hell of a doctor, Doctor," Wallis murmured, drawing back to look Shannon in the eyes. "If you should ever need a good reference, or anything else, you can reach us through the Imperial Anthropological Society." She grinned. "That's just one of our covers, of course, but His Royal Highness is a patron. Any message will be forwarded at highest priority."

Shannon nodded, and Wallis, with a slight wave of her hand, turned to follow Mather up the ramp. Both of them paused at the top to wave a final time before the ramp telescoped up and the door closed.

With a sigh, Shannon withdrew behind the airtight doors and watched them close, waiting as the warning lights came on and the atmosphere was blown around the *Shantar*'s shuttle. She had not noticed until now that it was painted in the Imperial livery colors. Gracefully the shuttle lifted off its pad and floated out of its berth toward open space. Shannon watched until it was only a dark mote against the sea of stars.

"Pardon me, are you the ship's surgeon?" an unfamiliar voice suddenly said behind her.

A clerk from the Health and Immigration ship held out a bill of lading and a stylus as Shannon turned to look at him.

"I'm sorry," she said absently, looking for the place to sign. "Yes, I'm Doctor Shannon. What is this for?"

"We have a body to trade you, Doctor," the man said. He gestured with his chin toward the cargo bay of the coroner's shuttle, where a sleek, black plasteel coffin was being off-loaded down the cargo ramp. "Some rich eccentric wanted his remains shipped home for burial—all the way to Terra."

"But that's halfway across the galaxy."

"Sure is," the clerk said with a sickly grin. "So much for leaving anything for his heirs. The shipping charges and the kind of burial he's ordered will cost more than both of us probably make in a couple of years. It's all prepaid, too."

Shannon shook her head and looked at the document again, but there was no mistake: *Baron Relker von Strelgo, Sol III.* There was also a copy of a page of legal documentation—apparently an extract from the man's will—with all but part of a single paragraph blacked out.

. . . and all monies paid out first to ensure that my

body be returned to Terra, that I may be buried in my native earth.

Native earth.

Shannon felt a shiver run down her spine at that, and after she had signed off for the clerk, she turned suspiciously to follow the coffin with her eyes until it had disappeared on its way to storage in one of the lower holds.

And through she tried to tell herself there really *were* no such things as vampires, she still found herself with a most disconcerting urge to go back to her quarters and look for an old silver necklace she had worn as a child.

THE LEGACY OF LEHR